His resistance

"Michael?" Tris stood next to his chair, a tentative smile flirting with lips that didn't look entirely steady. "Will you dance with me?"

No, Tris, I can't dance with you, because holding you in my arms makes me forget friendship and remember kisses by the night-dark water... because your fingers on my shoulder make me think of your hand pressing fire into my skin....

Lord, how could he tell her these truths? She needed him as a friend today. She might be confused right now, might even convince herself she wanted something other than friendship from her old buddy, Michael. Hell, she'd nearly convinced *him* last night. Then, after their kiss, she'd said his name with that questioning note in her voice, and he'd heard the wistfulness. The wistfulness of someone longing to call another name....

He kept his face neutral as he stood up. "I'd love to dance with you, Tris."

How much could a man take?

He was about to find out.

Dear Reader,

Happy New Year! May this year bring you happiness, good health and all you wish for. And hopefully, helping you along the way, is Silhouette **Special Edition**. Each month, Silhouette **Special Edition** publishes six novels with you in mind—stories of love and life, tales that you can identify with—romance with that little "something special" added in.

In January, don't miss love stories from Barbara Faith, Christine Rimmer, Nikki Benjamin, newcomer Susan Mallery and veteran Silhouette **Special Edition**-er, Lisa Jackson. To round out this month, you are invited to a *Wedding Party* by Patricia McLinn—the conclusion to her heartwarming *Wedding Duet*! It's a winter wonderland for all this month at Silhouette **Special Edition**!

In each Silhouette **Special Edition** novel, we're dedicated to bringing you the romances that you dream about—the type of stories that delight as well as bring a tear to the eye. And that's what Silhouette **Special Edition** is all about—special books by special authors for special readers!

I hope you enjoy this book and all of the stories to come.

Sincerely,

Tara Gavin
Senior Editor

PATRICIA McLINN
Wedding Party

Silhouette Special Edition

Published by Silhouette Books New York

America's Publisher of Contemporary Romance

To memories and friends
from days along Lake Michigan,
especially Marion and Susie.

SILHOUETTE BOOKS
300 East 42nd St., New York, N.Y. 10017

WEDDING PARTY

ISBN: 0-373-09718-2

First Silhouette Books printing January 1992

Books by Patricia McLinn

Silhouette Special Edition

Hoops #587
A New World #641
*Prelude to a Wedding #712
*Wedding Party #718

*Wedding Duet

PATRICIA McLINN

says she has been spinning stories in her head since childhood, when her mother insisted she stop reading at the dinner table. As the time came for her to earn a living, Patricia shifted her stories from fiction to fact—she became a sports writer and editor for newspapers in Illinois, North Carolina and the District of Columbia. Now living outside Washington, D.C., she enjoys traveling, history and sports, but is happiest indulging her passion for storytelling.

Members of the Wedding Party

The Bride	Bette Wharton
The Groom	Paul Monroe
Maid of Honor	Judi Monroe *(Paul's sister)*
Bridemaids	Tris Donlin *(Paul's cousin)*
	Melody Saccardi
Best Man	Michael Dickinson
Ushers	Grady Roberts
	Ronald Wharton, Jr. *(Bette's brother)*
Father of the Bride	Ronald Wharton, Sr.
Mother of the Bride	Denise Kulaski Wharton
Father of the Groom	James Monroe
Mother of the Groom	Nancy Mulholland Monroe

Chapter One

Michael Dickinson continued efficiently sorting his mail despite the telephone tucked between his ear and shoulder. His calm, assured voice carried into the receiver over the noise of two dozen people pursuing three dozen tasks around him. As he spoke, he dropped envelopes, postcards, fliers and magazines into separate piles—discard, read immediately, pass on to someone else, read in that distant someday when he had time.

Another pile held one envelope. Addressed in a nearly illegible masculine hand, it had been among the mail he'd picked up from home when he returned to Springfield this morning after another whirlwind sweep through Illinois.

"I understand your concern for the party," he said into the telephone. He listened a moment, then answered with no betraying inflection of dryness. "Yes, of course, and your concern for the candidate, too. We all want Joan to win the election. If there is a perception among the voters that she tilts at windmills, you're right to say that could hurt her candidacy. It's my job to ensure they don't have that misperception." As Michael spoke, his eyes rested on the single envelope.

"Yes, I will mention that to the candidate. Thank you. I'll let you know. Goodbye."

He hung up and reached for the envelope. Without making any move to open it, he turned it over in his hands.

Paul never wrote. Not even at Christmas. The phone was invented for a man like Paul Monroe. Michael suspected that if Bette hadn't insisted, the formal wedding invitation he'd received two weeks ago would instead have been delivered in the same manner as the request to be in the wedding party: "Hey, Michael, we're getting married. Why don't you leave your sleazy politics for a while and come join Bette and me? I want you to be best man. Bette suggested co-groom, but I told her that'd be a little kinky for a straight arrow like you."

Michael had heard Bette affectionately admonishing her fiancé in the background. He knew Paul well enough to recognize the invitation as a way to tease Bette, tease him and mask the sentimentality of the request, all at once. He'd been touched. And honored. And he'd said yes. So it was hard to imagine what Paul could be writing about now.

If he had been a cynic, he might have wondered if Paul Monroe had decided he'd prefer Grady Roberts as his best man, since Grady was well on his way to making millions, while Michael was only chief aide-de-camp for long-shot United States Senate candidate Joan Bradon. But Michael wasn't a cynic—he had that on the authority of Joan Bradon, who had overcome plenty of cynics in her fifty-odd years. What he was, said Joan with her usual precision, was a skeptic. "A cynic presumes the worst. A skeptic suspends judgment until the proof's in," she'd told him once. "And since you're never easy to persuade, you're our resident devil's advocate, finding the holes in time to plug them before we face the light of public scrutiny."

Michael accepted her label, but for his own reasons. A cynic would remember too many weddings, ceremonies whose memories outlasted the love they were supposed to celebrate, and say this one would be no different. A skeptic could look at Paul and Bette and believe there was a chance it could be different.

Before Paul's call, if he'd had cause to think about it, Michael probably would have assumed Grady would be best man. After all, Paul and Grady went back to grade school. Michael was the latecomer in the group. He'd met them in the first hour of their first day of college.

Without ever saying much, he and Paul had seemed to understand each other from the start. Grady...well, Grady was Grady. But for all Grady's astounding good looks, easy charm and moneyed background, Michael had envied him only one thing. And he'd buried that resentment so long ago and so deep he didn't think even Paul had gotten more than an inkling of it. Certainly Grady hadn't.

Michael looked again at the return address sprawled haphazardly in the corner of the envelope and shook his head at his own hesitation. Ripping open the envelope, he skimmed the letter with the same quick comprehension he used to attack press releases, position statements and news reports. He understood it all with his first glance through. Still, he read it a second time.

A week. All of them together again for a week. The way it had been back at college, with the addition of Bette.

No, not the way it had been at college. That was romantic foolishness. There was no such thing as recapturing the past. Or altering it. That was all over with.

A week.

Since Paul owned his own business—appraising collect-
ibles—he could clear his calendar for a week before the
wedding as well as the two honeymoon weeks after. And
he wrote that he'd talked Bette into turning over her temp
agency to her assistant for the extra time.

But how could Michael consider taking a week off in
August with the election coming up in November? A
weekend to be best man at a friend's wedding, yes. But a
week? How could he take that much time?

But he knew he would. Because Paul had offered a
temptation Michael wouldn't pass up.

Tris.

"Aha! I thought so!"

Leslie Craig's triumphant tone gave Tris an irrational
rush of guilt. Her co-worker and friend made it sound as
if Tris Donlin had just confirmed her worst suspicions. In
a way, maybe she had. But really, being at the office first
thing in the morning was nothing to feel guilty about. Her
flight had arrived at Dulles Airport so early that she'd even
gotten to her downtown Washington, D.C. office before
peak rush hour.

"It's good to see you, too," said Tris, her fingers stilling in midsentence on the keyboard. She had been com-
posing a memo on the conference, since there were a
couple of points she wanted the staff to consider over the
weekend. Even if they didn't give it conscious thought,
they'd come in Monday with ideas.

"Yeah? Well, it's not good to see you. You look like
death."

"Thanks!" Tris tried for outraged sarcasm, but the
chuckle behind it ruined the effect. Leslie never failed to
make her laugh. Even when she didn't want to laugh,

something about the blunt statements delivered with a slight Southern drawl appealed to her.

"Couldn't expect any different after taking the red-eye from the West Coast, could you? That trip could make next year's Junior Miss look like a hag. So go home and get some sleep, like you're supposed to."

Leslie was thirty-six to Tris's twenty-nine, and the most direct, most sophisticated mother hen Tris knew. "I will. I had just a couple things I wanted to do."

"A couple things you wanted to do—a couple things that'll take you all day and a good part of the night. Just because you were named after some indestructible, he-man football player—"

"Baseball," Tris corrected automatically; she'd had to explain this often enough. "Tris Speaker. Center fielder for the Indians in the twenties."

Leslie waved off the distinction and kept on talking. "—doesn't mean you have to be some superman. Good heavens, woman, first you spend three days in Cincinnati researching that facility for the homeless, and then go straight to a week of twenty-four-hour days at that wretched conference in L.A. Give yourself a break."

"I will. Honest. Just leave me alone awhile so I can get this done." A little tiredness wasn't too high a price to pay for what she'd found out. The Cincinnati project had fired her imagination, and the conference had produced solid proposals for how the historic preservation association she worked for could encourage more such projects. What could be better than turning endangered buildings into shelter for those who had none?

Leslie Craig consulted her gold-braceleted wristwatch. "You have forty-five minutes before I come back to turn you into a pumpkin. And that time includes a few minutes to check your messages."

Tris flipped through the pink slips she'd been handed, noting that two men she occasionally dated had called. She wouldn't mind catching a movie or going to a play this weekend with either Brad or Dave—after she finished this memo and got some rest.

"And read your mail," Leslie continued, plopping a stack of envelopes on Tris's desk before heading out the door. "I'll be back in forty-five."

Tris had already checked the basket that held her business mail, so this stack must have been culled from the deliveries to her house, which Leslie had been looking after for her. Since her house was five blocks one side of the subway stop and Leslie's apartment three blocks the other way, they exchanged house-checking duties when one traveled, as well as sharing the commute to work. It was just like Leslie, first, to know that she would appear at the office before going home and, second, to choose the most interesting of her week's mail to deliver to her.

She glanced at the envelopes splayed on her desk, but delayed opening them. First, she'd finish her report on the conference. They had to come up with ways to find funding for these projects. Somehow.

When Leslie returned in exactly forty-five minutes, Tris had opened a letter from her mother and another from her sister. She held a third letter open in her hand, almost as if she were still reading it. But she was staring out the window, past its narrow-slatted blinds to something no one else would have recognized even if they'd seen it.

"Bad news?"

"What?" Tris refocused, looking at the paper in her right hand as if she had no idea how it had come to be there. "No. Not bad news."

"Good news, then."

"I—I don't know. Not exactly either."

Leslie's thin eyebrows arched dramatically. "That sounds fascinating. Tell Leslie all." She propped herself on the edge of Tris's desk and waited expectantly.

"It's just a letter from my cousin. Paul."

"The one getting married in August. And you're in the wedding, right?"

"Yes. He says he and Bette have arranged to take time off from their businesses, and he wants me to come and spend the whole week before the wedding."

"I bet the bride loves that idea."

"Actually, Bette probably does. She's not the type to get too uptight—probably because she'll have everything done a month ahead of time. She grew up in the area, but her parents retired down to Arizona a few years ago, so I'd imagine she and Aunt Nancy are doing most of the arranging, and I can guarantee between the two of them they'll have every detail organized way ahead of schedule. Besides, Paul says it's the only wedding present he's asked for."

"Emotional blackmail." Leslie nodded. "I like his style."

Tris grinned halfheartedly. "He says Aunt Nancy and Uncle James are looking forward to having us all stay at the house. And he has all sorts of plans of things to do together. All of us. Ball games, sailing, parties."

"Sounds like fun," said Leslie without much conviction. Then she straightened. "What do you mean, 'all of us'?"

"Paul and Bette, his fiancée. And...um...some of the rest of the wedding party."

"*Some* of the wedding party?"

"Bette's brother's in the wedding and he can't get away until the weekend, and neither can one of Bette's childhood friends who's the other bridesmaid, but the maid of honor is Paul's sister, Judi, and I'm sure she'll be there along with, um, the other guys in the wedding.''

"Ah-ha! Meaning Buddy Michael and Gorgeous Grady.''

"I wish you wouldn't call him that.'' They both knew Tris's protest was aimed at the description of Grady Roberts, not Michael Dickinson.

Leslie ignored her protest. "Sounds great to me. It's about time you showed Gorgeous Grady that little Tris has grown up. A week ought to be plenty of time.''

Leslie had first heard of her college friends five years ago when, over a series of after-work dinners, they'd exchanged life stories and forged a friendship. Sometimes Tris thought that in those long sessions she'd talked herself through postdivorce trauma and right into maturity. And Leslie had listened. If she'd somehow also directed the conversations and the growth—and knowing her as Tris now did, she suspected Leslie definitely had directed—it had been very discreet and very deft.

Tris laughed, partly in genuine amusement, partly in exasperation. "Leslie, I don't know how many times I've told you that I'm long past my infatuation with Grady Roberts. I was a freshman in college and—''

"And Juliet was thirteen when she went gaga over Romeo.''

"It's hardly the same thing.''

"No,'' Leslie agreed with abrupt and uncharacteristic seriousness. "I've often thought that if Juliet had stuck it out a little longer she would have seen that Romeo really wasn't the right man for her. But she never had a chance to grow out of it, to find out if she'd really found love, or only infatuation. It's kind of the same thing for you, Tris. Grady Roberts was a major college crush that you've never had a chance to check against adult reality.''

Tris said nothing. What could she say? Leslie was right. As a freshman in college she had fallen for Grady Roberts with the depth and breadth of her seventeen-year-old soul. But Grady—a handsome, popular senior and part of the triumvirate, with her cousin Paul and Michael Dickinson, that had adopted her as a little sister—had never seen her as anything but a kid.

The infatuation belonged to the distant past. It had waned even before she left school, and certainly had been over before her brief, ill-considered marriage had knocked the inclination toward infatuations out of her for good.

But some questions about Grady Roberts had lingered. What would it be like to meet him now, now that the four-year age difference had narrowed to a blink of experience rather than a gulf of worldliness? Would there be any spark if they met now? Not the infatuation of twelve years ago, but perhaps something different. Maybe Leslie had a point. Maybe it was time to get the questions answered.

And it would be wonderful to spend time with Paul and Bette before their wedding.

And to see Michael, of course.

"Goodbye. Enjoy your stay in Chicago."

As Tris stepped from the airplane, the airline attendant's professional farewell started her heart pumping fast. She'd spent the flight pushing thoughts of the past few difficult weeks at work from her mind. If thinking about the worries would have solved them, they'd have disappeared weeks ago. She'd done what she could for now; pushing too much too soon could in fact undo her efforts. So she waited and hoped and tried not to worry. She'd promised Leslie that much, and she'd do her best to keep the promise.

But she hadn't been as successful avoiding thoughts of the coming week. As the plane had circled across Lake Michigan and slipped lower to show her the familiar settings of her college days, she'd played a game with herself, naming the buildings as fast as she could before the campus disappeared from sight and the plane continued west to O'Hare. Much safer than thinking too much about memories.

As she passed through the walkway connecting plane and terminal, she couldn't put the thoughts off any longer, because the memories were about to merge with the real-life people who'd created them.

What if I don't recognize them? The thought hit her with enough impact that she almost stumbled when her heel ticked a metal strip on the corridor's floor. Eight years. That was how long it had been since she'd seen Grady. Since the day all three of them had returned to campus for her college graduation.

She'd seen Michael only once since then, a little more than a year later. Just before her marriage. But she'd talked to him at least three times a year—his birthday, her birthday and Christmas. Some years those calls had been oases. And from them she knew Michael was still Michael.

Paul kept her posted on what both Michael and Grady were up to in their lives, the way, she knew, he kept them posted on her. But he never said anything about such mundane items as looks. Michael she could imagine changing, but what if tall, burnished, blond Grady looked totally different?

What if he'd gotten fat?

What if he'd gone gray?

Or bald?

That image pulled a chuckle from her tight throat, shaking Tris out of her momentary panic and propelling her through the entryway and into the glass-arched waiting area.

"Tris!"

A strong hand took her carry-on case from her and an equally strong arm wrapped around her shoulders, corralling her out of the stream of passengers behind her.

"How are you, Tris?"

"Michael?"

The voice was familiar but, without the telephone's distortion, deeper than she remembered. And the hard band of arm around her, surely that was different.

She tipped her head to look up at the eyes just a few inches above her own. Michael's eyes. Oh, yes. With a faint creasing at the corners as they smiled at her. The pleasure not quite masking signs of weariness and— And what? A shock quickly masked? She dismissed the puzzled surprise in his eyes to focus on the light of warmth and friendship in their hazel depths. Definitely Michael's eyes.

Michael with his slightly unruly, thick, dark hair, his little-boy's grin, his reliable salt-of-the-earth nature. Michael with his generous heart.

"Michael! It's so good to see you!"

She stopped their progress to throw her arms around his neck. "It's been too long, Michael."

She felt his arms tighten around her, drawing their bodies into firm alignment. His voice sounded even deeper when he said, "Yes, it has been too long, Tris."

Her blood gave the most peculiar lurch through her veins. Almost as if his hug had set off some sort of shock wave. Which didn't make sense.

She started to pull away from him with a vague feeling of discontent. Over his shoulder, she saw three figures hurrying toward them.

As burnished and blond and handsome as ever, Grady definitely hadn't gotten fat. Or gone bald. Fleetingly, she wondered if she'd sensed his presence without even knowing it. Somehow that didn't seem to fit.

"Tris!"

Paul's arms formed a vise around her ribs for an intense second. Bette Wharton's more gentle embrace gave way to a hug from Grady. How many times had she dreamed all those years ago of these long, muscular arms around her?

Maybe after all those dreams, this feeling of anticlimax was normal. Especially with everyone else around her discussing the mundane subject of getting lost in the airport.

"Should have known you'd get here first, Dickinson," grumbled Paul.

"I thought you were going to park the car," said Grady over the top of her head. He still had his arms looped around her waist, but it seemed almost absentminded.

"I did. Then I came straight out here. Where were you guys?"

Identical looks of embarrassment came over Paul's and Grady's faces, and Tris had a sudden impulse to hug them all again. It was all so familiar. Count on Michael to be the organized one.

"I knew I should have stayed with Michael," said Bette with a long-suffering sigh.

"Whaddya mean?" demanded her fiancé with a fine show of huffiness. Which none of them believed. "I got us here, didn't I?"

"Yes," Bette acknowledged. "You got us here. By way of the international terminal and just under thirty-two miles of walking."

Grady gave Tris's shoulders a final squeeze. "Aw, c'mon, Bette, it wasn't that far out of the way."

"No, and certainly not without its rewards," she said.

Paul guffawed and Grady looked ever so slightly abashed. But neither did any explaining.

Tris sent a raised-eyebrows look toward Michael, but he responded with a small shrug and a half grin that indicated he didn't know what they were talking about, either.

"Tell, Bette," she demanded of the most susceptible of the trio.

Bette Wharton cast her a searching look that rather surprised Tris. On the way to a Caribbean vacation late last winter, Paul and Bette had stopped in Washington for three days—to get Tris's approval, Bette teased. If her approval had been required, Tris gave it wholeheartedly. The two women had hit it off immediately, and Tris had seen how well Bette and Paul complemented each other, sharing basic values but with enough surface dissimilarities to keep the mix interesting. Between Bette and Tris, an understanding and honest affection had sprung up immediately.

Now Tris wondered at the appraising look being sent her way, a much more serious look than the topic seemed to warrant. And, if she wasn't mistaken, a look that Bette had been careful would be unobserved by any of the three men.

Bette's deep blue eyes abruptly changed from thoughtful to mischievous, but her face stayed neutral. "Oh, it was just another of Grady's conquests."

A spurt of laughter escaped Paul.

"Aw, Bette..." Grady made the appeal with little apparent expectation that it would be heeded.

Another of Grady's conquests. Tris felt herself waiting for her smile to freeze to stiff discomfort. It didn't happen.

Catching Michael's frowning glance at her, she even nudged the smile another notch brighter without any effort, to reassure him. Of course Michael had known immediately how that casual comment would have hurt the old Tris. How many times had he soothed those old hurts? But this time, there was no need. Amazing what eight years of maturity could do for you.

"Only this conquest informed Mr. Roberts—after he'd graciously helped her translate the directions to downtown from English to her oh-so-native French—that she was a nun. You should have seen the look on Grady's face when he finally got that bit of information!"

"Well, how was I supposed to know?" complained Grady amid his friends' laughter. "She didn't have on one of those nun uniforms. How'd I know there was a nun convention in Chicago this weekend?"

"Oh, poor Grady," Tris got out between giggles, "all that charm going to waste..."

She saw surprise in Michael's face as he looked at her this time. She felt rather surprised herself. She didn't mind. She really didn't mind. She felt like doing a cartwheel down the long, straight expanse of O'Hare Airport hallway. Only there were a lot of people in the way, and some might wonder what she'd found to celebrate. Even if she told them, they wouldn't understand how it felt to finally know, really and truly *know,* that she was no longer little Tris Donlin, waiting for a scrap of attention, of approval, of interest from the great Grady Roberts.

Leslie had been right. It was time. Well past time to shake off the adoring girl and the distant idol and replace them with the people they'd become—a woman and a man.

"Thanks for the sympathy, Tris. I knew I could count on you," said Grady. But his voice didn't sound as certain as his words. He looked a little puzzled as he met her smile.

A man and a woman, that was what they were now, Tris thought behind her smile. And who knew what might happen when a man and woman got together.

She turned to Michael to share the moment, but he had turned away, apparently focusing on a plane backing away from the opposite terminal.

"Luggage ought to be at the baggage claim by now," he said, staring in the opposite direction.

Another pang of anticlimax slid through Tris, similar to the one when Grady hugged her. Probably natural. Despite her efforts to keep her thoughts off the reunion, she must have built up unreasonable expectations.

"Yeah, we'll get the luggage and get you settled at Mom and Dad's, and then we can go see the campus," said Paul. "Show Bette all our old haunts. She's been asking to see them."

"Begging to see them," concurred Bette, deadpan. "You know how Paul hates to dwell on the past. But for my sake he's willing to relive some of the moments from his four horror-filled college years. The sacrifices the man makes for me."

She was still shaking her head, when her husband-to-be wrapped an arm around her waist and started her down the corridor toward the baggage claim. "That's right, woman. Horrible sacrifices."

Looking at the way they fit together, Tris felt surprisingly alone as she followed, walking between Grady and Michael.

Michael welcomed the details of getting the luggage, loading the car, paying the parking fee, maneuvering through the toll-road traffic, following the route to the Monroes' Lake Forest home. All the details that kept him from dwelling on what had happened when Tris walked into his arms.

He checked the rearview mirror before changing lanes and caught sight of her sitting in the corner of the back seat next to Paul and Bette.

Little Tris had grown up.

Her legs, once coltish and invariably clad in jeans, now stylishly filled a pair of sheer stockings beneath a pale float of a skirt.

Her hair, once a waist-length, sun-streaked tangle, was pushed from her face in casual sweeps that turned under just above her collar, leaving a tantalizing sliver of nape exposed and framing ears decorated with oblong gold earrings.

Her Wedgwood-blue eyes, once vulnerable and shy, now studied the world with self-confidence tempered by good humor.

Her body, still as youthfully slim as it had always been, now moved with graceful assurance . . . and had fit against his for one instant as if it belonged there. The way he used to dream it would. Long ago. Before he knew better. Before he realized that unlike the world he'd grown up in, there were worlds where some things didn't change. Some people who didn't shed their loves with each season's wardrobe. People like Tris.

That very stability of heart—so different from what he'd grown up with—was part of what had drawn him to her in the first place, all those years ago. Even while part of him had longed for her to have a change of heart. But Tris Donlin—girl or woman—still looked at Grady Roberts with dazzled eyes. Looked at Michael Dickinson as friend and buddy.

The damnable surprise was to find that his feelings hadn't changed, either.

He'd been so sure he was over her years ago, that the spell was in the past. Ancient history. He sure as hell *should* have been over her. Good Lord, he'd fallen for a seventeen-year-old girl who was now a twenty-nine-year-old woman. How could he still feel the same way about her?

But the instant she had come through that doorway, framed by the opening and with the light slanting sun highlights into her hair, he had felt it with a slam to his chest as if he had been tackled by the Chicago Bears' defensive line.

Great, the guy renowned for seeing the tiniest of flaws in a plan hadn't spotted a weakness in himself the size of the San Andreas Fault. Despite all his inner warnings about the emotional dangers of trying to recapture the past in this reunion, he'd plunged headlong into a pit he would have sworn he'd long ago escaped—wanting Tris.

Those first few minutes hadn't helped any. The little jolt of surprise in her eyes when she first looked at him, as if she were seeing him anew. The way she melted against his body, the rightness of the feeling. The glances exchanged that said their old communication still operated.

Then he'd seen the smile she focused on Grady.

Yes, Tris Donlin was definitely a woman. But she still wanted the man that the girl Tris Donlin had longed for, so hard and so long.

With his grip on the wheel only slightly tighter, he eased into the left lane to pass an overloaded van, the move so smooth no one else in the car noticed. But beneath the disciplined muscles, anger surged through him. Silently, he swore to himself, at himself. He'd be damned if he'd let himself go on this way any longer.

In this world of inconstancy, he'd always valued the things that didn't change. But his feelings for Tris Donlin didn't have to count among the unchanging. He would get over her, once and for all.

Chapter Two

"Everything looks different. That building wasn't here, was it?"

Bette put a consoling arm around her fiancé's shoulders and linked her other arm with Michael's. "Things change, Paul. It's natural."

"Yeah, but why didn't they leave any of the old things?"

Tris grinned inwardly at the plaintive note in his voice. From the parking lot where they'd piled out of the car, it did look as if the once familiar campus had been transformed. "We just haven't gotten there yet, Paul," she said. "Newer buildings are usually built around the core of older ones, like the rings of a tree."

"That's right," said Bette. "And we just have to go all the way back to prehistory to get to the buildings you'll recognize."

Paul got halfway to a scowl, but his chuckle disrupted it as, three abreast, he, Bette and Michael led the way down a tree-shaded path between new buildings.

"By the way, how goes the building-saving business these days, Tris?"

At Grady's offhand question, she glanced at him, and the way the blue of Lake Michigan formed a backdrop for his sun-glinted golden hair caught her attention. He really was a hunk. And he'd just asked about her job, her life. She should take the opportunity to introduce him to the grown-up Tris. So why didn't she feel any inclination to pursue the opening?

"It's fine, Grady. Busy and challenging."

"Not a whole lot of money in it, though, is there?"

"No. Not a lot. But I hear from Paul that you're hip-deep in million-dollar deals these days."

He grinned at her. "Yeah, the business is going great guns. But we can talk business later. C'mon, we're getting left behind."

Tris let out a long breath as he hurried her after the others, then wondered fleetingly whether it resulted from the warmth of Grady's hand wrapped around her elbow or an ignoble relief that he hadn't gone into a detailed explanation of his thriving business brokerage company.

"Now here's a building you should save, Tris." Paul stood, hands on hips, considering a century-old pseudo-Gothic structure.

"Oh, Lord! University Hall. Do you remember—?"

"That night we put up the banners—"

"For the Phantom Party—"

"It was the last building to do—"

"Tris climbed across from Harris—"

"I was the only one who could get in the window—"

"And then when she twisted her ankle, she couldn't get back and—"

The four-way words and laughter tumbled over one another until Bette begged them to stop.

"Wait! One at a time. This is one story I want to hear. Michael, you tell me. That way I'll get the straight story."

"We'd planned a party for this campus service group we all belonged to. It gave tours and welcomed new students, things like that. The four of us were assigned to come up with a fund-raiser. We decided on a Phantom Party."

He spoke seriously enough, but Tris noted a dimple high on his left cheek. How could she have forgotten how that single dimple would appear, so unexpectedly, to leaven his otherwise solemn face?

"What's a Phantom Party?"

"It was a ploy, that's what it was," said Paul. "We figured nobody'd come if we just advertised another fundraising party. So we made it a Phantom Party. We started wearing T-shirts saying Phantoms and put ads in the paper saying 'The Phantoms Are Coming.'"

"Then we decided to string up banners around campus," resumed Michael. "The idea was to have all the banners show up overnight, adding another mystery. Getting people so curious they had to go to the party."

"And it worked. We raised a bundle," said Grady.

"Which Tris wanted to give to the bums down on Maxwell Street," Paul interposed.

"That would have been a lot more of a service than chair cushions or whatever we bought for the student union."

"Yeah, just think of all the cheap wine they could've bought with that money," Paul answered.

"You can't know they would have—"

"You were always coming up with these wild ideas to solve the problems of the world overnight, Tris. Admit it.

Giving money to some derelicts in a one-shot deal doesn't solve anything.''

"It's better than buying chair cushions!''

"Trees,'' murmured Michael.

"What?''

"Trees. We bought trees with the money. If I'm not mistaken, these trees.'' He pointed to the tree-lined path.

"Hah! Trees help the ozone layer, so the money *was* put to good use.''

"Quit gloating, Paul,'' said his fiancée. "And tell me the rest of the story, Michael.''

Tris crossed her arms at her waist and leaned against the stone balustrade, remembering how they'd refused to listen to her back then. She'd wanted to do something meaningful with that money. Sure, her idea hadn't been practical, but she'd wanted so badly to better the world. She looked down the path canopied by trees bought a decade ago.

Turning back, she met Michael's eyes, and saw that light in them that had always made her feel he looked right into her. Her mood mellowed in familiar comfort at the sensation. She *had* been rather naive back then, thinking she could help people so easily. And trees weren't a bad investment.

"So what happened with the banners, Michael?'' Bette prompted again.

Tris watched the dimple reappear before he turned away to answer Bette. "We'd gotten into the other buildings—''

"What that means is Michael had finessed the janitors into letting us in.''

"And hung the banners,'' Michael continued without any indication he'd heard Paul. "But we had one building left—this one—and no way to get in.''

"Because the University Hall janitor had gone home by the time we got here," explained Paul.

"Tris said she could get in through an open window on the third floor by climbing out of Harris into that tree and across to that other branch."

Tris followed Michael's gesture to the venerable oak. It had seemed so simple that night, looking out from Harris to the beckoning open window a few yards away. Now, standing on the ground, looking up at the tree and looking back in time, she wondered if she'd been crazy.

"Good Lord," said Bette, obviously following the same line of thought.

"Michael, of course, said she shouldn't do it," said Paul.

Tris suddenly remembered how stern Michael had seemed that night and how she'd thought he didn't have much faith in her to think she couldn't reach the other building. She'd waited until he'd gone to the door to check out a noise, then she'd slipped out of the window and started across before he could stop her.

"But I made it," she said, half to that long-ago Michael, half to herself.

"Yes," Michael confirmed a little grimly, with no sign of the dimple. "You made it. And she hung the banner. Only when she tried to climb back out to the branch, she got her foot caught." Tris remembered how the old-fashioned steam radiator had seemed to grab at her, the pitching sensation as she lost her balance, the endless moment of teetering on the windowsill, then collapsing into the room with a sickening twist of her ankle. She also remembered the three shocked faces staring at her—Paul, Grady and Michael—framed in the window across the way.

"I had to haul Michael back in from the tree branch," said Paul with a half chuckle. "We would have had him splattered on the sidewalk. That branch never would have held his weight. But we sure were glad to hear Tris's voice coming from that other window—even if it was just to complain how much her ankle hurt.''

"I'd sprained it, but I could hop around," she told Bette. "Only the doors to the lecture room I'd gone into were all locked from the outside, so I couldn't get out."

"And we couldn't figure out how to get *in*," said Paul. "I thought Michael would throttle that poor janitor when he told us he didn't have keys to University Hall. We were really getting worried."

"Oh yeah? I don't remember you seeming too worried, cousin dear. I remember you standing over there, laughing."

"It was pretty funny with you hissing at us from the window to get you the hell out."

"How did you get her out?" Bette asked.

"Michael wormed it out of the janitor that the buildings were connected by an underground venting system. So he crawled through, found the master key, unlocked the room Tris was in, helped her down the stairs and they walked right out the front door." Paul gestured dramatically at the carved panels of the heavy wooden door. "Actually, Michael walked. Tris hobbled."

She grimaced at him. "I hobbled all right. I needed crutches for two weeks. Didn't get to dance once at the party." Instead, she'd perched on a table with Michael bringing her drinks and munchies, and making her laugh even while she watched Grady dance the night away with his latest date.

"Poor Tris," Paul said with briskly fake sympathy. "Didn't get to dance and didn't get to give the money away to one of her causes. Tris was always trying to change mankind and save the world then."

Tris thought Michael muttered something about "leading with her heart" and "impractical."

"Now I'm just trying to save an old building or two," she said, laughing and patting her cousin on the arm. "So old geezers like you will have something to remember—if you're not too old to remember."

"Hey, who're you calling old? I'm no older than—"

Paul started to wave his arm, but stopped when his broadly encompassing gesture included a couple of apparent summer school students, one a boy who looked as if he'd never shaved and the other a girl with go-on-forever legs beneath barely-there shorts. The stunned look on his face drew unstifled laughter as his friends shepherded him along the path.

"We were never that young, were we?"

"Tris was."

She made a face at Grady, not caring if it wasn't the most mature reaction. Of all the world, these people would accept her as she was. Feeling Michael's eyes on her, she grinned at him. It didn't matter anymore that Grady had thought of her as a kid. She'd grown up.

"Oh, good. Here's the spot. Now I want you all to line up for the same pose as that picture," announced Bette.

"What picture?"

"You know, the picture of the four of you together. Paul has a copy in his office, and so does Grady. I know Tris has one in her house and I bet Michael does, too. So don't try to tell me you don't know what picture I'm talking about."

Tris knew exactly what picture, and from the slightly sheepish grins of the others, so did they. They'd had it taken on the library steps the day before the three guys graduated, when they were all feeling more than a little wistful about the end of their wonderful year together.

"I keep it in my office to disarm unsuspecting clients into thinking I'm approachable and nice," said Paul.

"Baloney," disputed Bette affectionately. "You keep it in your office so you can look at it ten hours a day, and you'd break anybody's arm who tried to take it away. Here, Michael, you sit there, and Tris, you were up behind him. You know, Tris, I think the main reason your cousin is marrying me is so he has an excuse. Now he can say I'm the one who likes all the sentimental stuff and pretend he's just indulging me, when he really loves it."

Paul looked away from the knowing grins of his three companions on the front steps of the old library.

"Aw, c'mon, Bette. I don't get all misty-eyed about Christmas tree ornaments."

Tris caught the look he exchanged with his fiancée, and had no doubts about the love their banter covered.

"No, but you're the one who spent three hours searching your mom's attic for the box with the ones you'd made in grade school, so I could get misty-eyed. Now, you sit there beside Tris and, Grady, you get a little behind."

Bette assessed the grouping through her camera lens. "Something's not right." She lowered the camera. "I know. Tris, you had your arm around Michael from behind."

Tris complied. Beneath her arm, his chest felt familiar and yet different. This was Michael, her friend, her confidant, her companion. Yet his shoulders were broader than she remembered Michael's being, his chest harder underneath the thin shirt. And hotter. So much hotter.

"That's right. Now lean forward a little over his shoulder."

She could smell the soap on his skin, and the scent of the sun in his hair. A wholesome scent so much like Michael she found herself leaning closer.

"That's great!" Bette clicked a shot.

Michael shifted immediately, bringing his right hand up to where Tris's rested on his upper chest as if he were about to remove the hand she'd spread wide over his shirt.

"No, wait. Everybody hold still and let me get another, just to be sure."

Michael's hand stilled, squeezing around Tris's. Squeezing so hard that as soon as another click sounded, she said his name with a question in it, wondering what was wrong.

He half turned, but she had the impression he meant to move away from her hand rather than to face her, though that was the result. He almost seemed angry at her, and she didn't understand why.

"What's wrong?" His eyes held a sharpness she didn't remember ever seeing there before. For the first time, she had an understanding of the determination and relentlessness that drove him. She'd known on some level that it had to be there because of what he'd accomplished, but to her he'd always before shown only the gentleness.

"Nothing."

He moved farther away from her and gave her a half smile. A smile that made him look close enough to the old Michael that as they continued their tour of the campus, she could almost believe she'd imagined the other look. But not quite.

Why the hell did I agree to this week? Michael wondered disgustedly as he watched Tris, walking ahead of him, turn toward Grady. He shouldn't have come. He should have made some excuse to Paul and Bette. He should have just come in for the wedding weekend, left early. Maybe it wasn't too late. Maybe he could manufacture an emergency with the campaign, disappear for a few days, then return Saturday morning and . . .

Tris tipped her head to follow Grady's finger pointing out across the huge boulders forming a bulwark against the lake. Her hair swung to the side, exposing more of the soft, vulnerable skin at the nape of her neck. His heart slammed against his chest with the strain of controlling the urge to put his lips there.

No, dammit. He wouldn't flinch from this. If he left now he might never rid himself of this stupid, nonsensical desire for the unattainable. He sure as hell couldn't let it survive this week. Come hell or high water, it was time to face the reality. Tris Donlin apparently had been a ghost in his heart a lot longer than he'd thought. Too damn long.

A piece clicked into place in his mind, and for the first time he saw how that wraith of a memory might have been part of what had stood between him and Laura. Maybe he'd known that on some level at the time, but never clearly enough to admit it, even to himself and certainly not to Laura. As much as he believed in the concept, he hadn't been able to make any promises of forever to her. In the end he'd backed away, and she'd gone to another job, another state, another life. He'd missed her these past months, but he couldn't blame her for leaving. In a way, he'd even been a little relieved.

Automatically he stopped when the others did, aware of their talk as a distant muttering.

It was time to face down this ghost. Time to turn the light of day on it. To see it for the insubstantial, impossible thing it was. Tris might have become a woman, but her heart wouldn't change. She still wanted Grady.

It didn't matter that Laura hadn't been the right woman. Others had shown an interest in trying out for the role. When this reunion and wedding were over maybe he'd make some time to see where some of those implicit invitations might lead.

What he could do this week was enjoy the friendships he valued—Paul's, Bette's, Grady's. And Tris's.

What he *had* to do was exorcise a ghost.

"White shirts, Bette?"

Grady held up the garment he'd been handed by the proprietor of the formal-wear shop with an air of dissatisfaction.

Tris turned from examining the sleek royal-blue dress she would wear as bridesmaid. They'd trooped into the shop en masse first thing Monday morning for final fittings—the only one for her. She'd sent her measurements several months ago. The remainder of the wedding party—Bette's brother, Ron, and her longtime friend Melody—were to be fitted when they arrived in town Friday morning.

Right now Michael was being fitted in one cubicle and Paul's younger sister, Judi, in the other. All the men had decided to buy tuxedos rather than rent them—Michael saying he needed one for political functions, Paul grumbling that Bette would probably drag him to formal functions now and Grady saying he could use a spare.

"Did you have something else in mind, Grady?"

Bette's calm voice held just a trace of something other than inquiry in it. Tris became aware of Paul listening intently and realized that Bette seemed to be making a point of not looking at her fiancé.

"White seems rather bland, maybe a little stark," said Grady, his hand hovering over a rack of sample shirts.

"What do you think would be less stark, Grady?" Bette was quietly, unobtrusively leading him on, Tris decided.

Grady's hand settled on a robin's-egg-blue model, pulling it out. "Something like this would be nice, something—"

"Hah! I told you, Bette! Do I know Grady Roberts, or do I know Grady Roberts!" Paul's crowing drew a reluctant smile from Bette and a confused stare from Grady.

"What do you mean?"

Paul ignored Grady. "I told you, didn't I, Bette? I was right, wasn't I?"

"Yes, yes, you were right," she acknowledged with a half laugh. "You even picked the shirt."

"What are you two talking about?" Grady demanded.

"About your vanity, good buddy."

"Vanity? What do you mean?"

"I told Bette that you'd want the blue shirt instead of the white. No, I *guaranteed* you'd want the blue shirt."

Grady studied the shirt in his hand. "I think it would look nicer, less—"

"Stark. We know," interrupted Paul. "The fact that it matches your eyes has absolutely nothing to do with it, right?"

"My eyes?" Grady seemed genuinely puzzled how it came to be that the shirt matched his eyes perfectly and set his golden hair off to perfection. Then a small smile tugged at his well-shaped mouth. "It does match them, doesn't it?"

"Beautifully," Bette said. "But it would steal some of the spotlight from the dresses for Judi and Tris. That's why I chose the white. You'll still look wonderful, Grady."

"Miss Donlin?" The seamstress held the royal-blue dress and indicated Tris should follow her into the back.

Judi passed her with a definite glint in her eyes. "Wait'll you try it on, Tris. It's great. It's so-o-o sexy. It's almost *slinky.*'' That clearly constituted high praise in Judi's twenty-year-old mind.

The seamstress led the way down the narrow corridor. As she pushed aside the curtain on the right side for Tris to enter, the dress she held caught the material of the opposite curtain and pulled it aside as well.

The opening framed Michael, half-turned toward the doorway, finishing the motion of shrugging off his tuxedo shirt. His skin looked bronzed against the white fabric. She'd been right during that picture-taking session on the library steps—his shoulders were broader, his chest was harder than before. She could see that in the defined muscles across his shoulders and at either side of the hair-dusted valley that arrowed down his chest, disappeared into the waistband of the tuxedo pants, where it probably continued beyond, over the flat stomach and—

Tris snapped up her head at the inexplicable direction of her thoughts and slammed right into Michael's stare.

She couldn't read the look in his hazel eyes, though she recognized its intensity, brighter and sharper than the warmth she associated with Michael. It seemed almost...what? A challenge?

"Oh, I beg your pardon." The seamstress bustled around Tris to remedy her mistake. Just before the curtain closed, Tris thought she saw Michael's lips form a smile. At least she thought it was a smile.

She puzzled over that expression for the long minutes of standing still while the seamstress adjusted the dress's soft lines that crossed the bodice to leave a deep V neck that flowed into the clinging skirt. Not that she felt any need to avoid considering her own reaction. But that had been such an odd look on Michael's face.

By the time the seamstress stepped back, declaring the dress would need only the slightest work to fit to perfec-

tion, she'd decided she'd read much too much into a simple look of surprise. He'd been startled; anybody would
have been.

"May I come see how it looks?" Bette asked from beyond the curtain.

"Of course. Come in." Tris executed a model's turn in
the cramped cubicle as Bette entered and the seamstress
exited. "You have great taste, Bette. It's wonderful."

"It looks terrific on you, Tris. I knew it would. I didn't
want bridesmaid-y dresses for you. But maybe I made a
mistake, having you and Judi wear such knockout
dresses," she said with a mock frown.

"Afraid you'll be eclipsed, huh?" Tris teased as she
started to ease out of the dress. A little reluctantly. It did
make her feel marvelous.

"Well, I *am* supposed to be the star." An impish grin
pushed aside Bette's frown. "That's why I won't let Grady
wear a blue shirt. I don't want to be outshone by one of the
groomsmen!"

Tris smiled back, but not with full attention. In fact she
hardly noticed the seamstress's return with her arms filled
with the white satin of a wedding dress. Bette's comment
reminded her of the question that had been pushed out of
her mind by that sudden revealing view of Michael.

"Bette, do you really think Grady's vain?"

Bette spared her a glance over her shoulder, then finished removing her slacks and shirt in preparation for trying on the gown. Despite being muffled by the dress easing
over her head with the seamstress's help, Bette's voice
sounded light, almost casual.

"Of course Grady's vain."

"But..." But what? *But vanity's a flaw?* Wouldn't she
sound like a ninny if she said that! As if she expected
Grady Roberts—or anyone else—to be without flaws.

"It's part of him, just as teasing's a part of Paul and reserve's a part of Michael. Sometimes the individual part can be irritating as heck, but on the whole they're great guys." Her voice mellowed and her eyes softened, and Tris knew she was thinking of one great guy in particular. "Wonderful guys."

"Reserve? You think Michael's reserved?" Now why had that characterization caught her so unaware?

Bette turned at the seamstress's request and met Tris's eyes in the mirror. "Mmm-hmm. All that calm good sense on the outside, and inside . . ."

Inside, what? Wasn't there more calm good sense? That was what she'd always expected of Michael.

"Sometimes Michael makes me think of a pot simmering on the stove," said Bette. "Nothing much showing on the outside, but under the cover all sorts of potent things churning around."

"Michael?" Tris gave a half laugh. "I think your prewedding imagination is getting the better of you, Bette."

"Maybe," Bette conceded mildly. "Maybe."

The word seemed to echo in Tris's head long after they'd left the tiny fitting room.

"Everybody ready?"

"No, wait. Where's Michael?"

Tris's question stopped Grady with his hand on the doorknob. They were all set to head out for the rest of the day in downtown Chicago, with stops planned at his office, Paul's office, Bette's office, a couple museums and as many favorite shops as they could pack in. But one member of their party was missing from the Monroes' front foyer.

"Did he go to his room after we got back from the fittings?" Paul's insistence that they all stay at the Monroes' house had filled every bedroom, with one person leftover. Aunt Nancy had resorted to assigning the room—not fancy, but boasting its own bathroom—over the detached garage that had been Paul's teenage lair. Paul had volunteered to take that room for the week, but Aunt Nancy had said she wanted somebody out there whom she could trust to be on time for the wedding, and that meant Michael.

"He's in the den, on the phone," supplied Judi. "Somebody called about ten minutes ago."

"I'll go get him," volunteered Tris.

The den's door was open. Michael, his hips propped against the edge of the desk, stared out the French doors toward the lake.

"No. No, you were right to call, Sharon." He shifted the receiver to his left hand, freeing his right hand to drive through his thick hair. Tris felt a tightening of her throat in a sudden rush of affection, as if the once familiar gesture were a friend rediscovered.

"I just wish to hell she had an ounce of ruthlessness in her," he said into the phone. Then he gave a low chuckle. "Yeah, I know, that's why she keeps me around."

Tris blinked at the idea of Michael as ruthless, even as part of her recognized that element in him. Before she could consider the contradiction, his next words caught her attention, bringing with them a swell of disappointment.

"Maybe I'll come back for a few days." After listening a moment, he spoke into the phone again, apparently intent on soothing his listener. "No, the situation's not worse than you thought, Sharon, and you were right to think I can probably handle it from here. It's just that coming back for a few days has its attractions."

The grimness in his voice seemed directed more at himself than at either the bad news he'd received or its bearer.

Just then, he turned his head and met Tris's eyes. She couldn't tell if he was listening to a voice at the other end of the line or if his caller was letting him consider his own words in silence. Tris had the sudden certainty that holding his look was very important, though she didn't know why.

"No." He spoke into the phone, but Tris thought he hadn't aimed the curt word at the caller, or even at her. Maybe only at himself. "I should stay."

He broke the look, and she let out a long breath, somehow relieved.

"Don't worry about it. I'll give it a shot at handling it from here. Yeah, I think so, too. No, I wouldn't want to miss all the fun here. And there are some things I need to accomplish." The very flatness of his voice seemed to give an edge to the words that Tris didn't understand. "Thanks, Sharon. I'll get back to you as soon as I know more."

He hung up the phone and looked at Tris, his legs stretched out, his palms resting on the edge of the desk to either side of him, only his head turned toward her.

"Work."

"So I heard. Problems?"

"Yeah." His short, sharp sigh had a caustic tinge. "Problems."

"Anything I can do to help?"

His eyebrows rose slightly, as if she would be the last person who could help, then he seemed to realize his surprise might not be too flattering and his face became more neutral. "No, but thanks."

"You were thinking about leaving?"

"Yes."

"But you think you can take care of it from here?" She wanted to come out and ask why he'd considered leaving if he didn't have to, but something in his stillness dissuaded her.

"Probably. But I won't know until I try." He half smiled at her. "Think the Monroes would mind me tying up their phone all day?"

"Oh, I think they'd survive. Nobody's going to be home anyway. Uncle James is at work, Aunt Nancy's going to a charity luncheon, and the rest of us are headed downtown."

He sighed again, this time with regret, she thought. "I can't go."

"I know. Maybe you could meet us for dinner?" She named a favorite Near North pizza restaurant.

"I'll try. But..."

"I know," she repeated. She knew all too well how problems at work could consume a day's hours or a night's sleep. She smiled and started to the door, then stopped and turned back. "Don't work too hard. And, Michael?" She waited until he looked at her. "If you can't handle it from here, promise not to leave without saying goodbye, okay?"

She didn't know why it seemed so important to wait for his soft "okay," but she didn't move until she had it.

Chapter Three

"I thought we were going to leave all the packages in the car." Grady grimaced as the sharp edge of a smallish box banged into his leg for the third time.

"Sorry." Tris shifted the bag to her other hand. They'd parked several blocks from the restaurant and the narrow sidewalks provided little room. "It's for Michael."

"All the more reason to leave it in the car." And away from my poor leg, his tone seemed to add. "He probably won't come up for air from that political stuff for days, so you could have waited to give it to him back at the Monroes. Unless he's already left."

Annoyance seeped into Tris. Michael wouldn't leave without saying goodbye; he'd promised. And he'd be at the restaurant if he could. And if he were there, she wanted him to have a piece of the day all the rest of them had spent together, to feel included, to know he'd been missed. But she wasn't about to say any of that to Grady, because he wouldn't understand. He wouldn't...

She stopped in midthought. She had just found Grady lacking. Grady Roberts. Gorgeous Grady.

She would have found that unthinkable twelve years ago. Now she had an irrational urge to giggle.

"There he is. There's Michael," Paul announced from just ahead of them.

Tris transferred the urge to giggle into a welcome as Michael met them at the short flight of steps that led to the half-basement restaurant. Exchanging greetings and questions, they effectively clogged the entrance. Noticing a couple trying to pass, Tris hooked her hand through Grady's arm and tugged, trying to clear the sidewalk at the same time she asked Michael if he'd solved the problems.

His grin evaporated. "This one. But there'll be others."

"What do you mean?" she asked, a little startled by his grimness.

"Joan's got one of the sharpest minds I've ever encountered, but sometimes she leads with her heart instead of her hard political head. That's where the problems come in."

Remembering he'd used that same phrase, *leading with her heart,* about her, she bridled at his tone. "That's also where compassion and caring come in."

"Compassion and caring don't do a whole lot of good if you don't have the wherewithal to implement them," he shot back.

"So it's better to forget your heart and just lead with your head? Until perpetuating your power becomes more important than using that power to accomplish something? Isn't that exactly the sort of end-justifies-the-means thinking that has earned politicians the rotten reputation they have now?''

''Hey, right now I want to lead with my stomach,'' interrupted Paul. ''C'mon, we'd better get our names in to get a booth.''

''I put my name in twenty minutes ago. It shouldn't be much longer,'' said Michael.

While the others thanked him heartily, Tris hung back. Had Michael really become the sort of man he'd just sounded? He'd always believed in founding goals on reality, but had the years solidified that into something more rigid, less caring, less...Michael?

Or was she being overly sensitive about this because she'd been burned by a politician doing what was politically expedient recently enough to have the unhealed scars to show for it?

The hostess announced their booth was ready, and led them single file through the long narrow restaurant. Tris slid in first, followed by Grady and Judi. Directly across a table not much more than a single board's width, Michael shared a bench with Bette and Paul.

''Ow! Tris, there's that damn bag again.''

''Sorry, Grady.'' She extracted the bag from between them, then hesitated. Uncertainty turned her voice abrupt when she pushed the bag across the table to Michael. ''Here, this is for you.''

He looked at the Marshall Field's bag, then back at her.

''Go on, open it, Michael. We want some, too.''

''Some?'' Amusement lit his eyes and echoed in his voice. Tris relaxed. This was Michael.

He slipped a hand inside the bag and slowly extracted a box, recognition dawning on his face before more than a corner came into view. ''Frango Mints!'' He smiled, and his dimple appeared high on his cheek.

"We were in Field's and I couldn't resist," Tris said, absurdly pleased by the appearance of that dimple.

"My favorite candy in the world."

"You going to open your favorite candy in the world, buddy, or are you just going to look at the box?"

"All right, all right, Monroe."

Michael leaned over to pass the box to Paul and, under the table, Tris felt his denim-clad shin through the sheer hosiery covering her legs. The sensation bolted through her like lightning. She couldn't move. Tingles seemed to run over the surface of her skin, prickling along her legs, arms and neck. Michael abruptly twisted away, and she couldn't be sure if he meant to tease Paul by pulling back the box or to break the contact with her.

If it was the latter, he failed.

In the cramped quarters under the table, his movement put his other leg between Tris's. Instinctively she tried to close her knees against the intrusion, succeeding only in tightening them around the denim invader that brushed against the soft skin above her knees.

For an instant not measurable by any clock, she had the strangest sensation that everything else receded, until her friends' conversation became distant echoes, their faces faded to pale shadows. As if she'd left behind the familiar world and stepped into one more vibrant, more intense. A world that centered on the contact between her legs and Michael's.

So fragile, though, was this world, that she couldn't even breathe. The prickling of her skin turned into something pulsing deep in her. She stared at Michael's free hand, which was clenched on the table in front of her, seeing the straining tendons of the wrist, noting the strength of the fingers, concentrating on the pale slashes of taut skin marking the knuckles.

Slowly, as the slashes turned whiter, she felt the withdrawal of his knee as a slow, gentle friction against her skin.

Her breath came out in a quick, uneven exhalation. Then as quickly as it had started, the feeling of unreality shattered to the sound of Paul's laughing voice.

"Hey, Dickinson, you going to let me have some more of those mints or not?"

"Sure." She heard Michael clear his throat, then start again. "Sure, everybody have some more."

She shook her head at the offer of the candy box, and at her own foolishness. Where had all those thoughts of a private, vibrant world come from? Craziness, absolute craziness.

Embarrassment, surely that had been the source of the strain she heard in his voice. And that had to be the source of the heat she felt burning her skin.

For the first time in what seemed hours, she looked at the man across the table. This was Michael, her friend. What had gotten into her? Over an innocent brushing of knees under a table, too. Nothing more. Absolutely nothing more.

She looked at him more fully and saw the old Michael warmth in eyes tinged with a ruefulness that could only be the result of their mutual embarrassment. She smiled at him, and felt the world kick back into place in time to realize Bette was directing a question at her.

"Is this the kind of place you save in your business, Tris?"

Tris considered the polished and mellow surfaces of the old wood and older brick.

"If we're lucky they look this good when we're done, but most are pretty decrepit when we start. You have to see beyond the deterioration to what the builders created and what you hope you can recreate."

"Like your place, right, Michael?" Judi leaned around Grady. "You should see it, Tris."

"Oh, yes, Paul's told me about your Victorian in Springfield, Michael."

"We all thought he was crazy to buy this dingy, ramshackle place, but he's turned it into something great."

"Yeah, after practically blackmailing his friends into weekends of slave labor," Paul told his cousin. "At least when you got that row house in Washington, you didn't expect us to help fix it up."

"Only because I couldn't get you to come out to D.C. Michael was just smarter than me, that's all. Sweat equity is definitely the way to go."

"Especially if it's somebody else's sweat." Paul reached into the candy box.

"Looks like you're taking it out in Frango Mints," said Bette.

"Damn right. You should have seen the things he had us doing. That's why I figured he couldn't refuse to be my best man, even though we all know Michael would prefer a three-week hiking tour of the Sahara to going to a wedding."

No movement betrayed him and they no longer were touching, yet Tris somehow felt Michael's withdrawal. An instinctive defense, she thought. And perhaps also indicative of surprise. They did know how Michael felt about weddings, and she had long ago guessed it stemmed from his parents' far from successful marital history, but it occurred to her that he'd certainly never volunteered anything on the subject. It was something they'd all seemed to tacitly understand, and avoid.

She wondered if Paul had broken the taboo on purpose. If so, he either changed his mind or had achieved what he'd been after because he shifted the conversation, and she sensed Michael relax. A glance around the table left her doubting that anyone else had even noticed.

"One time he left me holding up a wall all by myself. For hours. I thought I was going to choke to death on plaster dust."

Paul's account of the work on Michael's house started them on a laughter-filled conversation that lasted until the restaurant closed up around them.

As they slid one by one from the booth, Tris wondered if Michael took special care not to brush against her legs. It was almost impossible not to make contact, but they didn't. And she quickly dismissed the fragment of thought that tried to label her reaction as disappointment.

"This has been nice." Tris settled back against the passenger seat with a pleased sound.

"Driving on the tollway at rush hour is nice?" Wry disbelief threaded through Michael's question.

She chuckled, but stubbornly maintained, "Yes. It is. As much as I love everybody, it's been nice to get away for a while. To be alone."

"Alone?" She hadn't really hurt his feelings; she remembered his inflections well enough to know that. "If I'd known you wanted to be alone, I wouldn't have volunteered to drive all the way out to Elmhurst to double-check Bette's old house before the landlord inspects it. You could have done it all by yourself."

"Volunteer, nothing. You were drafted, because Aunt Nancy knows you're reliable and she didn't want Bette to worry about it while they were at the luncheon this afternoon. I'm the true volunteer." In fact, she'd surprised herself a bit by asking if she could go with him rather than attend the luncheon with the combined staffs of Paul's and Bette's offices. But as soon as the words were out, she'd known that was how she wanted to spend the afternoon.

Driving to Elmhurst, the conversation had been sporadic and easy. They'd stopped at a neighborhood deli, then eaten the juicy sandwiches at a dilapidated picnic table and watched people go by. Once at the house Bette had rented, they'd poked around companionably, double-checking the items on Bette's list—all of which were already done—but mostly trading home ownership stories and speculating on where and when Bette and Paul might find a house to meet their divergent specifications.

They'd puttered around so long that their return had landed them in the midst of a steamy summer evening rush hour. She didn't mind the slow going, though.

She'd enjoyed herself thoroughly. Not once did she have to stop and think before she spoke. Not once did she have to worry that her words might be misconstrued, or repeated inopportunely. Not once did she think about work.

Only Michael could do that for her.

"Reliable?" Michael's insulted tone brought her back to their conversation. "That's as bad as describing a prospective blind date as having a good personality."

She laughed at that, but she also surveyed the man next to her. He drove with an easy smoothness that belied the alert concentration she knew he gave the heavy traffic. Bette's assessment of him ran through her head: *All that calm good sense on the outside, and inside . . . all sorts of potent things churning around.*

"I think any woman who opened the door to you as a blind date would be thrilled, Michael Dickinson."

"Oh, yeah?" His asymmetrical mouth lifted into a grin that seemed to be directed at himself. It made him look very young.

"Oh, yeah."

And even though he changed the subject then, she knew her unpremeditated words had pleased him a little, and that pleased her. What didn't please her was the peculiarly unsettled feeling that lodged in her stomach at the image of another woman opening the door to Michael Dickinson.

"You're an early riser."

Tris turned and looked up at him. "Morning, Michael."

He almost hadn't seen her sitting on the end of the small deck over the water. He'd just returned from running and was headed toward his room over the garage when an early ray of morning sun caught a glint of gold in light hair, and he recognized Tris. Since one force behind his run had been the hope of clearing his mind, still fogged by dreams that stubbornly ran to blue eyes and long legs, it would have made more sense to slip up the stairs than to walk over to her. But what the hell, the run hadn't succeeded anyhow.

"I must still be on East Coast time," she continued. "I've been up before everybody in the house all week. If I'd known you were up, I would have come over to your room and bothered you."

Bothered was the right word, all right. Tris in a room dominated by a king-size bed, in the soft light of morning, wouldn't have done a thing to chase away either old ghosts or his recent, and unwelcomed, reaction to accidental touches such as brushing knees under a table. On the other hand, he hadn't escaped those by running through the quiet suburban streets, either.

"Why don't you sit down?"

"I'm sweaty. I need a shower."

She slanted a look up at him and invited again, "Aw, c'mon, sit down. I've had enough of my own company."

Against his better judgement, he sat on the edge of the deck, swinging his legs out over the water as she did. The sun had crested the horizon of Lake Michigan and was turning the surface into dazzling fragments. He couldn't seem to prevent his eyes from going to Tris, to see the effect of that clear, soft light on her. But something in her face and the way she was turning a small stone over and over in her hand caught him in a way he hadn't expected.

"What is it, Tris?"

"What do you mean?"

"It's not just a matter of early rising, is it? I thought yesterday there was something... There's something on your mind that got you up so early, isn't there?"

He saw her prepare to put him off with a denial, but then she sighed and gave a half smile. "I promised a friend at work—and myself—that I'd give it a rest for a week, but my subconscious doesn't want to cooperate. I wake up every morning with my mind going ninety miles an hour."

"What is it, Tris?"

"There's a project I've been trying to put together at work, taking historic buildings that might otherwise be razed and fixing them up as facilities for the homeless. Last spring, I saw a place in Cincinnati that's really making it work and I knew I had to try to create more. It's the most worthwhile thing I've ever been involved in, Michael. Do you know how many cities could use something like this? And how many have buildings that are going to waste? But there's a problem."

"Money."

She nodded. "As always."

Still turning the stone, she described how she'd campaigned for the backing of the preservation association she worked for and how she'd lined up funding for several prototype projects around the country, based on the one in Cincinnati. But a major backer had pulled out—"for political reasons," she said, with a pointed look at him—even after the first project had been started, leaving both the project and the association in the financial lurch.

Leading with her heart. He could see exactly why the project appealed to Tris, and how she could have rushed into it without adequate preparation. Going out on a limb, as surely as she had when she'd tried to get from Harris to University Hall all those years ago.

"If we don't come up with funding in the next year, it could mean a major retrenching for the association. There could be a lot of buildings destroyed because there's no money to fight for them. And it's my fault. I sold the association on getting involved."

"You were the only one?"

"No, not alone." She gave him another half smile as if she recognized and appreciated—but also dismissed—his attempt to make her see she wasn't solely responsible. "But I was the driving force. And some others expressed reservations, concerns about exactly what's happened. I thought they were being too cautious." She made a soft, scoffing sound at herself, then slung the stone into the lake. "You know the really frustrating thing? There are federal agencies that could help us fund this, but they can't decide exactly whose umbrella this falls under, so we're left standing out in the rain."

"That's a bitch, when other people can't see the value of what you're trying to accomplish because they're looking at their own narrow view. But I know you, Tris. When you believe in something you never give up." Not even the times when she probably should have, he added to himself. He'd hate to see her hurt by this.

"No, I won't give up."

Her matter-of-fact tone surprised him, but he had little chance to consider it as she turned and the startling blue of her eyes caught him once again. He jerked away from her look, staring out over the placid water toward the horizon. "Would you help, Michael? Paul tells me that with this campaign you've made good connections in D.C. I could use advice from someone with your political savvy. And if Joan wins, she'd be a great ally to have in the Senate. This is just the sort of project she's been campaigning on."

He knew that. It was what had drawn him to Joan in the first place five years ago and it was what frustrated him mightily as she fought for election. He was having enough trouble keeping her campaign geared to the pragmatists in the party without this sort of issue being introduced.

Two long-standing instincts warred within him—the instinct to help Tris Donlin and the instinct to keep Joan Bradon as far as possible from lost causes. Lost causes like the ones Tris Donlin invariably backed.

"We'd look at any official proposal you send us, but not until after the election," he said. That might have sounded too formal, too harsh. "I have a responsibility to Joan," he added, hoping to mitigate his first response. "Personally, I'll help you as much as I can. The thing is, you might want to consider compromising, backing off a little. If you looked at just saving the buildings first, then maybe down the road fixing them up for the homeless, that might be one way to safeguard the association's investment."

There, that was clear. A careful expression of a moderate position, treading between the extremes of his two instincts. He'd kept Joan out, but he'd offered to help her as her friend—even knowing her propensity for hopeless causes—and he'd added sound, practical advice.

Tris gave him a rather odd look. "I understand. Political issues." He felt a prickle of discomfort at the look and the flat tone, but then she added, "Maybe we should get back to the house," and she sounded nearly normal. His imagination must have been working overtime.

He walked along next to her, feeling more at ease than he had since he'd gotten Paul's letter. How many times during her freshman year had she come to him for talks like this? He'd done a pretty good job of helping her then and he'd do his best to help her now. He'd also done a good job back then of keeping his feelings under control; surely he could do as well now. The intervening years almost seemed to have slipped away. No, that wasn't exactly true, because he'd certainly changed with the years. He was stronger. Strong enough not to let feelings run away with him.

Still, the comfort with each other remained. He felt the mutual acceptance and affection, even in the silence.

Impulsively, he took her hand.

"Seven years... In some ways that's a long time, but in some ways it's hard to believe it's been seven years," she said, and he knew her mind had followed the same track. "After that one time you visited me in Washington, Paul told me several times that you had trips planned to D.C. for that law firm you started out with. But you never called me when you were in town. Why?"

The question rocked his tranquillity. How many telephone talks had they had since the times he'd been in and out of D.C. without contacting her? Fifteen? Twenty? She'd never asked then. Why now?

"You had a new life. It seemed like a good time to, uh, back off. I didn't want you to think I was checking up on you or anything." He could have said: You had a new husband, and I couldn't stand to see you unhappy with him. Or happy. He'd believed for years just what he'd told her—that he'd thought it was time to back off, let go of a college friendship. But his mental answer was the real one. He'd been fooling himself. All those years. At the realization, his hand clenched involuntarily before he consciously eased his hold.

She looked at him steadily for a moment.

"You didn't like Terrence, did you?"

Damn, that question cut a little too close to the bone. Well, the truth could be as good a camouflage as any.

"No."

"Why?"

Because he had you. "I didn't think he was good enough for you." He tried to keep the words bland. They were true, too. "I thought he leaned on you too much, used up your strength."

She laughed, a dry sound but not harsh. "You were right. That's exactly what happened. Too bad you didn't tell me all that before we married."

"You wouldn't have listened." She wouldn't have listened if he'd told her similar things about Grady twelve years ago, either.

Hearing Tris was getting married had jolted him back then. He *knew* she would always care for Grady, so how could she marry someone else? But one look at Terrence—tall and blond, handsome and charming—and Michael had recognized him as an obvious substitute. She might have been mixed up enough to marry Terrence, but in a way she'd still been loyal to Grady. "Nobody who thinks they're in love listens to advice or reason."

"So you figured the best you could do was stay away and not let me sense the disapproval," she said with conviction.

"That was some of it," he said. The part he'd admit.

"You're probably right, I probably wouldn't have listened at the time. I probably would have resented being told the truth before I saw it for myself. So, all around, you were your usual wise self, Michael Dickinson. And I think it's only fair now to tell you that you were totally right about Terrence."

For all the lightness in her voice, the words had the slightest edge and her eyes were solemn as she faced him.

She looked into the flecks of many colors in the depth of his hazel eyes, and wondered at her odd mix of feelings.

She recognized an element of irritation. He had said he knew her while she told him about the homeless shelters, and she'd always thought he did know her, in some ways better than anyone else. But then he'd talked to her as if she hadn't aged a day or learned a thing or suffered a hard knock since her freshman year in college. He'd actually suggested she safeguard ownership of the buildings, as if she hadn't done that immediately when the backer pulled out.

For heaven's sake, he acted as if she would hand him some pie-in-the-sky dream. Didn't he know she'd never risk something this important to anything less than a thorough, professional job? Couldn't he guess what even the severest critic of her proposal in the association had said—that the financial strain had happened despite her efforts, not because of them? He doubted her ability, her sense. Maybe he still looked at her as the Tris of all of those years ago. She couldn't stifle a pang of disappointment at that.

And he'd sounded so distant and unfeeling when he'd talked about being practical. His words had sounded more like that backer who'd found it suddenly expedient to pull out of his commitment, than the Michael she had known. She felt sadness at that.

But she also realized an overwhelming need to acknowledge that he had been right about her marriage and to make him understand why it had come apart. The urge was strong enough that she didn't stop to consider why it seemed important that Michael understand.

"I wanted a mate, a partner. He wanted someone to arrange all the practicalities of his life. Someday, for some woman, he may make a great husband, because he really is a basically decent human being. But it's going to have to be a woman willing to do a lot of the work. The kind of woman who has the patience to *enjoy* house-training puppies."

Michael chuckled, and rubbed his thumb across the back of her hand. Unexpectedly, warmth flooded her, swamping the disappointment and irritation. Warmth for his understanding and acceptance. She'd spent so long nourishing her crush on Grady in college that she hadn't seen clearly what a wonderful companion she'd had by her side. She'd come here thinking about showing Grady that she'd grown up; maybe she had another one to convince, too.

"He wasn't irresponsible," she said. "He just wasn't responsible. I couldn't count on him. He was charming and endearing. And utterly exhausting. I could never relax. That may be exciting at first, but after a while, it left me too weary to remember that first, wonderful feeling."

Without warning, an image of Grady Roberts flashed into her head. Grady and Terrence. They even resembled each other superficially, although underneath they were very different. No, *they* weren't alike, but what had been identical was her reaction to them, the same knee-knocking awe of them—so charming, so endearing, so handsome. For a college crush that was fine, but as a basis for marriage it stank.

Poor Terrence. She never should have married him. But barely out of college and caught in the whirlwind atmosphere of their brief courtship, she hadn't had the maturity to say no. She'd paid for that mistake with a lot of pain, but she'd also benefited from it. She'd grown up.

She felt as if she'd just seen her marriage through a window, long clouded but now clear. And there was more. Another window was clearing, another piece of her past would open. All she had to do was look and—

"The divorce must have been rough."

Michael's voice came low and gentle, but it made her blink. She felt as if she'd just cracked a code—the code to her own past. She not only saw past mistakes, she had a grasp on why she'd made them, and she could forgive herself for them. Everything, even the sensation that she'd just missed another insight, paled in the triumph of that. She beamed into Michael's puzzled eyes. "Yes. Hellish."

"You don't seem too broken up about it now," he said with a frown.

"Not anymore. I've grown up a whole lot since then. A whole lot."

"Yeah?" The note of doubt in his voice mixed with something else she couldn't identify as readily. Somehow she connected it with that look she'd seen in his eyes when they'd had their picture taken in front of the old library.

For an instant, she felt a heightened awareness of the sun warm on her face, the water lapping, the trills of the morning birds and the nearness of Michael. It beckoned her. Tempted her to step forward, nearer to some discovery.

"Yeah, so grown-up that I don't mind being a kid now," she said, stepping back from the edge. Not yet, a voice seemed to whisper deep in her mind. Not yet. "Race you back to the house—last one there has to wake up Paul and Grady."

She dashed across the morning-dew-cooled green lawn, trailing her own laugh behind her like a pleasant memory.

"Do you think four more sandwiches will be enough?"

"Aunt Nancy, I think you've already packed enough food for us to sail from here to Northern Michigan and back three times," Tris said, as she and Judi exchanged glances. Nancy Monroe had never allowed anybody to walk away hungry, and the prospect of her houseful of guests going sailing for the afternoon had spurred her to mammoth picnic activity.

"C'mon, Mom. They're waiting for us." Judi gestured toward the French doors to the patio, where Grady, Michael, Paul and Bette waited with towels and tote bags.

"Just let me finish wrapping these, and then I'll make some lemonade and put it in the big thermos."

"You already did that, Mom. And Michael took it outside with him, remember?"

"Oh, yes. Of course. Michael's so considerate. Some woman's going to be very lucky to snare him."

"Damn straight."

"Judi!"

"I was just agreeing with you, Mom. I'd take him in a second if I could ever get him to look at me as a woman. Though it's not his consideration I'd be after."

"Judi!"

Tris wanted to echo her aunt's admonition. Contemplating the frank admiration on her cousin's face as she looked out the door toward Michael and the others, Tris had the strangest sensation in her stomach, as if it had just dropped about three stories and she hadn't caught up yet.

"I'm just saying he's a hunk. Tris'll back me up, won't you, Tris? Don't you think he's a hunk?"

She looked at her cousin. "Hunk? Michael? Don't you think Grady...?"

"Grady?" Tris couldn't mistake the dismissive note in Judi's voice. "No. Michael's much more of a hunk. Those wonderful eyes. And the hair always a little messed up, and that smile. Definitely Michael."

"They're all three very attractive young men," said Aunt Nancy, with affection in her voice and face.

"I suppose," said her daughter, sounding unconvinced. "But Michael's the only one who makes me drool."

"Judith Marie!"

"All right, all right." Grinning, Judi soothed her outraged mother as she closed up one of the hampers and headed out, leaving the other for Tris to carry.

Tris looked out the doors to where Michael and Grady stood side by side. The sun brought out the golden glow of Grady's handsomeness. But she saw that it also showed off the thick shine in Michael's dark hair, outlined the strength of his facial structure and tucked shadows into those faint creases at the corners of his eyes. Michael. She found herself warming just at the sight of him.

"It's hard for Judi to see that her own brother might be attractive," said Aunt Nancy. "Or even Grady, since he's been around the house all her life. He's practically another big brother. I suppose it's natural under the circumstances for her to see Michael differently."

As she said goodbye and took the hamper, Tris wondered a little if there might be more to Judi's feelings than Aunt Nancy's explanation covered, but the thought disappeared as Michael came forward to take the hamper as she came out the door. She could understand Judi's view of Grady. She might even have a similar blind spot herself where Michael was concerned, seeing him more as a big brother than as a man.

He looked down at her as they headed for the car, his eyes seeming to hold a special glow of warmth. Hastily, she amended that thought: Maybe she'd *had* a similar blind spot.

Chapter Four

Michael turned his face into the wind and away from Grady and Tris laughing over a stubborn knot. He wished he had more to do. But once they'd gotten the boat launched from the community dock, Paul and Bette, with occasional help from Judi, had things well in hand. The soon-to-be-married couple worked well together, communicating with half sentences and sometimes just looks. The sort of communication he and Tris had always shared as friends, the sort that might be growing between Tris and Grady...not as friends.

Damn. Was this worth it? This could be a case where the cure ended up being worse than the affliction. What would be so terrible if he cut his losses and took off now?

He looked at his hands gripping the railing, the smooth wood biting into his skin from the pressure, but he didn't really see them. He saw a little boy in bed, with his father sitting on the edge and his mother at the doorway. No tears, no screaming, no scene. Just some phrases about things not working out, the echoing word *divorce* and then that expression about cutting losses. In the telescoped way of memories, he heard the expression again, and again, in other conversations, with even less emotion.

He'd been taught young and often the meaning of cutting your losses, and he'd sworn that would never be his way. He'd see this week through, and he'd cure himself of Tris Donlin for good. Forever.

"Hey, how about something to eat for your captain?"

Paul's shout gave Michael a reprieve from his thoughts.

"Why don't you go get it yourself and I'll take over at the wheel for a while?"

"Okay." Paul let go of the wheel as Michael took hold. "I guess it's safe enough. We've got a rare wind, so you won't need to do much tacking. Just remember, no right turns. No matter how tempting the sights."

Since they were sailing south, parallel to the shore, a right turn would have taken them into Oak Street Beach. Michael acknowledged the gibe with a grimace.

"I'll keep him on the straight and narrow," volunteered Judi. She ducked under his arm and came up in the small opening surrounded by his arms, his chest and the wheel. She twisted to give him a devilish, lash-fluttering look over her shoulder. "Best seat in the house."

He chuckled. They'd been playing this flirting game for as long as he could remember. He figured he'd been the first of Paul's friends to treat the then scrawny adolescent as something other than a kid sister, and a nuisance at that. She'd been honing her flirting skills on him ever since. He pitied the guys her own age.

"Are you commenting on the scenery or bragging, Judi Monroe?"

She leaned her back against his chest with a would-be sultry sigh. "I didn't think you'd ever notice, Michael darling." Then she giggled.

"Pretty good, kid. Except the giggle at the end rather ruins the mood."

"Rats. I thought I might finally have gotten your attention." This time her sigh was gusty. "Maybe I need a makeover—'Find the New You.' You know, like an image consultant. They have those guys in politics, don't they, Michael? You know anybody who specializes in sexy?"

"The old you is fine, Judi. And, no, I don't know anyone who specializes in sexy. They're usually more interested in creating illusions of things like reliability and integrity."

"That sounds despicable. Why are you involved in politics when it's like that?"

"Because not all politicians are like that, because some are trying to do good things." He thought of Joan. Then, unexpectedly, he thought of Tris's project. "But there are some hard, cold realities you have to deal with, too. It's part of being grown-up."

"Hey! Judi, come here and decipher Mom's handwriting. We can't figure out what's in which wrapping without taking them all apart."

Judi popped under his arm with a farewell grin, and left Michael alone with a few of his own realities. Like his lack of success as a ghost exorcist. Damn it, he *would* get over her.

"Want a sandwich?"

His hands tightened on the wheel at his private ghost appearing, very real, at his elbow.

"Thanks. I'm starving." He held the wheel steady with his hip before taking the sandwich from Tris and quickly consuming it.

"I'd have thought you'd ask Judi to bring you back something."

If she sounded testy, he barely noticed. Sun caught the lighter streaks in her hair and the breeze tossed it around to lick at her forehead and cheeks. A stab in his gut accompanied the errant desire to push back the hair and explore her face with licks of another kind. Disgusted with himself, his answer was curt as he stared straight ahead. "We were talking about other things."

"Oh, you weren't discussing mutual hunger?" Astounded, he turned to look at her. An angry glitter in her eyes and a pink in her cheeks beyond what the sun had put there proved that he hadn't imagined the edge in her tone.

"What are you talking about, Tris?" He knew the calm of his voice could be deceiving, and very useful in masking a lot of other emotions. He'd used it successfully many times in political settings. Never before had it been incendiary.

Eyes narrowed and hands balled into fists, Tris snapped, "Don't talk to me like I'm still seventeen years old or don't have eyes in my head."

He felt his calm facade slip, felt the anger that had simmered underneath all week surge closer to the surface. "I don't know what—"

"Don't you think Judi's just a little young for you? Taken to robbing the cradle these days, Michael?"

Anger spilled over the facade, swamping it and him. How dare she criticize him when she'd been practically falling all over Grady Roberts for four days—hell, more like twelve years! He'd had enough, more than enough. The hell with calm. The hell with being her friend, with being understanding, with being grown-up. The hell with Tris Donlin.

Wrapping one hand around her arm, he jerked her against him, so her slender body was wedged between the unyielding wheel and his own tense body. He lowered his head to glare into her eyes and snarl his words into her face.

"How about you, Tris? Isn't that what this whole week is about—trying to pretend you're still seventeen? Trying to live out your girlhood fantasies? It didn't work with your marriage, but—"

"My marriage?" The confusion in her eyes couldn't check the frustration—at her, at himself, at fate—that had accumulated over twelve years, piling up even when he'd thought he'd left it far behind.

"—now you can try it again with the real thing, can't you? Having any luck? Is he worth the wait? Or are you finding the reality less enthralling than the dream? Is that why you keep running to old pal Michael?"

She tried to push free of him, but he pressed her more tightly against the wheel. Somewhere inside, he was aware of a sharp, tearing pleasure even now at the feel of her body against his, the slender length of it a brand through clothes and skin and muscle, right down to the bone.

"No, not my old pal Michael. You're nothing like him. You're—"

What might have been a stifled sob cut off the rest of her speech. Automatically he eased back from her, and she wrenched her arm out of his grasp to push free of him. For an instant he thought she might slap him. He might have preferred that to the hurt he saw in her eyes before she turned on her heel.

The string of curses he muttered under his breath would have astonished most of the people who knew him. But not the one who came up next to him at the tail end of the self-directed tirade.

"About time to get things turned around, don't you think, Dickinson? How about letting me take the helm a while?"

Michael looked at Paul blankly a moment, then focused on the shoreline. They'd come farther than they'd planned. Without a word he handed the wheel over to Paul to maneuver the boat for the return trip. But he didn't move away. There wasn't much space on the boat, and Tris already had staked out the opposite end of the deck.

When Paul finished bringing the boat about, he looked at Michael. "I meant what I said about it being time to get things turned around."

"What do you mean?" Michael's hope that the other occupants of the boat might not have noticed his exchange with Tris ended with Paul's next words.

"You and Tris."

"You heard?"

"No. But I could see. That was enough. I hate to see it. You two were always so close."

Michael shrugged, the facade nearly in place again. "It happens. People grow apart. Friendships die."

Even friendships with people you thought had given you a permanent corner of their heart—a small, platonic corner, but given forever. Even that could change.

"Bull."

"You can't expect to come back to reunions like this and have everything the same." Lord knew he hadn't expected his feelings to still be the same. He didn't *want* them to be the same. He wanted to be perfectly happy with the friendship he and Tris had shared for so long. Now even that might be gone, maybe for good.

"Bull," Paul repeated without heat. "Not all people grow apart. Don't go judging everyone by your mother and father, Michael. I understood it when we were kids in school, but you know better now. There are plenty of people around who take a while to figure out exactly what's right for them, but that doesn't mean they necessarily jump from marriage to marriage.''

Perhaps he sensed Michael's stiffening because Paul's next words shifted the conversation's course. ''And it's bull that all you've ever wanted from Tris was friendship.''

In the silence that followed, Michael wondered a little at his own lack of surprise. Maybe some part of him had already suspected that Paul had known how he'd felt for Tris back in college. In some ways it was a relief to have it out, at least with one person.

''That obvious?'' He managed a wryness he didn't feel.

''Obvious? Yeah, you've been practically shouting it from the rooftops,'' Paul said with heavy sarcasm. ''So obvious that nobody else has even got a hint of it. That I— renowned for my acumen in such matters as everyone knows—wasn't really sure until...'' He hesitated, then added in a very different tone, ''Until Bette.''

Until he'd met Bette, and fallen in love himself—the message was clear. But Michael couldn't accept what it said about his feelings. He met Paul's eyes directly, and saw empathy and more than a hint of impatience.

''Dammit, Paul, whatever you saw—thought you saw— it's gone, if it ever existed at all. All that's left is putting the ghost to rest, once and for all.''

''You can't put to rest a ghost of something that's not dead.''

Michael shook his head, trying to free it of Paul's words and the stupid, crazy hope that the words bred. ''There's never been anything more than friendship between us, and now that's hurting.''

"Maybe there hasn't been anything more than friendship in the past, but maybe it's time that changed. Maybe friendship isn't right for the two of you."

"What do you mean?" He wasn't sure he wanted to know, but he'd asked the question, and he didn't have time to retract it before Paul was answering.

"You know another term for putting a ghost to rest?" He glanced over his shoulder to where Judi and Bette were heading for them and didn't wait for Michael to shake his head.

"Laying a ghost."

"Play ball!"

Tris added her perfunctory cheer to the roar of the Wrigley Field crowd. Blue sky, hot sun, cool breeze, bleacher seats with good friends and the Cubs on a winning streak. If that didn't make for a perfect afternoon at the ballpark, she didn't know what did.

So why did she feel as if she'd just been scheduled for an IRS audit?

She didn't have to search for that answer as she munched on hot dogs and chips and watched the batters come and go. It sat three seats away. Michael Dickinson.

They hadn't spoken two words to each other since their exchange on the boat. She kept waiting for something, some sign that he was sorry he'd said those terrible things to her. But all she saw was a hard, stubborn man she'd only had glimpses of before. She remembered his telephone conversation with his office and his reference to himself as ruthless. For the first time, that element of him was directed at her. She didn't like it.

At last night's cookout at the Monroes' they'd managed to stay at opposite ends of the patio. By accident or by design, the group had sorted out to form buffers between them at breakfast, in the drive to the ballpark and for sitting in the bleachers. She was relieved that her parents were arriving for the weekend and would be taking her out to dinner tonight. It would be good to get away from this oppressive atmosphere. No one had said anything, but it was clear that Bette, Judi and Paul sensed the strain between her and Michael. The silences were longer and the rush to fill them more noticeable, the laughter louder and the causes for it smaller than she could ever remember. The only one who seemed unaffected was Grady.

She turned to him with a rush of affectionate gratitude. Thank heavens for the sense of normalcy he provided.

But Grady's attention remained all on the game and, as he started rising from his seat, she became aware of the roar of the crowd and the surge to their feet of the people around them. A ball was headed in their direction. If it reached them it would be a home run, and put the Cubs ahead by three runs.

She came to her feet, caught in the game's excitement for the first time. She could see it! The ball was coming, a home run for sure. And it was coming right at them!

"I've got it! I've got it!"

"It's yours, Jason! Get it, Jason!"

She heard the passionate shouts of a young boy and his father in the row behind them and felt a tingle of goose bumps. This would be a memory the boy carried with him his entire life.

She half turned to watch the joy on the youngster's face as he reached up to cradle the ball in the glove he'd so hopefully toted to the game. But the ball didn't reach the glove. Inches away, a pair of long arms stretched up, and a bare hand snared the ball. Grady Roberts's.

"I got it! How 'bout that! Did you see that catch, Tris?"

"Grady! You took the ball away from that little boy. You can't do that!"

"I didn't take it away. I caught it. Whoever catches the ball and holds on to it gets to keep it, and I'm the one who caught it." He tossed a grin over his shoulder at the crest-fallen boy and his father. The father patted his son's arm, still holding out his glove, waiting for the ball that didn't come.

"He's right, son. The ball goes to whoever makes the catch."

"That's terrible! You're two feet taller than him! What's fair about that?"

"Aw, Tris.."

"Give it to the boy, Grady."

"What? You're kidding."

She shook her head. "I'm not kidding. Give it to the boy."

Grady tried a charming smile on her, but it faded as he seemed to read the determination in her face. Perhaps seeking reinforcements, he turned to the others. Bette and Judi wore identical reproachful stares. Michael's and Paul's expressions held a bit more sympathy—he who catches keeps *was* the rule of the bleachers, but...

"He's only a kid, Grady."

Grady didn't respond to Paul's words, but he did turn and place the ball into the boy's glove.

"Gee thanks, mister! You see that, Dad? I got the ball. Maybe I can get it autographed after the game. I nearly caught it myself, didn't I, Dad?"

"You did catch it," Tris told the boy, who was all grin and freckles. "You had your glove right on it."

The father beamed at his son, then spread a wide thanks to their entire group. They all smiled back as everyone settled in for what looked sure to be a Cubs victory.

Tris glanced at Grady from the corner of her eye. Even he had managed a smile for the boy, but now he sat a little slouched in his seat. He shouldn't have snatched the ball away from the boy in the first place. Maybe he had acted purely on instinct, but still...

I'm annoyed at him. The realization seeped into her. Annoyed at Grady Roberts. She couldn't remember ever being annoyed with Grady before, not in all the years she'd known him. Awed, infatuated, overwhelmed, but never annoyed.

The hero had fallen off his pedestal. No, not fallen. If there'd been a pedestal, she'd built it under him; he hadn't stepped up on it on his own. He'd always been the same Grady; it was her view that had changed.

She turned to stare at him. The breeze ruffled his hair attractively and the sun brought out its gold. Healthy color underlined the clean lines of his handsome face. None of that had changed. Yet she saw more. She saw a charming man, not perhaps totally grown-up. Used to having things, large and small, go his way in life. A good man. Yet enough the not-right man—for her—to irk her now and then. She wasn't even surprised. It was as if she'd finally articulated something she'd long known.

Grady Roberts was a major college crush that you've never had a chance to check against adult reality. Leslie Craig's words, spoken weeks ago, floated into Tris's mind, along with something she'd told her friend: *I'm long past my infatuation with Grady Roberts.*

Maybe she hadn't even realized then the truth of those words, but she did now. She'd needed this week—not to get over Grady, but to remind herself why her long-ago feelings had never developed beyond that college crush.

She thought of her feeling of anticlimax when Grady hugged her at the airport and of times the past several days when she'd avoided openings to tell him about the things that were most important to her. At one level she must have recognized this all along. It just took her conscious mind a while to catch up.

Down the row, she saw Michael lean forward in intense concentration on the game. She'd told Michael about her past and her present, about her home and her work, about the problems with the project and her fears. That was what it meant to be a true friend. And she knew she couldn't love someone she didn't share that kind of closeness with. She'd also told Michael about her marriage....

Her marriage... Something Michael had said about her marriage yesterday during that horrid exchange on the boat. What was it? Something that niggled at her, something that left the impression that he thought she'd married Terrence because he was like Grady.

But he wasn't. What had been alike was her reaction to them: infatuation. Heady stuff, but like mist burned off by the sun, unable to survive exposure to reality.

She'd been a fool—a young fool—to rush into marriage with Terrence before her feelings took the test of reality. But she'd never been fool enough to marry one man because he reminded her of another.

No matter what harsh words they'd exchanged, surely Michael Dickinson knew her too well to believe that.

She sat back and raised her face to the blue, blue sky above her. A single tear slid from the corner of her eye. Maybe it was for the touch of sadness at the final letting go of her long-ago hero. Or maybe it was the last farewell to the girl she'd once been. Or possibly it was for the pure joy of knowing that she was, truly, a grown-up woman named Tris Donlin.

But it might also have been for an estrangement from someone she suddenly wasn't sure she knew at all.

* * *

Tris clicked off the outside light Aunt Nancy had left burning for her, slipped off her heels and headed for the kitchen, where a single light glowed in the dark house. She wasn't surprised everybody was asleep. After a long, chatty dinner with her parents, she'd gone back to their hotel room for more talk—until her father's snoring informed mother and daughter that they'd talked well into the early-morning hours.

She eased open the refrigerator door in search of something cool to drink. They'd talked of many things, she and her parents. She'd caught them up on details of her life, too small for phone calls or letters, and filled them in on the activities this week. They remembered Michael and Grady from her college days and were interested in how the years had treated them. And of course they had family news to discuss—a tooth for her niece, a new job for her sister-in-law, a boat for her brother, a less-than-charming boyfriend for her sister, a health update on a longtime friend of the family.

About the only topics they hadn't touched on were a certain coolness in her relationship with Michael Dickinson and her recognition of her long-changed feelings for Grady Roberts. Her hand closed around a plastic jug of lemonade.

"'Bout time you got home."

Tris clutched the container to her chest like a shield and swung around with an inarticulate cry.

"Quiet! You'll wake up the whole house."

"Paul! You scared me to death." She put the lemonade down and placed a hand to her heart to check if it could possibly be beating as fast as if felt. It was. "What are you doing down here?"

"Waiting for you." He closed the refrigerator, then pulled two glasses from a cabinet. "I remembered how you always had to have something to drink before you went to bed, ever since you were a little kid, so I knew you'd come in here."

Recovered, she lifted her brows as she poured the lemonade. "Aw, how sweet. You were worried about your little cousin being out late at night—and with her own parents! Aren't you supposed to save that role for your little sister Judi?"

He snorted. "Hah! Worried? Even if it hadn't been with your parents I know better than to worry about you or Judi. Only thing I'd worry about with either one of you is the poor guy you'd set your sights on."

Tris felt her face tighten at the mental image of Judi, encircled by Michael's arms on the boat the day before, laughing up into his face. Had her young cousin set her sights there? "So if it wasn't worry, why did you stay up, Paul?"

He carried the glasses to the breakfast-room table and waited until they had both sat before answering. "I figured you could use somebody to do some listening."

"What do you mean? What gave you that idea?"

"Everybody needs somebody to listen to them, a sounding board. I know you've had other people for that before." He slanted a sharp look at her over the top of his glass as he drank, and she concentrated on keeping her face expressionless. They both knew he meant Michael. "But sometimes, for whatever—um—reason, you need somebody else, and it turns out I'm not half-bad at it. Bette's been working with me."

Tris softened at his pleased-with-himself grin. "That's a generous offer, Paul, but I don't have anything right now that I feel I need to talk about, or bounce against a sounding board.''

He made a noise resembling "Humph," but didn't argue. "We can just chat then. It's been a nice week, hasn't it?"

"A very nice week."

"Good to see the campus again, and hit some of our old haunts. Sure enjoyed that pizza the other night. And of course the sailing. There's nothing like being out on the lake." Tris thought she saw where this conversation was headed and tensed. Perhaps he sensed that, because Paul continued on. "Heck of a ball game this afternoon."

"Yes, it was," she said, willing to cooperate in steering the conversation away from sailing trips. "It's always great to see the Cubs winning."

"And to have a home run hit right to where we were sitting—that's pretty rare."

"Certainly is."

"And to have one of us actually catch it, boy, that's something."

"Yes."

"Hard even for a grown man to give up something like that."

"Yes."

"But the kid was awfully excited, wasn't he?"

"Yes, he was." Tris fought the urge to grin at him, and took a long swallow of lemonade.

"Probably made that kid's day. He'll be talking about the home run ball he caught at Wrigley Field for years."

"Yes."

"'Course, so will Grady." Paul chuckled. "Eventually he may even forget he didn't give the ball to the kid right away."

Tris smiled back at him. "Probably."

"Are you in love with him, Tris?" Her heart seemed to hold its breath. "With Grady?" he added, and her heart scurried to catch up with itself.

"No."

He exhaled long and deep before lifting his head to look her in the eyes. "I thought from the way you were acting this week that you'd seen things more clearly, but I was a little worried you'd gotten so used to agreeing to everything I said in this conversation that you'd just keep saying yes."

More curious than anything else, she tipped her head to study him. "You didn't want me to be in love with Grady? Why not? He's been your friend forever. He may not be perfect, but he's a good guy. And he's one of your dearest friends in the world."

"So's Michael."

"We're not talking about Michael." She didn't think she succeeded in keeping her voice completely steady. The conversation's unexpected shift made her feel as if one of her old buildings had collapsed on her, weighing her down, making breathing impossible.

"Aren't we?"

"Well, I'm not."

"Maybe you should be."

"That's crazy. Michael and I...I mean, our, uh... relationship has been..." Dammit! Why was she stumbling over these words? "Michael has always treated me exactly the way you and Grady treated me—like an overgrown younger sister. Only Michael's been a little more polite about it."

"Maybe that's how he acted."

She tried to ignore the emphasis he put on the final word, but her question wouldn't stay unspoken. "What does that mean?"

"It means how he acted and how he felt are not necessarily one and the same thing. I don't think I'm flattering myself to say I'm the only one who knows him well enough to see it, but let me tell you, little cousin, the way Michael Dickinson looks at you is not the way a man looks at an overgrown younger sister."

"No." But the whispered word didn't carry any weight of denial. Tris feared it was simple vanity, but something in her was thrilled. Still, she rallied enough sense to protest more strongly. "We don't even seem to be friends the past couple of days."

She would have ruined the cool effect of that statement if she'd let fall the tears that filled her eyes so unexpectedly at the reminder of her estrangement from Michael.

"You've been giving him a pretty hard time, you know."

"Me? I haven't done anything." Except a single comment about robbing the cradle.

"I know it's nosy as hell, but I figure a cousin's got a right to ask—besides, this is my wedding week, I should get to be nosy if I want to be." Tris gave a rather damp chuckle at his reasoning, but amusement quickly faded at his next words. "What did you guys fight about yesterday?"

"I wouldn't really call it a fight...." Paul gave an impatient grimace and she decided not to argue semantics. "It was silly really."

"What did you say?"

Tris considered telling him it was none of his business, but she'd never been very successful at holding out against a determined assault from her cousin Paul. This time, she didn't want to hold out. She told him. And when he asked what Michael had said, she told him that, too.

"Geez, you two take the cake. Here you are accusing him of making up to Judi when he's doing his damnedest not to want you, and he's accusing you of going after Grady when you've finally, totally recognized the fact that you don't want Grady Roberts!''

She stared into her nearly empty glass and tried for a light tone. ''That's presuming your crazy theory about Michael's feelings is right. I mean, he's never...'' She let it trail off, but her question was obvious.

''Told me? No, not in so many words. But I'm right. If you don't believe me—'' He broke off. When she raised her head to see why, he was staring at the window, whose dark surface reflected their images. ''I wish Bette were here,'' he muttered to himself. ''I probably shouldn't have told you any of this, but I have. So I might as well go all the way.''

He turned to face her, his face almost stern. ''Why don't you test it out? You women know all sorts of ways. See if I'm right about how he feels about you—but only if you want me to be right. You wouldn't be the person I think you are if you played around with the emotions of a man like Michael Dickinson. He's seen enough reasons in his lifetime not to believe in love, don't give him any more.''

''You really respect him, don't you? I always knew you liked him, but I never realized you admired him.''

''He's the man I want standing next to me at that altar day after tomorrow when I tell the whole damn world that Bette's mine and I'm hers.''

''I...I don't think I've ever heard you talk the same way about Grady.''

Paul shrugged. ''Grady's Grady. I love him like a brother, maybe better. He's been part of my life as long as I can remember. Sometimes I think that if he'd had a few hard knocks now and then, just enough to make him grow up a little...'' He shrugged again. ''But I don't expect him to be any different than he is.'' He stood up, stretching his back with his arms high over his head. "And if there were such a thing in a wedding as a best buddy, I'd have chosen Grady in a flash. But that wasn't what was called for. Think about that, little cousin. Think about what Michael Dickinson will be at my wedding."

The best man.

He dropped a hand on her shoulder and leaned over to say three more words before walking away. "Think about it."

Michael watched Tris flick off the kitchen light and shifted his position on the top step leading to his room over the garage. What could Paul have said to her that left her staring into space like that after he left the room? For that matter, what had they been saying to each other during that whole, intense conversation?

Not that it was any of his business. As long as he'd seen Tris return safe and sound, he could tell that badgering voice in the back of his head that wouldn't let him sleep exactly where to go. Maybe it would listen now. It sure wasn't the kind of voice to listen to reason. Not even when he'd pointed out that she was a grown woman, out with her parents, for heaven's sake, and that there had been nights, months, years when she could have been out all night long in Washington, D.C., and the badgering voice hadn't known a thing about it. Logic made no dent.

The voice had lowered a decibel or two when he'd pulled on a pair of sweatpants and come out to the steps where he could see the back of the house. But it hadn't quieted totally until he'd seen the kitchen light go on and saw Tris head to the refrigerator. There'd been that heartbeat-suspended instant when a man's form appeared, but he'd started breathing again and walked back up the steps he couldn't remember descending when he recognized Paul.

Now, pondering that long conversation between cousins, he wondered if his relief at the sight of Paul had been misguided.

Paul Monroe could be a dangerous man. He seemed so easygoing and uncomplicated on the outside, but he noticed things. And he knew things about Michael Dickinson that no one else did. Like how he felt about the fact that his mother and father totaled seven marriages between them. Like how he felt about Tris Donlin.

Michael drove his right hand through his hair. This week wasn't going the way he'd planned, not at all. He'd thought he'd simply see a friend. Instead, he'd discovered that the ghost of a long-ago emotion not only continued to haunt him, but seemed to be as vital and alive as ever. Maybe more so.

Only now he and Tris weren't even friends. And Paul was dropping crazy ideas in his head about forgetting being friends with Tris, forgetting driving other thoughts of her out of his mind. About the heated possibilities that whispered in his blood when he felt her arm around his chest, the touch of her breath on his ear, the rub of her leg on his.

He rose quickly from the step, as if to escape such thoughts. And closed the door firmly behind him, as if to close out the influence of Paul Monroe. Crazy. And dangerous.

Chapter Five

"And they say women are always late," Bette grumbled, shifting from one foot to the other in the Monroes' front hall. Tris gave her a sympathetic look. The day before the wedding, the bride was entitled to a jittery moment or two, especially with a groom like Paul. After last night's conversation she'd been feeling a little jittery herself. Even after deciding, as morning's light seeped into her bedroom, that ignoring his preposterous theory was the only possibility.

Paul had insisted on adding one last activity to the week's agenda, a volleyball game with their group plus longtime friends who'd arrived for the wedding and local friends. He said, with some logic, that he and Bette wouldn't have enough time to visit with everybody as much as they'd want to at the reception, and with the rehearsal dinner tonight, this was the only opportunity. Aunt Nancy had refused to have the impromptu party in her backyard the day before the wedding, so the word had gone out to meet at a nearby park.

But now Tris, Bette and Judi stood in the front hall waiting for the three men to make an appearance.

"Grady said he wanted to take a nap, Michael said something about taking a shower after he'd been out running and Paul was muttering something about his lucky ball when he disappeared into the attic," Judi offered.

"Oh, no." Dismay sounded in Bette's groan. "I promised Paul there'd be no set schedule all week, but today— We'll never get there, and that means I'll never get him to come home, and then we won't have time to get ready for the rehearsal and if we don't have a rehearsal they probably won't let us get married tomorrow. Not to mention that we'll be late for the rehearsal dinner at the country club and they'll throw out Paul's parents after thirty-two years of membership."

"No way, Bette. And no matter what happens, you know Paul won't let you get out of this wedding." Tris's teasing brought a vaguely dreamy look to Bette's eyes for a moment before it seemed to spur her to action.

"I tell you what, each of us should go corral one of them. I'll lure Paul out of the attic if I have to tie him up and drag him. Judi, why don't you—"

"Go find Grady, and I'll get Michael," filled in Tris. She didn't like the prospect of sending Judi off to Michael's private room over the garage. But she might have spoken with too much emphasis, because the other two women looked at her with surprise.

"Okay, We'll meet back here as quickly as possible."

At the steps to Michael's room, Tris hesitated.

They still hadn't healed over the harsh words they'd spoken on the sailboat Wednesday. The odd thing was that in all the years of their friendship, they'd never had a fight before. Neither seemed to know how to proceed now. She resolutely ignored the whispered memory of Paul's suggestion on that score.

She'd started this week looking forward to recapturing the old days with one significant difference—Grady Roberts's view of her as a kid. She hadn't expected so many other changes. She saw Grady, and even Paul differently now, probably saw them more accurately and certainly felt closer to them. That was all to the good. But the break in her relationship with Michael...there wasn't anything good about that.

She wanted to be friends again. *Friends.* That was all.

She straightened her shoulders and marched up the steps, knocking loudly on the door.

"C'mon in. The door's open." The words were muffled, but decipherable.

She pushed open the door and stepped into the room, which was dominated by a king-size bed and had windows looking toward the deck and the water. Once inside, she could hear the shower running. She swallowed nervously as she realized he hadn't closed the bathroom door all the way. All she could see at the moment was steam billowing out, but when that cleared...

The water was turned off. "Who's there?"

"It's Tris. Bette sent me to hurry you up." Only a slight revision of history.

"Okay. You can tell her I'll be there in a minute."

With the water off, the steam started to dissipate, and through the half-open door she could make out movement reflected in the fogged mirror. Something that looked like broad shoulders and a tanned back. She remembered how she had felt the heat and hardness of that back when they posed on the library steps. She'd told herself at the time that she was aware only of the feel of his chest under her arm, but her body had been attuned to the way that position had brought her breasts up against his back. She'd tried to ignore the tightening, filling sensation she'd experienced, but the memory was stronger than her will. Even now she felt the hardness against her softness, felt the tenderness, the . . .

Abruptly she pivoted away, bumping into the counter of the tiny kitchenette before making her way to stand by the love seat, looking out the windows.

His words and tone had given her the option to leave him to follow on his own. But she had a chance to try to mend the break in their friendship. She wanted to take it. She would take it.

"Michael." The word came out through her tight throat as a mutter.

"Tris? Are you still there?"

"Yes." Silence filled the room, as palpable as the moist air. "I . . . I, um, wanted to talk to you. I'm sorry, Michael. About what I said on the boat. I shouldn't have said that. I don't know what got into me. I know you'd never do anything to hurt Judi." She felt a small stab at her conscience; she was fairly sure the possibility of his hurting Judi hadn't been the sole cause of her words. She heard the bathroom door open wider and thought Michael stepped into the room, but she didn't look around.

"I'm really sorry, Michael. And I hate this awful coldness between us. I feel . . . I don't know— Lost?" She swallowed at the burning in her throat and tested out a wry smile on the glass in front of her. It wobbled. "I'm used to thinking we'd always be friends."

She knew Michael had come up behind her before he touched her shoulder. "I'm sorry, too. I was out of line, way out of line, saying those things. I hope we can forgive and forget this whole thing, because I haven't much enjoyed the past few days either."

"Oh, Michael, me either." She turned to face him and stopped. He stood in front of her, the same Michael she'd known, trusted and counted on for all these years, yet somehow different. His hair, usually so unruly, was slicked down by the shower's water, taming it, molding it to his head and revealing more of his bone structure, showing more of its strength. Showing the skeleton of a strong and fine man.

Her gaze slipped lower and she saw he wore no shirt, just a pair of cutoffs that hung low on his slim hips. The water had curled and darkened the hair that marked a path down his chest. She remembered the dressing room curtain pulling back and her mental tracing of that path. All she'd have to do now would be to raise her hand to span the six inches that separated them. Just to touch him. Just to know the feel of him.

She never knew if she'd actually started the movement when he turned away and went to the dresser. She thought he yanked a drawer open with unnecessary force, but she couldn't be sure. Expelling the breath she'd been holding without giving way to a sigh—would it have been shaky or wistful?—took all her concentration. Because his back was to her, she couldn't read his expression, but his voice sounded calm and even.

"Well, I'm glad that's taken care of. Now we can play on the same team without my having to worry about being spiked from behind by my own teammate."

Count on Michael to say the right thing to put her at ease. She appreciated that . . . but at the moment it also irritated her. But why? Because she wanted to be kissed, not put at ease. Why hadn't he kissed her?

She became aware of his eyes on her. Dismissing her disturbing thoughts, she chuckled at the memory. "If we're talking about forgiveness, isn't it about time you forgave me for that? It was an accident, you know."

"Forgiveness was no problem," he said, pulling on his second sock and reaching in a drawer for a shirt. "But forgetting's something else. I had a bump on my head for weeks. It's human nature to remember attacks from behind like that."

His last words were muffled as he pulled a T-shirt over his head. She ignored what might have been a twinge of disappointment at that covering of the smooth muscles and planes of his back.

"It wasn't an attack. It was a great shot gone astray. If the ball hadn't—" She broke off as he turned and she caught sight of the tattered lettering on the front of his shirt: *Phantoms*. And then she laughed. "Michael, I can't believe you still have that shirt! You're even more sentimental than Paul."

He grinned that little boy grin at her, tinged with self-directed amusement. "It's really starting to fall apart, but I can't bring myself to throw it away."

"How about using it for rags?" She lifted one brow at the holes that had worn through where the letters attached to the T-shirt's thinned fabric. "It looks like it's halfway there anyhow, and that way you could still have a piece of it around. So to speak."

"That's sacrilege, even suggesting such a thing."

She moved closer and caught glimpses of tanned chest through the holes. "I guess it is." Maybe she wanted to touch him so badly because touching the shirt would be like touching a beloved piece of her past. Maybe.

Had she been so blind to Michael? Was she just now discovering what Bette and Judi had seen long before her? Had friendship blinded her?

Almost absently, she smoothed her fingers across the surface of the shirt and absorbed the sensation of warmth and hardness beneath it. Dipping inside one of the larger holes, she reveled in the texture of a dusting of hair over firm skin. She could feel his heart beating strong and hard and the lift and fall of his breathing, faster now than only an instant before.

She could smell the soap and the water on him, and wondered, if she put her lips to one of those holes would his skin taste of soap? Soap was supposed to taste terrible, so why did the idea of discovering the flavor melded of soap and Michael send a zing through her blood?

Because she wanted to be kissed.

By Michael.

Now.

"Tris." Michael's voice sounded deeper than usual. Almost a rumble. Low enough and soft enough to easily pretend she hadn't heard. Even when he spoke a second time.

"Tris. Don't."

She ignored him until he wrapped his fingers around hers, stilling her hand.

"Don't what, Michael?" She heard the words, but had no recognition of having said them. Her mind, like her gaze, still rested on the tantalizing view through those holes. She wanted the shirt gone.

"Don't touch me like that, Tris."

The roughness in his voice drew her eyes up at last. There was that same look she'd seen outside the library when they posed for the picture. A tautness. A sharpness. And, yes, a hunger. Almost as if...as if—the thought stunned her, but she couldn't help completing it—almost as if he wanted her.

Without warning, he dropped her hand and spun away, pretending he needed to devote all his attention to piling a towel and spare pair of socks into a tote bag.

Astonishment swallowed her. Michael Dickinson desired her. The rough need in his voice was for her. *Her.* But that didn't shock her nearly as much as her own reaction. A bit of relief that he'd backed away, more than a bit of disappointment, plenty of confusion... and triumph so strong she was dizzy with it.

When Paul had suggested Michael cared for her as more than a friend, had felt that way since they'd all come together twelve years ago, she'd tried to tell herself she wasn't thrilled by the idea. But she couldn't deny this reaction.

The question was, what had caused it?

Was she so shallow that she would glory in such a conquest? So vain that the idea of a man wanting her that way appealed to her? So cruel that a wonderful, caring man being hurt, even inadvertently, didn't bother her?

"All ready. Let's go." He turned to her with a neutral expression, and she allowed him to usher her out the door and down the stairs, pretending nothing had happened.

Maybe nothing had. Maybe Paul was out of his mind, and maybe she was becoming the kind of woman who read more into a look from an old friend than was there. But, good Lord, how she wanted it—all of it—to be there.

"Uh, Tris. How about swapping spots so you're playing in front of me?"

"You're not going to start that again, are you?"

Hands on hips, she glared at him, but he read the humor in the depths of her eyes.

He'd been trying to coax that look from her ever since his reaction to her touch had produced a cloud of awkwardness between them. He'd seen the puzzlement in her face, probably wondering why he'd made such a big deal out of a friendly, affectionate touch. And he'd felt her withdrawal as she must have realized that to him it had other implications. Well, at least now she seemed to have returned to their usual easy camaraderie, even if he hadn't. But he would. Dammit, he would.

"It's all for the good of the team," he said, guiding her into position in the row closest to the net. "You're a much better digger than I am."

She eyed him with mock suspicion. "No ulterior motive?"

"Certainly not. It's just from this position you can get those drop shots and set them up for me." He gestured across the net to where Grady, on the opposing team, was poised to serve. "You better get ready."

Tris gave him one more searching look. If he'd been fooling himself he might have been able to pretend it had more meaning than the little game of words they were playing. "All right, I'll be the digger so you can feed your male ego by being the spiking star," she grumbled. She turned toward the net as Grady made contact with the ball.

"Plus, this way you can't hit me in the back," Michael said just as the ball skimmed the net, the words low enough that only Tris could hear.

"You rat!" she hissed back, but her eyes didn't leave the ball, which their teammate in the far corner returned rather weakly.

"A mere matter of self-preservation."

Across the net, Grady leaped to meet the floating return and drove down the ball at a fearsome angle, destined to land right at Tris's feet.

She crouched low, getting her locked hands under the ball, preparing for the perfect setup. Michael couldn't deny a rush of pleasure at their teamwork as he moved in to turn her set into a winning spike. Nor could he help a more basic pleasure at the sight of her rounded bottom, stretching smooth the fabric of her shorts as she rose, sending the ball high and easy for his shot.

Already going up to spike the ball, he was amazed when he felt his balance thrown off by an unexpected impact with Tris. She'd been clearly out of his path. The only way they could have collided . . .

He twisted his body in midair to compensate and still make the hit, sending the ball across the net with less force but a devastating spin, but he couldn't save himself from falling to the ground, hitting hard on his side, then rolling to his back.

The only way they could have collided was if Tris had deliberately knocked into him.

"So much for self-preservation." He heard the devilment in her voice even before he looked up into her mocking expression, and concluded that he hadn't lost his mind. Tris had deliberately thrown her hip into him.

Curling to a sitting position, he heard a squeal from the other side of the net, and saw that his shot had left the other team in disarray. Grady was on the ground, with his arm firmly around the waist of one of his teammates, the dark-haired woman named Melody, a longtime friend of Bette's and the other bridesmaid. Neither Grady nor Melody seemed in much of a hurry to get disentangled as they exchanged accusations about the missed shot and their fall.

He looked up quickly to see what Tris's reaction would be, but she was laughing and holding out her hand to help him up. Maybe she hadn't seen— No, he saw her eyes flick to the pair still on the ground, the laughter never dimming, and come back to him. Almost as if she didn't care.

No. Of course she cared, of course it bothered her that Grady was showing another woman such attention. She had to care because if she didn't still care for Grady—

He grasped her hand hard and pulled himself up, the abruptness of his move propelling him a step too far, so he brushed against her, feeling the smooth, long line of her leg against his, the curve of her hip just below his. Immediately, he let go of her hand. He saw the slight questioning in her eyes as she unobtrusively flexed the fingers he'd just crushed in his own. He ignored it.

"C'mon. Let's get this game going. Our serve."

Concentration on the game kept other thoughts at bay until it came his turn to rotate out and sit on the sidelines, trying to watch the other players. Paul, Grady, Bette, Judi. Paul's longtime secretary, Jan, and her husband, Ed, taking turns chasing nearly ambulatory Ed, Jr. Bette's high-school friend Melody. Former neighbors, a smattering of relatives. All the people who'd gathered to share this wedding with Paul and Bette.

He hardly saw them. Watching just one player, really, kept him fully occupied. That and trying his damnedest to ignore the voice from so deep inside him that it could barely be heard, asking exactly how to label his reaction to the idea that Tris didn't still care for Grady.

The momentary elation was understandable, but had that been fear mixed in? Fear? No, it couldn't be. Why fear? It wasn't fear. What could he be afraid of? Nothing. Absolutely nothing.

If Tris didn't still care for Grady... Then maybe what Paul had said wasn't so crazy after all. Then maybe what he'd seen in Tris's eyes this afternoon really had been dawning desire. But... but if Tris didn't still care for Grady, how could she be the Tris he'd always known? The Tris whose heart was steady, constant? So unlike his family.

He shook his head, trying to clear the questions. It was all moot, because Tris *did* care for Grady, had always cared for Grady. He repeated the words to himself with the emphasis of a curse.

He watched her laugh at Paul's ungainly lunge for a ball, then lavishly praise him when he managed to connect with it.

"C'mon, team!" he shouted. "How about winning a point, so I can get back in there?"

"Why do you think we're losing all these points, Dickinson?" Tris shot back. "We want to keep you on the sidelines where you can't do any damage."

Damage. If he'd done damage to their friendship these past few days, he'd repair it. If these past few days had done damage to his belief that he could treat Tris as strictly a friend, he'd repair that, too.

By God, he would.

Michael had expected that he'd be escorting Judi, as maid of honor, at the various formal functions of the weekend. But with everyone getting ready to leave for the rehearsal, Nancy Monroe came up to him with a preoccupied smile and said she'd decided to go against form. She wanted Tris and him riding herd on Paul for the next twenty-four hours.

"Paul will be less likely to get one of his wild ideas with Tris around than with his little sister. You don't mind, do you, Michael?" she asked with a smile. "After all, you see Judi all the time. This way you and Tris can catch up on old times more. That will be nice for both of you."

Nice. If he were a cynic, he'd believe that being paired off with Tris for the wedding activities constituted one of fate's nasty jokes. "Of course, Mrs. M. No problem." No problem, just a bit of torture.

His gaze slid to Tris as Nancy Monroe explained to the group who would be driving with whom. That dress she was wearing... At first look he'd thought it conservative enough, with its nonplunging V neck between staid lapels. It didn't cling, although the way it slid over her curves certainly indicated that what was underneath was worth clinging to. But the color was another matter. A distinctive deep peach. It had him thinking of lush, ripe peaches and the sweet coolness of their flesh, and that had him thinking of other lush, ripe, sweet flesh and that had him thinking...

"All right, everybody ready? Shall we go to the cars now?"

"Gentlemen, start your engines!" Judi intoned.

Michael was congratulating himself on disciplining his errant thoughts into hibernation as they started out to the cars. Then he got a closer look at Tris's dress. Good Lord, the thing had only one button. One pearly, white button. He'd been opening buttons since he was three years old. How easy... No, there had to be more holding it together than that. He felt sweat slide down the center of his back and film his forehead as he held the car door for Tris, ignoring her slightly puzzled look.

Tris slid into the car gracefully. He couldn't have looked away from the deepening V at her neck and the rising slit over her leg at that moment if it had meant guaranteeing Joan the election. Something hot pooled in his throat so he had to swallow an extra time, but the reasoning part of his mind insisted the dress had to have undercover fastenings of some sort or a lot more would have been revealed than a few inches of sleek thigh and a hint of a shadow that

might or might not have been the curve of a breast.
Though that was more than enough for him in this state.

Driving to the church gave him an excuse for silence
while Paul, Bette and Tris chatted, and that gave him a
chance to deliver to himself a stern lecture. By the time
he'd listened to instructions on the next day's preliminaries and escorted Paul, Grady and the other groomsman,
Bette's married brother, Ron, to the front of the church to
practice the actual ceremony, he figured he'd reasoned his
hormones into submission.

It was understandable. When they'd been in college,
he'd kept a constant alert against thinking of Tris in those
terms. In the years apart his willpower had gotten out of
shape, and the strain of this week was showing. Especially
since this afternoon. Since hearing Tris's voice, not quite
steady, apologizing and saying she wanted to be friends
again. Since watching the sunlight through the window
gilding her.

When she'd turned, he'd seen that look in her eyes. It
resembled what, in another woman, he would have recognized as desire. But he knew that couldn't be. Because
Tris wanted—would always want—Grady. Because con-
stancy was a part of her he'd always valued.

So it couldn't have been desire that had had her finger-
tips sending heat to his skin through the tattered shirt. It
could only have been his reading something into it. He
would keep his body firmly in check if he had to devote
every spare minute to exhausting runs or numbing show-
ers.

He focused his attention to where Bette's friend Melody was practicing her role as the first bridesmaid in the
procession. Then Tris started down the aisle, and he knew
what aching was all about.

Chapter Six

Tris walked slowly down the aisle toward him. The evening sun sent its last rays through the stained glass, igniting shimmering colors that surrounded her but could not dim her light. Michael felt stunned, immobilized. Tris was walking down a church aisle, and for a moment, senseless but undeniable, he let himself believe she was coming to meet him.

Near enough now to read her expression, he watched her exchange a quick grin with Grady before shifting to a smile as she looked at Paul. Then her eyes met his and he wasn't ready for the jolt that hit him. He couldn't bear to look at her, but didn't have the strength to look away. Only when he saw the uncertain quiver of her lips did he realize what his eyes might reveal.

He jerked his head away, staring unfocused toward the back of the church where he was vaguely aware of Judi starting down the aisle.

Sanity hinged on his ability to count his breaths, making each a little steadier than the previous one, and letting nothing else into his mind. By the time Bette had joined them and they all faced the minister to listen to the plans for the ceremony, he had his lungs under control. But that was about it.

He tried to concentrate on the details of his duties for the next day. But he'd had too much experience at doing that with one level of his mind while another level wrestled different issues. Like how to get through the next forty-eight hours.

Bette and Paul led the way back up the aisle. He turned to offer his arm to Judi as they followed.

"There, that wasn't so bad, was it?" Judi grinned at him.

No, not so bad. Just hell. But at least he'd been disciplined enough not to look at Tris again.

"Seems pretty straightforward," he said. Very straightforward. As long as he didn't see, hear, touch or smell Tris Donlin.

"Yeah, Bette and Paul wanted to keep it simple. I like it. Someday..."

Absently, he patted Judi's hand where it rested on his arm. As they reached the back of the church, Paul looked up from whispering something into Bette's ear and cocked a grin at him.

"Hey, Dickinson, I know you're not crazy about weddings, but you could look a little more cheerful, you know."

Michael longed to tell him in no uncertain terms to shut up, but with the Monroes and Whartons gathered around he had to make do with a glare and a muttered, "It was hot."

"Oh. Oh, dear. Did you think so, Michael?" Mrs. Wharton looked toward the front of the church with concern. "Maybe I should talk to Reverend Siles about turning up the air conditioning tomorrow. We don't want people to be uncomfortable."

Guiltily, Michael listened to Bette and Nancy Monroe calm the fears he'd raised. He could practically feel Paul's unholy amusement at the scene. With some sense of urgency, he used the excuse of bringing the car around to escape. He used his chauffeur role as an excuse again when they arrived at the country club for the dinner, dropping off Paul, Bette and Tris, and saying he'd be in after parking the car.

Instead, he slipped past the room they'd reserved to a quiet patio bordered by garden and overlooking the lush green golf course. Michael pulled in a lungful of twilight air heavy with the scent of just-watered grass and a day's worth of summer warmth. In a minute or two he'd join the others for dinner and then dancing, but for right now he needed a little solitude and a megadose of equilibrium.

You don't mind, do you, Michael? After all, you see Judi all the time. This way you and Tris can catch up on old times more. That will be nice for both of you. This time Nancy Monroe's innocent words had an inflection of unintended irony.

Right. Mind? No, he didn't mind. Why should he? Spend time with her, watch over her, see her walking down a church aisle toward him . . .

"Michael?"

The soft voice accompanied a light touch on his sleeve, but he froze instantly.

Tris jumped at his abrupt reaction. "Michael, are you all right?"

"Fine. I'm fine."

"I...I, uh, thought I saw you come out this way and...and I thought I'd make sure you were all right."

"All right? Why wouldn't I be all right? I said I'm fine, didn't I? So I'm fine."

He turned to face her with pugnacious indignation, but looking into her eyes was a mistake. Dammit, she looked as if he'd just told her that he personally had blown up a historic building in each of the fifty states plus Puerto Rico and Guam.

"All right, Michael. I'm sorry to have bothered you." Her voice trembled at the edges.

Aw, hell.

"Tris." He stopped her retreat with a touch on her arm, then couldn't resist sliding his hand down the soft material, trying not to think of what the skin underneath might feel like. "I'm the one who's sorry. You were being nice to a friend and I was a jerk."

A hint of her smile flickered across her lips as she studied him, looking for signs, he knew, that he might really be ill. In a way he supposed he was, and she'd just been treated to a symptom—overwhelming irritability. Right now he was irritated at himself and fate, at the squeak of a door farther down the patio and the sound of a giggle.

"We seem to be apologizing to each other a lot these days."

"Yeah. We do."

He felt it then, almost as if she'd spoken the question aloud. She might not even be aware of it herself, but she was beginning to wonder about the odd eruptions over the past few days in a relationship that had been placid for so long. Her probing gaze skimmed over his face. He had to stop her; he couldn't afford to have the full force of Tris's perception trained on him. She could see too damn much.

Without much hope, he looked around for a reason to leave her. There had to be some excuse, some explanation she'd accept. Then, over her shoulder, he caught sight of Grady. At the far end of the patio, Grady was in a deep and obviously romantic conversation with a dark-haired woman. Melody. The other bridesmaid. She'd been at the volleyball game this afternoon, too. He should have recognized the signs then, he'd certainly seen them often enough during college—Grady was in the throes of one of his intense flirtations. He reassessed his priorities. Tris came first. The best thing old buddy Michael could do for Tris now was keep her occupied.

"Just a couple of cranky old-timers, that's us," he said with a fair assumption of wry humor. "Guess the job pressures get to both of us."

"I guess so," she agreed, but he heard her doubt.

"I really am sorry, Tris. And I promise to be on good behavior tonight and tomorrow. No more moods. I swear."

He held up his right hand in a botched Boy Scout salute.

She chuckled. "Promise accepted, as long as it includes dancing every dance tonight."

"Every dance?" he groaned.

"Well, maybe not every dance." He thought she'd truly relented until he caught an echo of something in her voice, part mischief, but another element not so easily identified. "You can skip some of the fast ones. But you have to dance all the slow ones with me."

"All . . . all the slow ones with you?"

"I thought, uh, I thought that would be a way to prove for sure that we were—are back to, uh, normal."

Color streaked into her cheeks and her eyes slid away from him. He wanted to kick himself, hard. His awkward reaction had made her think he'd rejected her—how was that for irony?

Even if she hadn't seen them together just now, Tris had probably picked up the vibes between Grady and Melody. That was why she had asked him to dance with her. At least dancing with him would prevent her having to sit and watch Grady.

He felt a strange mixture of relief and disappointment. Disappointment, he understood. He was disappointed for Tris's sake, that Grady still hadn't woken up to what—or who—was right in front of him. And maybe, yes, just a little disappointed for himself now that he realized why she had asked him to dance. But why relief? Quickly, he pushed the question aside as he turned back to her.

"You're right. We should dance every dance, Tris. We have a lot of years to make up for, right?" He put a hand to her hair, stopping somewhere between the fond ruffling he'd intended and the soft caress he wanted.

She gave him a look with a question in it, but answered firmly, "Right."

He was going to die. Right here on the dance floor, from the unadulterated pain of not allowing himself to take too much pleasure in the much too pleasurable sensation of holding Tris in his arms.

Remember what this is all about, Dickinson. A friend needed a partner, that's all. A friend who might feel a little fragile emotionally right now because the guy she'd adored for years had another woman snuggled up to him as the band played another song about falling in love forever.

Almost as if she'd read the word *snuggled* in his thoughts, Tris slid closer to him. Another inch and a half and there'd be no air between them at all, just his suit and her dress. That dress with its one button.

He backed away a safer inch. He had enough trouble convincing his body not to make its demands all too clear. Not that an inch would do much good. Maybe a plunge into Lake Michigan. His willpower was just out of practice, wasn't that what he'd said to himself? Out of practice, hell. More like dead and buried.

The band slid effortlessly from one ballad to another. Damn! How much more of this could he take? Involuntarily, he tightened his hold on Tris's hand. She looked up, her expression half smile and half question.

"It's another slow dance," she said.

"So it is."

"There've been a lot."

Lord, what got into him, reading satisfaction into her voice? "Yeah."

"Can somebody cut in, or is this a private party?"

Michael turned around to meet Judi's glinting look of mischief and an identical expression on the face of her dance partner, Paul.

"How about a partner swap, you guys? I haven't gotten to dance with my cousin all night. Seems somebody's been monopolizing her."

Fighting a perverse instinct to tell Paul to go to hell, Michael swung Tris into Paul's arms as Paul twirled Judi into his. He'd just been wondering how much more he could take, so why did he feel bereft? His eyes followed the progress of Tris's peach dress, and he watched her laugh up at Paul. Part of his mind knew that Judi had said something to him, but the words didn't register.

"What?"

Judi's dramatically gusty sigh finally pierced his fog. "I said," she stated with pained emphasis, "that it's pretty rotten of you to make me feel like a wallflower even when I'm actually on the dance floor dancing with you."

He cocked an apologetic grin at her. "Sorry. I guess my mind was wandering."

"Yeah, I could see that." She shot a sideways glance to her cousin and brother. "Guess I'll have to wait until tomorrow to hone my flirting skills."

"What do you mean?"

"I've danced with my father, Mr. Wharton, Bette's married brother, my two uncles and my brother. That's a pretty boring lineup, you know. If you take away the guys who are married or a relative of mine or both, the only ones left here tonight are you and Grady. And you both seem thoroughly preoccupied elsewhere."

She gave another gusty sigh as Michael considered for the first time how onlookers might interpret his dancing so much with Tris. He'd been too busy quashing his own reactions to consider anybody else's. He hoped nobody said anything to her. If she became self-conscious about what people might be thinking she'd stop dancing with him. That would be better, of course, but all he could think of at this moment were the ways it would be worse.

But he also felt a small stab of guilt for ignoring Judi. "Maybe the reason I've been preoccupied is because Grady's so preoccupied."

"Huh? That doesn't make . . ." Her words trailed off as she looked from him to Tris to Grady, at the moment slipping out the terrace door with an arm around Melody. She raised one speculative brow as her gaze lingered on the door that closed behind them, then swung to Tris and finally back to him.

"You mean, you think Tris is hung up on Grady, so she's consoling herself with you?"

Damn, she didn't have to be that blunt about it. He used the movement of the dance as an excuse to duck her searching look. Evasion, however, didn't do any good.

"No." She shook her head emphatically. "I don't think that's the reason."

To his everlasting gratitude, the band wrapped up the song with a flourish. He stepped away from Judi—and her probing look—to applaud. That was how he caught sight of Paul passing the keyboard player a bill, just before he escorted Tris back to where Michael and Judi stood.

"Here's your partner back, Michael. Boy, I sure hope I didn't take up the last of the slow dances."

Michael looked from Paul to the band. "Somehow I don't think you have anything to worry about on that score." As if on cue, the first strains of a slow, dreamy number started.

Paul's eyes glinted with suppressed laughter. "It looks like all your slow dances are taken, Tris, but next time there's a fast one you really ought to dance with my dad. I bet if anybody could convince him to try something more than a waltz, it would be you. C'mon, Judi, I'm going to deliver you back to Dad and track down my bride for a little prewedding slow dancing." Paul's tone was airy, but Michael noticed his friend didn't risk meeting his look.

Michael could feel Tris's eyes on him, and now he was the one avoiding eye contact.

"They are playing an awful lot of slow dances. And Paul's probably right that I should dance with Uncle James, and...and maybe some of the others. Like Mr. Wharton and my dad. So if you don't want—"

"Guess it's the wedding atmosphere."

He took her into his arms nearly as abruptly as he'd interrupted her. She'd been about to give him an out, an excuse to stop this acutely painful pleasure. But, dammit, he couldn't let her, not when she sounded so hesitant, so vulnerable.

"I'm not sure what you mean."

He shrugged, the resulting movement of her hand on his shoulder almost feeling like a caress.

"Everybody's thinking about Paul and Bette, and getting married, so it's natural to come up with songs about love." Just as it was natural to think about the way she fit into his arms, the way her hair tickled his cheek, the way her dress swung just wide enough to flirt with his legs.

"Like subliminal advertising?"

"That's right."

Silently, they danced. He altered their path to avoid another couple and their bodies momentarily brushed along their lengths. Immediately, he restored the distance between them, but he knew it was too late. He felt the curve of her breast and hip as if it had been imprinted on his skin, and his body tightened in response. Staring over Tris's head he mentally repeated every lecture he'd given himself earlier.

Sure she'd paid attention to him at dinner and sure she'd danced with him. But he understood. He'd seen the way Grady had been turning the blaze of his charm on Melody. Nobody in the room could miss it. It had to hurt Tris.

A wave of protectiveness swept into him. That was nothing new. What bothered him was the undertow of possessiveness.

For a moment of intensified pain and pleasure, he strengthened his hand on her back, pulling her to him so her breasts pressed against his chest and her hips nestled near where he most needed them. With the song winding down, she moved deeper into his arms as if she belonged there, and for a heartbeat he accepted the feeling of having her body against his, tight and warm.

The band's last note echoed into conversations around them.

"Michael?"

He looked into her uplifted face and he knew he'd kiss her if this went on any longer. He wouldn't be stopped by the people around them, or even by the shock he'd feel on her lips.

"Maybe we should get some fresh air," she said.

"Air?" He knew he should be able to figure out what she'd said, but suddenly breathing had become a complex maneuver. Thinking was out of the question.

"Michael, do you want to go out on the terrace for a little while?"

"The terrace?" The terrace? Some instinct for self-preservation kicked in and his mind started operating again. Alone, in the balmy dark of a summer evening with the sensation of holding her in his arms like this too new even to be called a memory—that would be suicide. He'd take his chances on the dance floor.

He dropped his arms from around her and backed away. "No. No, I think we should stay inside. Or we might miss one of our dances."

What was going on?

Tris stood in the darkened kitchen, drinking a glass of water and trying to figure it out.

She'd told herself over and over in the twenty-four hours since her talk with Paul that he'd gone crazy to think Michael Dickinson had the kind of feelings for her that had nothing to do with buddies. *He's seen enough reasons in his lifetime not to believe in love, don't give him any more.* Love? Crazy. Obviously, crazy.

After all, look at the way Michael had reacted this afternoon when she'd simply brushed her fingers against his chest. Absently, she rubbed the tip of those fingers against the texture of her dress as if that would ease the remembered tingling in them. For just a moment, she'd thought she'd seen that, that *look* on Michael's face. But she must have been mistaken because if it had been there, he wouldn't have told her to stop. Would he?

It didn't make sense.

But neither did she. She had decided, absolutely, that Paul was crazy and she was nuts, and that look on Michael's face had been anything but desire. Absolutely, positively decided it . . . and then she'd heard herself suggesting they dance every slow dance together. No, not suggesting—finagling him into it. Granted she hadn't expected there to be quite so many slow dances. Or for it to feel quite so right to be in Michael's arms.

She gave her head a small shake and took a drink of water, as if to cool the direction of her thoughts. Be honest about this, Tris. At least with yourself.

She had felt something in Michael's arms. Attraction. There, she'd said it—at least mentally. She was attracted to Michael Dickinson. Not as a friend is attracted to a friend, but as a woman is attracted to a man. Very attracted to a man.

And she'd thought now and again during the evening, during those long series of intoxicatingly slow dances, that maybe Paul wasn't quite so crazy. That maybe Michael did want her. She'd sensed him reacting to her, physically anyway.

At least she thought she'd sensed that. But maybe it had been wishful thinking, because he'd taken none of the openings she'd offered. Despite her subtle signs that she wouldn't object to being held closer as they danced, he'd only tightened his arms that once, and then immediately backed off. He'd refused her not-so-subtle suggestion that they go out on the terrace as if it had been an invitation to streak the U.S. Senate.

She'd even tried one last time. When the party back at the house was breaking up and everyone heading home or to bed, she'd asked if he'd like to take a walk. Instead, he'd jumped on Aunt Nancy's preparing to call a cab for a guest who needed a ride as if it were a lifeline, insisting on driving the man back to his hotel.

What if he knew what was on her mind and was trying to avoid having to tell her he wasn't interested? She should have felt embarrassment at the notion, but her reaction was much darker and deeper than that.

But if he wasn't interested, what had that look this afternoon been? And that expression on the library steps? And for that matter, the response she'd detected when their legs had touched under the table at the pizza restaurant?

Oh, hell. The whole thing probably existed only in her imagination, spurred on by Paul's misguided desire to see everyone as in love as he was. Sure, that must be the answer. Just a bad case of wedding fever.

So why was she standing here in the dark waiting for Michael's return?

A car came to a stop outside, then she heard the quiet replace the sound of the engine. A car door thunked closed. She set her glass on the counter and pushed away.

From the French doors between the kitchen and breakfast room she watched Michael's moonlit shadow cross the lawn toward the room over the garage. At the bottom of the stairs, he hesitated. She saw him shrug out of his suit jacket and hook it over the railing, then follow that quickly with what must have been his tie. Without looking back at the house, he pivoted away and headed for the deck.

After a quick glance around to confirm no one else remained downstairs, she stepped out of her shoes and unhooked her stockings, sliding them down her legs one at a time and leaving them with her shoes on a chair seat. Quietly she slipped out the door.

Chapter Seven

Moist and cool, the grass curled around her feet as each silent step carried her closer to the water. The light seemed brighter here, away from the shadows of the house and intensified by the calm water's reflection. Propped up by his right shoulder, Michael leaned against the supporting post of the deck's arbor, staring out across the silver and black lake.

All in all, a most casual pose. But Tris didn't believe he was as relaxed as he looked. She hoped not, anyhow.

She thought she'd reached him without making a sound, but when she softly said his name from just behind him, he didn't start or show surprise. She thought the line of his shoulders did tense some before he shifted a little toward her, but she could have imagined that.

"Tris." Something about the way he said the single syllable set her heart racing. "I thought you'd be asleep by now. It's going to be a long day tomorrow. You should get some rest."

"You too."

"I will. I thought I could do with some fresh air first."

"Me too."

Stalemate. He didn't alter the posture that shut her out, and she wasn't about to walk away as he seemed to hope.

"Michael."

She took another step around him until his shoulder no longer formed a barrier between them, until she could see his face better. It told her nothing.

"Yes."

She longed for daylight, floodlights, any light to let her see the secrets of his heart. What if Paul was wrong? What if she was wrong? What if...

"I..." I, what? I wonder if you feel the change in our relationship the way I do? I wonder if you want it as much as I do? I wonder if you wonder how my lips on yours would feel? "I enjoyed dancing with you tonight."

His gaze met hers a beat longer, then flicked away, over her shoulder. "I enjoyed it, too."

His voice was too impossibly flat. It couldn't be that flat if he felt nothing; only if he were trying to suppress what he felt.

"Michael..."

She waited until he looked at her again. Her heart banged against her ribs with the deliberate, spaced reverberations of a bronze gong being sounded. She gently touched his cheek, finding the slight indentation of that high, wild dimple. Her throat suddenly felt dry and tight. Trying to swallow down the uncertainty, she slid her tongue across her lips, not aware of the movement until she saw his eyes follow it.

"Tris, this isn't..."

She didn't want to hear what it wasn't. She wanted to discover what it was. She shaped her palm to his face as she stretched up to bring her mouth to his. Almost chastely, her lips touched his. Warm and firm. Not perfectly molded; she reveled in this imperfection, testing it with feathering contact along his lips. She'd always recognized that his asymmetrical mouth was part of the charm of his little-boy grin. Now she discovered it contributed to another charm, one that had nothing to do with being a little boy.

A ragged breath whispered through his parted lips. And she knew that her guesses hadn't been wishful thinking.

He *did* feel the change in their relationship. He did want it. He did wonder how her lips would feel on his. Really feel on his.

"Michael."

She tipped her head and brought their mouths fully together. For that moment she reached to him, the muscles of her calves bunched as she stood on tiptoe to keep sliding her lips along his, while he stood straight and stiff. This was right, she knew it. She wanted to laugh with the rightness of it. And cry.

Michael. All these years. Michael. Her friend, her confidant. Reliable, familiar, understanding. And now exotic, strange, unknown. She marveled at it all, at the same time a voice deep inside her, as old as woman, whispered, Of course...of course... This was how it was always meant to be, the voice seemed to say.

And then she no longer reached alone. His hands cradled her face. His lips met hers fully, with heat and demand. He bent to her until her heels could have come back to the ground...if she'd been satisfied to only accept. But she wasn't.

She curled her arms around his neck to bring him closer, then drove one hand into the thick hair that swallowed her questing fingers. It felt like coming home, only home was suddenly grander and more thrilling than she'd ever known. She felt the light demand of his tongue and parted her lips for him with a soft sound that seemed to spawn a groan from deep in his throat. The first touch of his tongue to hers tightened the need growing deep in her body.

He changed the angle of the kiss, deepening it, plunging his tongue into her mouth. Her hands tightened their hold on him as she arched under the weight of his desire. When he lifted his head she gasped for breath, though she hadn't been aware of not breathing until that moment.

He muttered something dark sounding. She didn't understand what or why, but the instinct to soothe him led her hand around to caress his cheek, touching that high dimple again before her fingers trailed down to the line of his jaw, then the length of his neck until encountering the stiffened collar of his shirt. With no thought, her fingers found the V of skin left bare by two open buttons and followed it to the barrier of another, unopened button. Nimbly she disposed of that button, another and started on another.

"Tris."

His voice sounded hoarse, as if it grated his throat to speak. She found it fascinating. She bent to touch her lips to the base of the throat making that amazing sound, and felt the jolt go through him.

"Tris—"

Whatever protests he might have been about to make, he cut off himself by hauling her close and taking her mouth again. This time she didn't wait for any demand from his tongue, but met it with her own, exploring, teasing, tempting.

She felt his fingers weaving through her hair to bring her closer. Then, as if satisfied that she wouldn't pull away from him if he loosened his hold on her face, he cupped her cheek with one palm, then slowly glided it down the side of her throat, echoing the path her fingers had taken on him. Meeting the collar of her dress, his descent paused, and she thought she might go mad. She pressed a slight demand against his mouth and felt his response. His hand slid under the material, following its diagonal path until it met the hindrance of the snaps at the point of the neckline's V. A small hindrance they proved as they popped open under his touch. His palm moved lower, its pressure and its warmth branding her through the silk of her camisole. He lifted his mouth from hers but only to press against the sensitive skin where her throat and shoulder met. She felt his fingers' slight fumbling at the button at her waist as if the tickling of nerves that she felt inside had a mirror outside.

And then the dress opened. She felt the material swing loose, felt the night-cool breeze touch her skin through the silk that still covered her, and felt the heat and stillness of Michael against her. It was the tense stillness of waiting, a holding of breath in preparation.

She didn't understand it, and she had no patience for it. She didn't want to wait, she didn't want to hold her breath. She wanted him. She curved her arm around his waist, finding an opening where his shirt had come untucked, and tunneling her hand under the material until she could feel the smooth hardness of his skin, until she could press him to her, until she could burrow closer to the heat of his body.

Again, he muttered. This time she didn't even try to make out the words. She didn't care, because he was twisting, shifting his body to brace himself against the arbor support and drawing her between his slightly spread legs, where she had greater contact with his enfolding warmth and full proof that he did, indeed, desire her.

"Michael." She whispered his name for the pleasure of saying it, but also with a bit of wistfulness. So much time she'd wasted. So much time when she hadn't been right here, like this, with Michael.

She felt the change in him even before his grip on her shoulders set her firmly on her own feet, establishing several inches of clearance between their bodies.

His breathing came ragged and harsh, and his fingers were tight on her. She couldn't read his face, not sure if it was because of the wavering light or his determination that she not see inside him. What had happened to their great communication?

"Michael?" Uncertainty and a little bit of fear came through in her question. She could hear it and she knew he had, too, when he wrapped his arms around her and pulled her against his shoulder, as if protecting her from something, or consoling her. But how could she need consoling when she could hear the strong pulsing of his heart against her cheek and smell the clean, musky scent of his skin?

He set her away again and started straightening and refastening her dress as if she were a child. But she could see the taut, strained lines of his face and knew he had reacted to her as a woman.

"Look, I know this has been a long day. Rough, and long." His voice sounded gruff, not like Michael's usual smooth voice, but somehow endearing. He took her hand and started back toward the house. Stunned by what had happened, what she'd wanted to happen and what hadn't happened, she followed.

"Don't let this bother you. It happened, it's okay. Nothing... I understand. All the emotions this week... Grady... I understand. It's all right."

Grady? For a long moment she couldn't think of who he meant. It took a few deep breaths for her to adjust to the idea that anyone existed in the universe beyond the two of them. What did Grady have to do with the two of them, with Tris and Michael?

He opened the French doors and urged her inside with a hand at the small of her back.

"Lock the door behind you and don't worry about this. Tomorrow it'll be like this never happened. It was just... just something that happened. Tomorrow it'll be like it's always been. We'll be best buddies, and you'll feel... you'll..." She absorbed one look from him, as brief and charged as a bolt of lightning, then he was shutting the door between them. "Good night, Tris."

Mechanically, she retrieved her shoes and stockings and headed upstairs to prepare for bed. But not for sleep. Not with her body still thrumming, not with her mind in turmoil.

Everything like it was? How could it be? How could she possibly want it to be? She'd wanted to know about the change in their relationship, and now she did. It had gone from seersucker to satin, from beer to brandy. How could it ever go back? How could she ever forget these new sensations and tastes of Michael that were now inextricably mixed with the old, familiar ones? Was that what he wanted? To pretend it never happened? Did he regret kissing her? Touching her? Very nearly loving her?

Grady. She sat up in bed. He thought she hadn't gotten over her infatuation with Grady!

That must be it. But why would he think that? Maybe she'd needed this reunion to put the final cap on her realization, but in fact that infatuation had ended long ago, and she'd have thought Michael, who'd always known her so well, would have guessed that. But even if he hadn't before, he must see that she'd spent hardly any time with Grady the past few days. She'd been too busy discovering this new feeling for Michael. And Grady... A vague image of Grady and Melody came into her head. Grady had been too busy, too. Just as had happened so often in college.

She could have used a cartoonist right then and there to draw the light bulb over her head. Of course! Michael was confusing this all with twelve years ago. Acting as if she'd be hurt and vulnerable because Grady had been flirting with someone else. As if she'd turned to him for solace, and then things had gotten a little out of hand.

She smiled a little, indulgently. Misguided as he was, in a way it was rather sweet. Like when her father had brought her a doll from a business trip years after she'd left dolls behind.

The smile faded. The doll from her father she had accepted with a hug, then quietly tucked away. She wasn't prepared to be as passive where Michael was concerned.

She could tell him, but actions spoke louder than words. So what she had to do was show him, oh so clearly, that a certain onetime buddy was the one and only man on her mind.

This time when Michael came back from his morning run, the figure on the deck watching the sun rise wasn't Tris, but Paul.

"Nerves?" He'd left his tone neutral enough that Paul could take it as teasing or a serious question—whichever he needed and wanted to answer.

"No." Paul smiled, slow and wide. "Eagerness, I guess. And amazement. And wondering what took me so damned long."

Michael chuckled. "Don't be so hard on yourself. You'd only known each other for a few months when you proposed."

Paul dismissed that with a shrug. "I knew almost right away, though. Was just too damned stubborn to admit it. And afraid."

"Afraid?" Michael echoed the word automatically, at the same time it triggered the memory of sitting watching the volleyball game and a mental voice asking him why he was afraid.

"Yeah, afraid. Just like you are now."

"Me?" His laugh had the right scoffing note. "I don't have anything to be afraid of."

"No?" Paul appeared unmoved by either laugh or words. "How about what's going on with you and Tris?"

"Nothing's going on with Tris."

"Because you're afraid to let it."

"Because Tris is who she always has been and—"

"Is she?" The challenge crackled in Paul's question. "Or do you just need to think she is?"

"What does that mean?"

"Think about it. Think about it, and think about Tris, and think about what you might be feeling if this were your wedding day."

He'd never had greater cause to hate a wedding. The day before had indeed been a mere rehearsal for today's agony. It would have been that way even without Paul's words, but they did their part. That was all he needed, to think about what it would be like to be marrying Tris....

He'd started with his resistance worn down in the first place. Lack of sleep could do that to a man. And who could sleep for the images tormenting him all night? Images of Tris with her hair wild from his hands, her lips swollen from his mouth, her body shimmering from his caresses. Remembered sensations and tastes and smells of Tris.

Memories he hadn't been able to run away from. Memories he couldn't afford.

He muttered a curse and caught a startled look from Bette, seated next to him at the head table.

"What did you say, Michael?"

"Nothing. It was nothing, Bette."

He was just grateful Paul, seated on the chair beyond Bette, hadn't heard, and grateful that etiquette had seated Melody rather than Tris on his other side.

He caught a significant look from Nancy Monroe and realized the waiters were moving among the tables, pouring champagne. Nearly time for the toast, another of his duties.

So far he'd fulfilled every one of his responsibilities with outward calm—he hoped. He'd shepherded Paul to the church on time and double-checked the rings, then stood in his proper place with Paul as the music began.

He'd been fine until he let his eyes follow Tris coming down that aisle again today. Even knowing what to expect, the impact had rocked him. *If this were your wedding day...* He figured the only thing that had saved him was pulling his gaze away just as hers came to his face.

Still, they were several minutes into the ceremony before he recovered his equilibrium. And not many minutes more before he realized his mind had wandered from the solemn, joyful words making Bette and Paul husband and wife to the question of whether it would be harder—or easier!—to get Tris out of the swirls of blue that covered her today than that peach dress from last night.

He swallowed hard and heard a ringing in his ears, then discovered he was the one making the noise, tapping his knife against the water goblet in front of him. Others took up the sound and soon the room hushed and all eyes followed him as he rose, champagne glass in hand.

He looked at Bette and Paul, smiling at each other, and he spoke the words in his heart about friendship and love, and the rare kind of people who made both last forever.

His mistake was letting his eyes meet Tris's over the rim of his glass as he raised it to the new couple. Tears shimmered in her eyes like sunlight on a clear blue lake. But that was only the surface, and there was so much more, so much deeper in her eyes. Promises of the kind of friendship and love he'd just described. The kind he'd longed for.

"Are you all right?"

He sat in the chair, without any memory of how he'd escaped the hold of Tris's gaze or of sitting down. But Bette was the only one looking at him, so apparently he'd accomplished it without any fuss.

"Fine. I'm fine." He saw concern in Bette's eyes, and concentrated on convincing her it had no cause. "Honest."

"Good, because I'd hate for our best man not to have a good time, especially after that lovely toast." She slid one hand over his. "It really was lovely, Michael. Thank you." She leaned forward to kiss him on the cheek.

"You're welcome, but I only said what I felt, Bette."

As he watched Paul lead Bette into the first waltz, he tried to pull together the shreds of his resolve with a a stern lecture. He could practically repeat it by rote now. Although the version he'd used during the ceremony had added a pithy commentary on inappropriate thoughts in church.

And that was before he'd seen what that look could do to Tris's eyes. His resistance was going—fast. Good Lord, how much could a man take?

"Michael?" Tris stood next to his chair, a tentative smile flirting with lips that didn't look entirely steady. "Will you dance with me? I don't expect all the dances today, but I'd like the first one with you."

No. No, Tris, I can't dance with you because holding you in my arms makes me forget friendship and remember kisses by the night-dark water. Because looking at you makes me think about watching blue material flow around you as I strip that dress away. Because your fingers on my shoulder make me think of your hand pressing fire into my skin.

Lord, how could he tell her those truths? She needed him as a friend today. Today and all days.

She might be confused right now, might even have convinced herself she wanted something other than friendship from her old buddy Michael. Hell, she'd nearly convinced him last night—or, probably more accurately, his own desires had nearly convinced him. Then, after their kiss, she'd said his name with that questioning note in her voice, and he'd heard the wistfulness. The wistfulness of someone longing to call another name.

He should have known. He *did* know, because he knew Tris. The one person in his life who had always remained constant in her loves. No matter what Paul said, she was the same Tris she'd always been.

All these years she'd longed for Grady Roberts, and now to watch him pursuing another woman once again...it must hurt. He kept his face neutral as he stood up. "I'd love to dance with you, Tris."

How much could a man take?

He was about to find out.

Chapter Eight

"May I come to your room, Michael?"

Lord, she was getting bold! She could hardly believe the words came out of her mouth. But then in the past few days she seemed to be making a habit of being bold, of touching Michael, of following him, of kissing him, of asking him to dance. What was one more request?

"My room?"

Her cheeks heated, and she couldn't prevent herself from stumbling over a few more words of explanation. "Uh, to talk for a while. The wedding and the reception were so wonderful, I'm not ready to call it a night yet."

He frowned at her. They stood in the deep shadows between the house and the garage, but she knew him so well she could feel his frown.

"If you're up for more partying, I'm sure we can catch Grady and Judi and the others. Grady usually favors a couple Near North spots. We shouldn't have too much trouble finding him.''

"No! I, uh, I'm not in the mood for someplace loud and smoky.'' She'd had a hard enough time separating Michael from the rest of the group in the first place; she wasn't about to go chasing a crowd now that she finally had him to herself. "I thought maybe we could have a drink and, um, talk. The two of us.''

She felt his imminent refusal like a thunderstorm on the horizon.

"Like old times,'' she added, as a personal lightning rod. It worked.

"Like old times,'' he repeated. His frown lifted as if he'd solved a puzzle to his satisfaction, but she wondered if he were aware of the peculiar flatness that came into his voice when he tried to mask his feelings.

"Mmm,'' she murmured noncommittally, as she followed him up the stairs and remembered those long sessions in the "old times.'' They'd been so unequal, so unfair. Certainly they'd shared their dreams, but when it came to disappointments, she'd poured out her feelings for Grady while he'd never mentioned his hurts, though even then she'd known he had them.

If Paul was right, perhaps she herself had been one of the hurts. But there'd been others. She'd always known he wasn't close to his family, not the way she was. And she recognized his pain over the unstable pattern of his parents' lives. She'd understood some of that from bits and pieces he'd let fall, and from the fact that his parents never came to school functions. But most of all she'd known it from what he didn't say. They were so open to each other about so many things, how could she not know when he'd closed part of himself off?

Now, tonight, she wanted to unlock those parts, to know him completely, to blend the familiar friend with the stranger who made her shiver with warmth when he put his arms around her.

Not exactly like old times, Michael. At least I hope not.

"You want something to drink?" He flipped on the light switch and headed toward the miniature refrigerator. "I think there're some soft drinks in here."

"All we need are glasses."

When he turned around, she displayed the bottle of champagne she'd masked from him with the folds of her skirt. She figured that if he'd known she had champagne drinking in mind, he might have maneuvered out of letting her come up.

"Uncle James gave it to me as we were leaving. He said to make good use of it."

The frown returned to his eyes, and he pushed his right hand through his hair with the air of someone trying to figure out how to deal with a thorny problem. He opened his mouth, but she hurried on, starting to unwrap the foil from the neck of the bottle.

"I, uh, thought we'd have another toast. To the bride and groom, of course, and—" She untwisted the metal clasp around the cork and lifted it off. Reaching around him, still standing in front of the refrigerator, she took a clean dish towel and covered the top of the bottle. Then she very deliberately defused his objections by adding, "To old times."

She could have opened the bottle, but instead she held it out to him, suddenly needing him to be a participant in this night, too. He looked almost solemn, as if about to deliver a lecture. But after a long, heart-thumping second, he took the bottle from her, and she imagined she heard the crumbling of one line of defenses—the first of many.

"Glasses are over the sink," he mumbled, steadily working the cork out.

She eased past him without touching, concerned he might yet turn her out of his room, and got out two old, scratched tumblers, turning around as the bottle emitted the satisfying *thwump* of a good champagne, opened well. He didn't waste a drop by letting it foam over the top, instead tipping the effervescence into the glasses she held out.

When he'd filled both glasses, he raised his tumbler. "So, here's our toast. To Paul and Bette, to old times, old friends and—"

"New beginnings," she interrupted, clinking her glass to his and taking a quick sip to make her addition the final words in their toast. He seemed startled for an instant, but then he nodded and took a drink.

She reached back to flip off the switch on the wall behind her, leaving a low-wattage bulb over the stove the only light in the room. At least the only artificial light, because moonlight silvered through the bank of windows, its glow doubled by the water's reflection.

"There, that's much better. Now we can see the lake from the windows. Shall we sit down?"

She took the bottle and headed for the love seat without waiting for an answer. Since his only choices were to sit there or on the bed, she was pretty sure he'd follow. Curling her feet to the side as she sat put her closer to the middle of the cushion than either end. She watched through her lashes as he hesitated, eyeing the narrow space she'd left before he joined her. She heard the long, soft breath he let out as he settled next to her, barely this side of being as far away as possible.

"It's been quite a week, hasn't it?" he started.

Ah, that was supposed to be her opening to pour out her heart about Grady. I remember your tricks, Michael Dickinson. "Yes, it has. Quite a week."

He eyed her, but when she simply took another sip of champagne, hoping the action would hide her smile, he shifted on the love seat and made his opening a little bigger.

"It hasn't been exactly what I expected somehow."

"No?"

Definitely frowning now, he seemed intent on getting a better look at her face, but she foiled him by twisting to slip off her shoes and then arrange them neatly by the end of the love seat.

"No. How about you? Has it been what you expected?" Since he'd abandoned finesse, she figured she could afford to be forthright, too.

"No. It hasn't been what I expected." She felt him start to relax, preparing for the conversation to follow familiar lines. "It's been much, much better."

"Better?" He stiffened, seeming as shocked, Tris decided with some glee, as he would have been if Pollyanna had turned into a siren right in front of his eyes.

"Much better," she said firmly. "But what I want to hear now, Michael, is about you."

"Me? What about me?"

"You've hardly talked about yourself all this week. I want to know what you've been doing these past years— more than the bare-bones outline I get from you on the phone or from Paul."

"There's nothing much to tell."

She saw the stubborn line come into his jaw. He didn't like this shift from their usual script. Too bad. Maybe there isn't much to tell, Michael, but there's plenty to ask.

"How's your family?"

"Fine."

"Everybody's well? Healthy?"

"Yes."

"And happy?"

"I guess."

"You guess? Haven't you seen them lately?"

"Not lately."

She opened her mouth to batter that flat note in his voice with another question, then stopped. Maybe this wasn't the topic for an all-out assault.

"Paul said you'd been dating someone regularly, someone in Springfield. I...I, um, thought you might bring her as a guest to the wedding." That was a lie. It had never occurred to her that he might bring a guest to the wedding, because back when Paul had told her about this woman in Springfield, she'd refused to listen to the details, refused to admit such a woman existed—a woman who could be important to Michael. *Oh, what a fool I've been, and for so long.*

"I was seeing someone." He put the slightest stress on the past tense.

"What was her name?"

"Her name? Her name was—is Laura."

"Laura." How could she feel such a clutch of jealousy over a name? It was a nice name; she wished it weren't. She wished she could hate the name, hate the woman. But she couldn't. She could tell by the way Michael said her name that Laura was a nice woman, someone worth liking. Michael wouldn't have been involved with any other kind.

"Did you know her long?"

"Six months, a little more."

"What happened, Michael?"

He looked away, and she felt a sliver of dismay that the memory of Laura had that effect on him.

"Happened? It didn't work out, that's all. Maybe, without even realizing it, I was too...too preoccupied with other things."

His words had significance, she knew that instinctively. But what significance?

"Like your job?"

"My job can be very time-consuming. And with the campaign there's been a tremendous amount of travel the past year."

"Tell me about the campaign, Michael. What's it like?"

It took more than that to get him to talk about his job, but in the end she prevailed. It was only while she listened to him talk about some of the incidents and misadventures of the campaign that she realized he hadn't truly answered her question about whether his job had interfered with his relationship with Laura. But right now that didn't seem as important as the fact that he was sharing part of his life with her, as she had so often done with him.

She had shifted sideways on the cushion to watch his face as he talked, so she saw the rise and fall of his chest with the deep sigh he gave.

"What is it, Michael?"

"Hmm? Nothing, really." She waited, willing him to tell her. "It's crazy, but sometimes I wish none of this was happening."

"The campaign?"

"Yeah, the whole thing. I mean, I know that Joan will be a terrific senator and she'll work as hard as it's possible to work to do good things for the state, and the country, but..." He shook his head, apparently at his own thought. "We've been doing good things in Springfield, too. And this...it'll be like starting all over in Washington. Everything will be different, and sometimes I think it wouldn't be so bad if she didn't win, if we didn't end up in Washington. Heck, then sometimes I find myself wishing the campaign would just go on forever, how's that for crazy? Because heaven knows I wasn't wild about the campaign when that started, either."

He shot her a sideways glance as he refilled both glasses. "If you ever breathed a word to the media that I said I wouldn't mind if Joan lost, I'd string you up."

"Oh, yeah, like I'd run to the media with the scoop." She was irked, but not as much as she might have been. His words came from his own self-consciousness, she knew, not doubts of her.

"Well, you've got to admit it would be a scoop. I can't figure out what gets into me sometimes."

"You don't like change, never have," she said promptly. He looked up quickly in surprise, a frown of concentration between his eyes.

"What do you mean? You think I'm afraid of change?"

"Afraid? No. Not afraid. And it's not that you mind the challenge of something new. Some people can't stand for their lives to be constant, they have to have change for the sake of change. You've never been like that. All things being equal, you always preferred to keep things status quo. It's more like you *distrust* change. Does that make sense?"

"I don't know. You're the one doing the analysis here." But his voice didn't sound as forbidding as his words.

"I remember when my sister was little and we shared a room, I desperately wanted to redecorate, but she wanted everything the way it had always been. Mom said to be patient, that she was still a little girl and she'd grow out of that. That eventually she'd accept that change happens all the time. And she did, and two years later we did redecorate the room and then we had this horrible fight because she wanted wallpaper with big, gaudy purple flowers.''

Facing her fully, his expression shifted to rueful. ''I'm not sure if you're saying I'm going to get over this when I grow up or if you're accusing me of having terrible taste in wallpaper.''

His voice held chagrin, but the sight of his dimple had her chuckling low in her throat. She saw the change in his eyes, and knew her own were showing some of her feelings.

''Michael.'' She loved saying his name. She loved the sound of it as a whisper, something soft and intimate between them. Could she make him understand what she was feeling? She stretched forward to brush her lips across the lingering indentation of his dimple, and felt him go still and tense.

Before he could exchange the stillness for movement— away from her; she knew if he moved now it would be away from her—she touched her fingertips to his mouth, then followed them with her lips. Ah, yes, she could be bold when it meant tasting Michael. With the tip of her tongue she absorbed the line of his lips, swept to the corners, then beyond to where faint lines echoed with the years' smiles.

But the lines formed now resembled pain. And his eyes closed tightly as if he were gathering strength. Her mouth whispered over the eyelids, the tickle of his eyelashes making her feel something hotter and deeper than laughter. She kissed the bridge of his nose and then his cheek. She came back to his mouth, but he made no move to cooperate. Did he think he could outwait her? Did he think she wouldn't notice the change in his breathing? The tension in his muscles? The intensity of heat from his body?

"Michael, will you kiss me?" Asking had gotten him to dance with her and had gotten them here, maybe asking would get her this, too.

"Tris."

If that one stern word was a clue, asking wouldn't be enough. She met his lips while they still formed her name, taking the sternness from them, taking the stubbornness from them, taking the denial from them and returning desire.

The tension stayed in his body, but the stillness was gone. He made a sound against her lips as he wrapped his hands around her arms to pull her abruptly against him. For a moment, she sprawled across him awkwardly, and their mouths slipped away from each other. But he shifted her closer still and twisted his body so she was layered against him, and he found her mouth again, delving into it in a sweeping exploration.

He turned her deeper into the cushion, and his weight seemed to surround her. He left her mouth to kiss a path of live sensation across her cheek, to the point of her jaw, then down the pulsing line of her throat. Her dress had dropped low on one shoulder, and she shrugged it farther down her arm to leave him freer access. The hungry sound in his throat made her shiver.

But accepting his caresses wasn't enough. She wanted to give, too. She circled his waist, holding him tightly to her, then slid her hands up his back in long, possessive strokes, feeling the bunching of his muscles under her palms. His hand skimmed over her bottom and hip, and then to her waist. Even before he touched her, she felt her breast tightening in anticipation. His hand still at her waist, he stretched his fingers wide until the thumb feathered the lower curve of her breast. At last his palm shaped to the roundness of her, and then he grazed her nipple, already

taut, but tauter still after his touch. She let out a breath in
satisfaction, but the need for more was growing in her.
Finding the buttons of his shirt, her eager fingers opened
them in no special order, but at each she lingered to explore the firm flesh they discovered.

His mouth took hers once more. The stroke of his
tongue in her mouth and the sweep of his hand on her
breast set up a beat in her body that built and built until
she had to answer it. Instinctively, she rolled her hips
against him, straining to match the rhythm. For one glo-
rious moment, he met her movement, pressing against her
in promise and hope. Then, abruptly, he pulled back, and
the promise and the hope were as quickly gone.

He sat up, taking her with him and turning her partly
away, though he kept his arms wrapped around her abdomen. Confused by his reaction, and still absorbed by the
sensations of her body, she felt grateful for that contact.
She heard his ragged breathing, then felt his lips on the
nape of her neck, caressing the sensitive skin above her
dress.

"I've wanted to do that."

The barely heard murmur and the shivering touch of his
lips seemed to liquefy the bones in her neck, so her head
fell forward, exposing more territory for him. She covered his hands where they rested on her rib cage with her
own, and wished she could reach more of him to touch.

"We have to stop. God. We have to stop now."

"I don't want to stop, Michael." Lord, she'd gone beyond bold to brazen. But this was Michael, and with Michael she could be her most brazenly vulnerable. She
twisted around to slip two more buttons open, until his
fingers caught hers, squeezing them into stillness where
they rested against the heated skin of his abdomen. She

could feel the silky prickle of his hair against her finger-tips.

"Tris. Don't."

"You always tell me don't, Michael. But I want to. I want to touch you. I want to know you, the feel of you without the shirt. Without anything between us."

He let out a harsh, uneven breath. She looked up from the fascinating sight of her pale fingers against the hard, tanned flesh exposed by his open shirt. The shirt she'd opened. And in his eyes, she saw the bright, hot light of desire. Ah, Michael.

Maybe he knew then that it was useless to pretend that this was an innocent kiss between friends that had somehow gone astray. The look in his eyes said all too clearly that his body knew exactly what was happening, and what more it wanted to happen.

"I want you, Tris."

That was supposed to shock her, she supposed. The bald statement, gruffly spoken with no embellishments, was supposed to frighten her off. "I want you, too."

He shook his head, but she didn't know if it was in denial of her words or in frustration at her reaction.

"Last night... Well, I don't think I have as much self-discipline as I had last night. You're not an innocent young girl anymore. You know what could happen—what will happen. If we don't stop now we won't stop at all."

"I know."

The hand that covered hers flexed, then loosened as if by force of will. She spread her fingers wide and flattened her palm under his to absorb as much of his skin as she could. He seemed unaware that his other hand stroked temptingly beneath the exposed line of her collarbone.

"Tris, you can't—"

"I can...I do." Something about the erratic beating of her heart must have affected her lungs, because the words came out breathless. Yet she knew there was no uncertainty behind them. There was only the rightness of being with Michael.

She was aware of a faint scent of soap that clung to his skin, aware of the smooth skin over taut muscle under her hand, aware of his breath against her skin. She leaned to him, brushing her lips across his, a sudden shyness keeping her from doing more. What if she were wrong? What if he didn't share this feeling?

"You're...God...I don't want you to be sorry about this."

His mouth came down on hers, hard, demanding, then he broke away abruptly.

If she could have laughed, she would have. Sorry? How could she be? How could she ever regret what felt so right?

"I won't be sorry." She kissed him gently, but he pulled away. Then immediately came back to her, kissing deeply before he backed away once more.

"Can't take any more...willpower...gone...God, I can't..."

She had no time to assess the ragged words slipping out between kisses, to decide if they were meant as a yes or a no, because his lips were on hers, his arms surrounding her, and his weight bearing her back against the love seat's arm. The heat of the kiss exploded her doubts, and wherever his hands touched, her skin felt as tender as if it had been singed.

Like a building brought down by a wrecker's ball, the crumbling of his resistance set off tremors. She felt them deep inside herself, and she felt them in him.

His tongue plunged into her mouth again, bringing new heat and sensation. His hand traveled down her leg to the edge of her skirt, pulled halfway up by their maneuvers. When he slid his hand to the bare skin above her stocking, the meeting of fingers and thigh drew a murmur from both of them, exchanged mouth to mouth. He shifted, and even through the fabric of the tuxedo pants, she felt the swollen, heated length of him, as blatant a statement of his desire as his words had been.

She skimmed her hands over his chest as he unhooked her stocking with enough expertise to make her determine to tease him about it . . . later. When he twisted to strip the stocking off, she took advantage to shift her attention to his back, pushing the shirt out of her way. Impatiently, he shrugged the rest of the way out of it, as she touched her lips to a band of muscle just below his shoulder blades. He took less care in removing her second stocking, reminding Tris of the elements of determination and willfulness in this man that she had not always recognized.

"Damn. This dress . . . Where the hell . . . ?"

Tris pulled herself away from the fascinating havoc his fumbling attempts had on her senses to find the side zipper herself. She stood, and he stood with her, moving her toward the bed even as she let the loosened dress slip off her shoulders. His hands hurried it, so it floated down her body and pooled at her feet.

His hands under her silk chemise made her draw in her breath, and at the feel of them on her bare breasts she let it out in a moan. He cupped them gently, then with more strength. His thumbs stroked across the nubs until her back arched in silent response. Now even the rub of silk was too abrasive, and the stiff fabric of his slacks became almost painful against her thighs and abdomen. She wanted nothing between them. She wanted nothing but him.

As if he sensed that need, he skimmed the chemise over her head, dropping it behind him and nudging her down onto the bed. She watched him shed pants, briefs and socks in one efficient movement. But she had no time to consider it, because then he had joined her on the bed, his hands and mouth feeding the fever that seemed to rage just under her skin.

She found herself lifting her hips at his silent command, to aid him in stripping off the final, lacy barrier between them.

This wasn't at all what she'd expected, this intensity, this hunger. This was Michael, her friend, her companion. Yet this wasn't Michael at all. This wasn't her reaction to Michael. This compelling need to have his kisses, his caresses, to have him inside her. To have him fill her. This was something she hadn't known about herself.

He muttered again as he leaned across her body, but her mind could make nothing of the words, not when her body reacted to the imprint of his arousal, hot and pulsing against her hip. There was a distinctive crackle of foil, and that registered on the small corner of her mind left for rational thought. Ah, yes, this *was* Michael. In at least one basic, caring way.

But his hands sliding under her drove out every thought, leaving behind only sensation, the splendid sensation of his first, sure thrust into her. She clutched at his shoulders for a stability that eluded her as he withdrew and thrust again, stronger.

She rose to meet each stroke, needing to have him deep within her. But still he didn't slow. The need became a frenzy as the tremors ripped through her. She felt his body tense, then heard his cry and echoed it with her own. Michael enfolded her as the tremors retreated, slowly, leaving behind an exhaustion so complete that only contentment had a share of her senses.

"Tris."

She awoke to the sound of her name, murmured against her skin. The softness of both sound and touch contrasted with the slightly abrasive movement of Michael's hair-coated leg against her thigh. The musk of their lovemaking lingered. In the faint moonlight brave enough to journey through the window and across the room, his face appeared taut and intense as he looked down at her.

The face she knew so well seemed as new and unknown in that light as the man who had been revealed in their lovemaking. She might have expected sweetness and patience, but she'd received power and passion.

The tightened muscle of the arm that supported him above her drew her fingers to test and explore it. He bowed his back to touch his tongue to her nipple, and she felt her response as a simultaneous tightening and lifting of breast and pelvis. His mouth closed on her, pulling until she arched to draw near the source of such pleasure. She wanted him again. As much, as urgently. As completely.

There were things they should say to each other. Questions to ask, thinking to adjust. But not now. She couldn't now.

Five senses, that was all anybody got. But to accept all the pleasures her body was absorbing now would require fifteen, twenty.

She reached to him, willingly contributing to the overload that would short-circuit her senses in pinwheels of electricity.

"Michael."

* * *

The bed seemed large and empty, the dawning sunlight overbright even before she opened her eyes.

He stood at the window, hands dug into the pockets of cutoffs that were the only thing he wore, staring out toward the water. She wished he were still in bed, near to her. But the next best thing would be standing by him. Sitting, she scooped up his Phantoms T-shirt from the nearby bureau, pulling it over her head as she eased out of the bed. He must have heard her. He didn't turn, but something about his posture indicated a new tension.

"Tris." His voice was low and a little hoarse, almost muffled as he continued to face away from her a moment longer. "I'm sorry."

"Sorry?" she repeated, unsure what he meant. Two more steps and she'd be near enough to run her hands down his back, along those planes and muscles that were usually so innocently masked in his conservative clothing.

Then he turned to her, and she stopped. Her movement, her breath, her blood—all stopped. Frozen by his expression. She knew that only the strength of his will had forced his muscles to obey the command to face her. The clarity of her knowledge stunned her, but that emotion was lost in the sweep of pain; he could barely force himself to look at her. If he'd been any less of the man he was, he wouldn't have. He would have turned away from her for good.

"Last night—last night shouldn't have happened. I'm sorry."

Shouldn't have happened...sorry. Through the pain she tried to make sense of it. "Sorry!" The repeated word came out a hoarse cry.

She remembered his words of the previous night. *I don't want you to be sorry about this....* She wasn't, but he was.

He was sorry about a night that shouldn't have happened. Sorry he'd given in to her...to her seduction, there was no other word for it. He'd made his reluctance clear, but she'd refused to hear it. And now he was sorry. Sorry he'd loved her.

He reached for her in what could have been an involuntary move, but she jerked her arm away just before his fingers would have touched her. She couldn't bear pity in his touch. Not after last night.

She couldn't bear it in his face, either. She wasn't as strong as he was. She turned away from him.

"You've always been . . . I shouldn't have—" His voice faltered, then started again, stronger. "I should have stopped it before . . . Last night was my fault."

The sound that came from her throat was supposed to be a disdainful laugh. Pain distorted it.

She'd been transported. He was sorry.

She'd felt the loose threads of her life coming together in a pattern that meshed with him to create something real. He felt regret.

He ground out a curse under his breath, and somewhere deep in her mind Tris recognized she'd never heard him swear that way before. "This was exactly what I never wanted to happen, Tris. I never wanted our friendship to suffer. Your friendship means too much to me—"

A slight sound behind her told her he was driving his right hand through his thick hair in that familiar gesture of frustration. But suddenly, he was a stranger. A stranger she had shared passion with through the hours of the night. A stranger she didn't know anything about now, here, in the light of a summer day's dawn.

"It was a mistake. I never wanted to risk your friendship. I never— Tris! What are you doing?"

She continued gathering her clothes, bundling them to her like pieces of her pride. Her heart would be harder to put back together.

Not to put them all on—that would take too long, and she couldn't bear to breathe the air that reeked of his pity and regret—but to ensure that no shred of her remained behind to remind him of his "mistake."

"I'll send the shirt back." Her words were jerky, mechanical.

He caught her at the door, and even though his hold on her arm kept her still, she wouldn't look at him.

"Tris, please . . . I didn't—"

"I know. You didn't want our friendship to suffer." Her voice shook a little on the last word. "Don't worry. It didn't suffer at all. It died a quick, painless death."

She jerked her arm away and was gone.

"I don't understand why you're leaving today, anyway," Grady grumbled. "And especially so early."

"Shut up and drive."

She saw the look he shot her from the corner of his eye, but felt perfectly safe ignoring it. Slightly hung over and more than a little short on sleep, he'd take the path of least resistance. That was what she'd counted on when she shook him awake and demanded he take her to the airport. He hadn't even realized what time it was until they passed the billboard digital clock flashing the numbers on the way to O'Hare.

"Don't park," she ordered as they came up to a fork in the entry road. "Just drop me off at Departures."

He didn't argue. But when he pulled to a stop in front of the terminal, he leaned over and clamped a hand around her wrist.

"Tris, are you okay?"

"I'm fine. Really." She turned to direct a smile at him, but it faltered at the concern in his eyes. "I will be fine. Honest. I just need to get away right now."

He continued to look at her. "I know I'm not always the most perceptive person, but it seemed like you and Michael were working on something this past week. If there's something I—"

"Nothing." She softened the curt word with a touch of her fingers to his cheek. God, wasn't this great for irony? Twelve years later, here was Grady consoling her over Michael. "But thanks. Thanks for your concern." She looked at him again, dark smudges of sleeplessness somehow managing to make him look even more handsome. But that wasn't what she saw. She saw a friend. "You know sometimes we don't give you enough credit, Grady."

"No, you don't," he agreed solemnly.

"You're really very sweet."

"Yes, I am."

She almost smiled at that. "Thanks for the ride, Grady."

"Take care of yourself, Tris."

"You, too."

She hefted her suitcase from the back seat and turned it over to a skycap, gave Grady a wave and disappeared from view among the people hurrying on to other destinations even at this hour on a Sunday morning.

Michael sat on the corner of the bed, his elbows on his knees, his hands clasped in front of him. The sun rose in front of unfocused eyes.

He'd known. He'd *known.* And still he couldn't stop himself. One night of loving Tris, and that was all he'd ever have again. No more out-of-the-blue phone calls. No more affectionate messages relayed through Paul. No more right even to ask how she was doing these days. No more...

Twelve years before, he'd known how it was between them. And he'd accepted it then. Not always gracefully, but he'd accepted it. He had never let her see the hunger in him for her. He had never jeopardized the friendship they'd shared. Until last night.

He hadn't had the strength to turn her away, even knowing the emotions that moved her. He'd even tried to rationalize it in that last, sane moment when he'd felt the framework of his resistance giving way. He'd told himself that making love to her once might be the answer, might be the way to finally still that ghost of hope. To get her out of his system.

What a fool. He should have known she would never be out of his system, and now the feel of her, the sensations of her body, the sounds of her pleasure, the smell of her hair, the taste of her skin were all memories imprinted in every cell of his body.

God, how sweet she was. He had never... No, of course, he'd never. Because never before had the woman been Tris.

He couldn't let her go out of his life like this, couldn't let go even those fragile threads to her of the past few years. If he could talk to her, make her see that their friendship could survive this. That she could trust him to never again let desire overrule his control, to never again let the taste and touch of her inflame his senses until he had to possess her, had to wake her to love her again. And again.

He bowed his head a moment, then pushed himself off the bed and hurriedly dressed. He had to face this, try to salvage something.

The sun was well up. Mrs. Monroe and Judi were already in the kitchen, their slippers slapping lightly against the floor as they moved around making coffee, pouring juice. Mrs. Monroe greeted him warmly.

"Good morning, dear. I can't believe you revelers are up so early."

"Where's Tris?" He saw her surprise at his brusqueness, and didn't care.

"Tris? Tris is gone, dear."

"Gone?" He heard the stupid note in his own voice. How could she be gone already? She'd just left. He caught sight of the clock over the range and realized more than an hour had passed since she left his room.

"Yes. To the airport. I had a note from her. She said she had to change her plans. The office needed her to get back early." She hesitated, as if faced with a small puzzle. "Although I don't know how she was going to get there. I didn't hear a taxi honk or anything—"

"Grady took her," supplied Judi. "I saw them leaving from my window."

"Tris left with Grady." He said it with detachment, as if he just wanted to verify the facts.

"Yes. I heard his car and saw her taking out her suitcase." Judi was watching him intently. "She looked upset."

"Oh, dear. Did she?" Nancy Monroe asked her daughter, a frown pulling her brows down. "Oh, I almost forgot. In her note, she asked me to give you this, Michael." Automatically, his hand closed around what she held out to him. His Phantoms shirt. He thought he could feel Tris's warmth still in the material; he crushed it in his fist, trying to absorb the sensation.

"Tris left with Grady," he repeated numbly. What a fool he was. What a damned fool.

"Are you all right, Michael?" He could feel Nancy Monroe's hand on his arm. He could feel the aged material of the shirt straining under his grip on it. But mostly he could feel pain.

"Fine. I'm fine."

Chapter Nine

"America loves an underdog," the newscaster intoned, "and especially when the underdog successfully pulls off a stunning upset. So, America, prepare to meet your latest darling.

"It's well past midnight here in Illinois, and for Joan Bradon and her staff, the day that started at dawn this morning is still a long way from being over...."

The television camera panned over the happy chaos of a victorious campaign headquarters on election night, centering on a tall, rawboned woman who radiated energy and determination. But in a darkened living room in Washington, D.C., the viewer's attention focused on the background, where a man with his loosened tie askew and a phone tucked into his shoulder used one hand to sign something held out to him by a teenage messenger, while he drove his other hand through his thick, unruly hair. He smiled at the teenager, a smile that didn't mask his weariness, but made it clear that no amount of tiredness would change the basic decency of the man.

In the living room in Washington, the watcher folded her knees more tightly to her chest, covered her mouth with a fist and tried to ignore the twin tears burning down her cheeks.

Tris subtly withdrew from the conversation. It wasn't impolite to do that when you wanted the other two people at the dinner table to get to know each other, as she hoped Leslie Craig and Grady Roberts would.

She deserved this slightly smug feeling. It had been a stroke of genius to insist Leslie come with her to dinner. She might not have done it with any ulterior motive where Leslie and Grady were concerned, but once she'd seen them together the idea had taken hold. They acted a bit wary of each other, but she hoped that would pass, especially if she participated less so they could talk more to each other. It didn't hurt that that also served her initial purpose in inviting Leslie—deflecting some of the questions she had a feeling Grady was dying to ask her.

She'd been surprised when he called last week and said he was going to be in D.C. a few days and wanted to get together for dinner. But not as surprised as she would have been a few months ago. He'd called her more in the three months since Paul and Bette's wedding than he had in the previous six years. Almost as if, for the first time, he felt comfortable being her friend.

Tris watched him laugh at one of Leslie's medium-outrageous comments, and thought again that maybe all of them underestimated Grady Roberts.

"Oh, look, it's the Filbertsons. I simply must go say hello to them on my way to the ladies' room. I'll be back in a bit," announced Leslie, significantly pressing Tris's hand. "That'll give you a chance to catch up on old news without an outsider here."

She looked from one to the other of them, then swept away. Tris watched her go with an inward grimace. She'd underestimated Leslie Craig, too. She should have known Leslie would maneuver it so she'd have to face Grady alone, at least for a while.

In the first weeks after the wedding, Leslie had plied her with worried questions about what was wrong and what had happened. When Tris had finally made it clear she didn't want to talk, they'd reached a tacit truce—Tris would pretend everything was normal, and Leslie would pretend she didn't notice anything different. That agreement, however, bent a little when Tris invited Leslie to this dinner. Leslie had given her a sharp look and asked if Grady Roberts was the cause of her unhappiness. She hadn't looked particularly convinced by Tris's terse "no," but at last she'd agreed to come along tonight. Now Tris wished she'd thought to get a promise from her friend on the issue of desertion.

She felt Grady's eyes on her and gave him a half smile.

"You look great, Tris." But he said it with an inflection of doubt, so she knew he could see the signs of tiredness that went heart deep.

"It's been a busy time at work." She answered his tone rather than his words. "It's always a little crazy with funding requests during an election year."

"I'll bet. Well, with the elections over last week, things should settle down some for you."

"Yes." She knew what would come next.

"I suppose you know Joan Bradon won the senate election."

"Yes, I know. That was great news. It must have made...everybody very happy." Lord, she couldn't even say his name.

"I guess. Although Michael acted pretty weird about it."

She looked up from the silverware she'd been aligning and realigning on the white tablecloth. "What do you mean? Is something wrong?"

"Wrong? I don't know. Would you call it wrong when a guy works like crazy for something for more than a year, something he really believes in, and then when it happens he acts like he's not totally aware of it? Would you call it wrong when someone looks like being miserable would be one hell of an improvement in his life?"

"Don't. Please, Grady." She blinked hard at the tears she thought had evaporated months ago, along with the hurt pride. She knew Michael must regret that she'd been hurt—of course he would. But how could she feel sorry for his pain when all she had left to feel for herself were weariness and sadness?

Grady covered her hand, stilling her infinitesimal straightening of her dessert spoon. "I didn't want to upset you, but it's hard seeing my friends hurting like this. Especially you two. You were always so...so close, I guess. You always seemed to understand each other so well. Don't you think if you just talked it out...?"

She shook her head. "There's nothing to talk out."

What could there be to talk out? She'd already forced the issue. If he'd once thought she still was infatuated with Grady, her actions surely had disproved that. How could Michael doubt that he was the one she wanted? Good heavens, she'd practically thrown herself at the man—no, she *had* thrown herself at the man. So, he'd been only human. He'd probably half convinced himself it was what he wanted, too, just because she wanted it. But in the morning, he'd seen it for a mistake—he didn't feel that way toward her, and he'd been too honest not to tell her.

Yes, he'd been only human and she'd been a fool. This time, their famed ability to communicate had been way off the mark. She'd been so sure she and Michael must be feeling the same thing that she hadn't even stopped to listen to the doubts he'd tried to express.

But now she saw exactly how he'd tried to warn her. She just hadn't listened.

"Nothing to talk about," she repeated.

Grady looked unconvinced.

"It was a mistake, that's all...a mistake." Her mistake. "We didn't know each other as well as we thought we did. It's all right."

He patted her hand a little awkwardly and released it, staring into space a long moment before turning back to her with narrowed eyes. "Joan Bradon could be in a position to help you with your homeless project. She's shown a lot of interest in things like that. And she's not the type to be afraid of plunging in."

"How did you know about the project?"

He shrugged. "I knew. And Paul told me some of the details, some of the problems you've had with it. Are you going to submit the proposal to Michael?"

"No!" She said it with enough vehemence that heads turned at neighboring tables, but Grady didn't seem to notice.

"Why not?"

"I don't think it would be, um, appropriate...taking advantage of our, uh, our connection."

"Baloney. I may not be a politician, but it can't be all that different from business. Of course it's appropriate to go to somebody you know. And you know darn well Michael wouldn't ever recommend something to Joan Bradon that he didn't think was right.''

She tried to meet his suddenly searching look, but when his eyes narrowed again, she found the sight of her salad fork too fascinating to ignore.

As much as she wanted this project to survive, as much as Joan Bradon's backing might help cut through the red tape and encourage the agencies to pool their money for it, she didn't want to go through Michael. She could tell herself it was because he wouldn't give the proposal a fair chance, judging by the way he'd reacted in August. She could even say she felt insulted at his treating her like an untried seventeen-year-old. But she knew those weren't the real reasons.

She didn't think she could bear it. Talking to him, seeing him. And knowing that the night of love and passion that had finally and completely opened her eyes to this man, had convinced *him* that what he felt for her wasn't deep enough, wasn't strong enough. He'd desired her, yes, but the feelings that had been a revelation for her had merely been an aberration to him.

Talking to him couldn't make her ache any more than she already did, but it wouldn't help her forget, either.

Perhaps if that had been the only way to get help for the project, she would have. But there were other avenues to bring it to the senator-elect's attention, avenues she was already pursuing. Over these past months, she'd deliberately thrown every bit of energy and emotion she had into work, vainly hoping that there would be less to devote to missing Michael. She'd honed the proposal, making it as practical and well documented as she could, with support and explanations and contingencies for every aspect of it. At each step, she'd heard Michael's voice advising and assisting. But that wasn't unusual, because she heard his voice all the time. She heard all the words and inflections stored up from a week in August and more than a decade of friendship.

"That stuff about appropriateness is an excuse, Tris. So what is it really? Do you think Michael would dismiss your proposal because the two of you have had this misunderstanding?"

"Of course not." The snap in her voice punished his temerity for suggesting Michael could be so unfair.

"Then you shouldn't handicap this proposal because of a 'mistake' you and Michael made."

Not Michael. Just me, alone, making the mistake. And paying dearly for it.

Relief swept into her as she saw Leslie slowly making her way back to the table. That would put an end to this cross-examination.

"I'll think about it, Grady." A promise easily made. As much as she'd tried over the past months, she knew that *not* thinking about Michael Dickinson would have been the promise impossible to keep.

"They're sending us home, Tris. Get your coat. C'mon, we'll brave the Metro together."

"What? Why?"

"Haven't you looked out the window? I know you've spent the past few months working like someone possessed, but I'd think you'd lift your nose from the grindstone once in a while, just long enough to note a little thing like a blizzard."

Tris spread the thin-slatted blinds that covered her office window to look out on the January sky. Shades of off-white colored the whole world, from the cloud-packed sky to the whitening ground below, and all the snow-filled air in between.

"That's no blizzard," she said with a Midwesterner's weather snobbery. "A blizzard is a precise term—you have to have very high winds and a lot more snow than this."

"Maybe not in the Great White Waste you used to live in, but in D.C., *that* is a blizzard."

Leslie's gesture pointed down more than out, and Tris craned her neck to view the street below. Cars skidded and spun in disastrous abandon. She became aware of the bleating of horns. Through the maze, she watched the blue roof of one sedan steadily work its way through the panicked traffic. Northerner, she thought. Probably a newcomer, maybe part of the administration taking office in ten days. Because there was something about Washington driving—a couple D.C. winters, and even the most hardened snow driver degenerated.

Leslie returned, draping Tris's coat over the corner of her desk and plopping her boots at her feet.

"Besides, the office is closing, so you've got to leave. The place won't fall apart because you leave a couple hours early, you know. You might as well come with me. You can brag about how you had to walk eleven miles to school in weather like this every day of the winter when you were growing up, and I, Virginia belle that I am, promise to be suitably impressed."

Tris considered the scene outside a moment longer. Going home meant too much time, too much quiet. Too much time to think and wonder and wish, and too much quiet to drown out her heart. But she knew this town and its reaction to snow. If she stayed, she could very well be stranded for a couple of days. She capitulated with a halfhearted laugh.

"My God, the woman laughs. I don't think I've heard that since the cherry trees were blooming. No, a little later

than that. August, I think. So it must have been the crape
myrtle blooming.''

Tris slanted a warning look at her friend, but didn't say
anything as she pulled on her boots.

"Let's go, Tris, or we'll never get a spot on the Metro.''

"You've got to be kidding. You can't think we're going
to get a seat—''

"A seat? Huh! I'm not talking about a place to sit, I'm
talking about a place to stand!''

The stinging wind-driven snowflakes and the pure
adrenaline of a simple battle against the elements brought
a tingling to Tris's cheeks. Fighting the elements provided
a welcome change from tilting against memories.

They were laughing together as the momentum of the
crowd carried them into the escalator entrance to the
Metro, down a short flight of stairs to the platform heading north and into a waiting car.

"Well, at least we've got a place to stand,'' she said to
Leslie as the flood of people behind pressed them into the
nearly full standing area. Already the body heat had driven
up the temperature. She pushed the snow-dampened wool
scarf back off her hair and froze.

"Yeah, a place to stand, all right,'' Leslie said. "I don't
think we could *not* stand. We're packed in here so tight I
think you could faint and still be standing up. I swear—
What is it, Tris?''

Tris heard Leslie's voice, but the words didn't make
sense to her. Nothing made sense with Michael standing
three feet away. Over the shoulders of the four commu-
ters who separated them, he stared at her.

"Hello, Tris.''

His voice was so low she shouldn't have heard it for all
the complaints and comments of the people around them.
But she did.

Her lips parted, but no sound came out. She should have been ready for this. She should have been prepared. Of course she knew his candidate had won the election back in November. Even if she'd never read every newspaper article about Joan Bradon's election or stayed up half the night watching the returns, Grady had told her. And somewhere in her mind she must have realized that meant Michael would be coming to Washington. But she hadn't allowed herself to consider it. She hadn't prepared herself to come face-to-face with him.

"Oh." She heard Leslie's soft sound of comprehension behind her. "Oh-ho!"

The train started with a jolt, and she wasn't prepared for that, either. She lurched forward, careening into the man nearest her. Michael's hand shot out to her shoulder, and between that and the close quarters, she quickly regained her balance. At least her physical balance. Her emotional balance still reeled from the double shock of seeing Michael, and the contact of his hand on her shoulder. The layers of leather, wool and silk between them didn't seem to matter to her tingling nerves.

Somehow Michael had gotten closer. She felt his presence like a source of heat in a cold room. At her side, Leslie wormed and wiggled two other people out of their way, and the three of them stood in a compact circle, isolated in a sea of backs.

"Hi, I'm Leslie Craig. I work with Tris."

Leslie pivoted the elbow tucked in against her side by a woman to her right, and offered her hand.

"Oh. Yes..." Shock thawed out of Tris. She could react again. And she could hurt. "Leslie Craig, this is Michael Dickinson. Michael, Leslie Craig."

"How do you do, Michael," Leslie said, squeezing his hand because there was no room to shake it, and openly appraising him. "Who are you?"

"Leslie—"

"I mean how do you know Tris?" Leslie clarified unrepentantly.

"We knew each other at college," Michael said, with a hint of a smile behind his good manners.

"Oh, did you?" Leslie seemed to feel his answer explained a lot. "You're a friend of Cousin Paul and Gorgeous Grady, are you?"

"Leslie—"

Tris ignored the look Michael shot at her, preferring to focus the full force of her glare on Leslie. But she nevertheless felt the impact of those hazel eyes on her face.

He turned back to Leslie, frowning. "Yes. I'm a friend of Paul's. And Grady's."

Leslie nodded, the way a teacher does at a student who has just answered a difficult question perfectly.

"And you were at Paul and Bette's wedding in Illinois in August."

"Yes." His frown started to slip.

"In the wedding?"

"Yes." Amusement edged the frown further aside.

"Best man?"

"Yes." He chuckled. "Is this part of the usual Washington greeting? Are you with the FBI, Ms. Craig? Demonstrating for me how futile it would be to try to hide any skeletons in my closet?"

"Do you have any skeletons in your closet?"

Again Tris felt his eyes on her. "No. None that would interest the FBI."

Leslie didn't seem to notice the strain in that answer. "Good, then you should call me Leslie. And let me say you're very welcome to Washington. Very welcome," she repeated with emphasis and a sidelong look at Tris, still the silent point of their triangle.

"Thank you, Leslie. It's nice to feel welcomed. I just got into town for good at the beginning of the week, and I haven't had a chance to do anything but work so far."

Tris wondered if that was partly for her benefit; telling her he hadn't had an opportunity to call her since he got into town. But what would they have said to each other even if he had called?

"Well, I can guarantee you won't be doing any work the next couple of days. D.C. does not function in snow. Where do you live?"

He mentioned an address two Metro stops past the one Leslie and Tris used.

Leslie tilted her head at him consideringly. "I hope you've got plenty of food supplies stashed away. The stores will be picked clean by now."

"Actually, no. I just moved into my apartment. My furniture won't arrive for a couple more weeks and I haven't had a chance to do much shopping yet."

"Then you better plan on staying with Tris."

"Leslie!"

Tris wished she had the power to make Leslie disappear. Or at least shut up. She was excruciatingly aware that her contribution to the conversation had consisted solely of speaking her friend's name in various tones of reproach. But she didn't know what else to say to Leslie. And every time she tried to think of something to say to Michael, her eyes burned with the horrible threat of tears.

"I mean it. You know what this town is like, Tris. The man could starve."

"Yes, but—"

"I'll just eat out, the way I have been— No?" He broke off as Leslie shook her head vehemently.

"No. You don't understand what happens to this place when it snows. The restaurants close. The stores close. The government closes. Everything closes when it's this bad."

"But it's not that bad," he protested. "I thought they were kidding when they said the offices were closing."

"That's what you and Tris think, but the rest of us think different. You two sound just alike. In fact—"

The crackle of the Metro's PA system interrupted her. Words popped in and out of hearing range, tantalizing the listener into believing someone really was saying something worth listening to.

"What'd he say?"

"Which station?"

"Did he say buses?"

"Closed for sure?"

"Shuttles."

"Oh, shuttles. I thought he said something else."

"Amounts to about the same thing."

The questions and comments eddied around them, the passengers piecing together the bits of the message heard, and extrapolating from experience.

"See!" Leslie was triumphant. "Our stop's the last one open. Michael can't get home."

"Maybe you'd better..." Tris looked up at Michael, and couldn't go on. Looking into his eyes reminded her too much of what she'd lost. She'd lost that warm look of her friend Michael that she'd relied on for so many years. She'd lost that hot look of her lover Michael that she'd reveled in for one brief night.

"It's all right, Tris. I'll make it to my place fine. It's really not that bad a storm. I can't believe everything would close up for this."

The Metro car came to a stop. As soon as the doors opened, people in front popped out like a champagne cork, with the rest of the passengers frothing along behind them. Everyone was carried away in the frantic eddy of those most anxious to get ahead.

"Where are the shuttles?"

"Which shuttle do you take to Bethesda?"

"Hurry up, or they'll all be filled."

Tris let the current take her up the stairs. Then she realized it wasn't just the crowd guiding her steps. Michael had a protective arm across her back, holding off the bumps of those hurrying behind them.

Up at ground level, Leslie eased away from them, waving and calling goodbye as she headed off on her three-block walk to her apartment.

Tris let Michael lead her to a corner protected from the crowd, the wind and the snow. The storm seemed worse, the snow settling down, preparing to fall steadily over the long haul. The sky was a uniform cloud gray that made it impossible to guess the time of day. It looked as if it might snow forever.

"Michael, I think Leslie might have a point."

"It's okay. I'll get one of the shuttles. I'll be fine, Tris."

She'd heard stories about those shuttles. Sometimes they got stuck for hours. In the cold and the snow. And even without that, it could take hours in this weather to go just the couple miles to his stop. And even then he'd be returning to a new apartment: no furniture, no food.

"Don't be silly, Michael. I can't let an old friend starve to death in the cold." She'd meant to sound brisk, but not so harsh. She tried to soften the effect with a gloved hand on his overcoated arm. "It really makes more sense for you to come to my place. It's just a few blocks and I have plenty of food and—"

She started to say she had plenty of room, thinking of the bed in the spare room. But she didn't want him in the spare-room bed. She wanted him in hers, spending all the nights the way she'd spent one unforgettable night in his. She wouldn't tell him the lie, and she couldn't tell him the truth.

"I'll be okay, Tris."

Without warning, the need to have him safely with her became urgent. She couldn't let him go off and probably spend days alone, maybe cold and hungry because her impulsiveness in acting on new feelings for him had made a mess of their friendship.

"And I could use some help with the shoveling," she added. "The lady next door's rather elderly, and I shovel for her, too. If I don't do it, she tries to get out there herself and she really shouldn't. She has a weak heart. It's bad for her. Especially with this kind of snow. Heavy."

She demonstrated by holding her gloved hand out, palm up and level, to catch the weighty flakes.

"Well, if I earn my keep shoveling . . ."

"You will," she promised. She looked up at him again, and saw the light in his eyes. Her heart somersaulted in a maneuver worthy of an Olympic gymnast. She didn't think it was the warmth of friendship, or the fire of love, but at least it was light of some sort.

They left behind the activity of the subway stop and the panicked whirring of tire wheels on the main road as their snow-muffled footsteps took them into a sedate neighborhood of tall trees, tiny yards and trim row houses. Tris turned one corner, and then another, wondering if Michael would ever talk again. Without a twinge over contradicting her earlier wish that Leslie would disappear, she longed for her friend. Leslie might not be the most tactful person in the world, but at least she filled the silence.

"I heard about Joan's winning the election," she said, and cringed to hear herself. Brilliant, Tris.

Of course, she'd heard about the election. She would have had to have spent the past months in a cave not to, since Joan Bradon had pulled off the upset of the election. And she hadn't been in a cave. She'd been following every report on the campaign, searching for a certain name in print, or a glimpse afforded by a television camera, even though it meant exposing emotions she'd tried to forget.

She bent into the wind-driven snow and forced herself to keep going. "Congratulations. It must be very exciting."

"Thanks. It has been exciting, and hectic."

"I'll bet. But you must have been elated election night, to pull off an upset like that." She remembered the image of him on the TV screen election night, and knew his elation had been mixed with many other things. "Of course, campaigning like that would be very unsettling. Tiring. Constantly having to adjust your life."

"Yes. Unsettling's a good way to describe it. Before and after the election. A lot of changes."

She risked a look at him, as he walked at her side, and saw that he was watching her, obviously remembering the same conversation his words had called up to her mind. It was safe to remember that, she told herself. It was only what had followed that she could not let herself think of. Ever. But especially not with Michael walking so close that his arm brushed hers now and again.

"I didn't have any purple-flowered wallpaper to leave behind," he said, and his voice seemed to deepen on the words, "but there were still a lot of changes, a lot of adapting to do."

She couldn't prevent smiling at him then, any more than she could help the flood of warmth at his answering smile.

Maybe the damage she'd done to their friendship wasn't irreparable. She'd never lose the emptiness of knowing that there couldn't be more between them, but to have some part of Michael was better than the past few months of having nothing. It had to be.

"And how have you been doing at adapting?"

"Pretty good, I think. I've had my moments, but Joan didn't have to threaten me more than once or twice to get me to agree to be on her staff here on Capitol Hill instead of staying in Springfield."

"Here's my house," she said, using memory to follow the walk obscured by snow. Barely three strides took them to the front steps, and she gestured for him to join her on the small porch, out of the hard-falling snow. She fitted the key to the lock. "So, you think you're going to like Washington?"

She looked up at him as she swung the door open, waiting for his answer.

"It's too early to tell."

He held the heavy outer door for her, standing so close that she could smell the wet wool of his overcoat, could see the creases at the corners of his eyes, built by humor and deepened by responsibility. She looked into his multicolored eyes, and she knew he was talking about more than a job.

Chapter Ten

Michael watched Tris stretch to hook the hanger over the back of the closet door, placing his coat next to hers to dry out before hanging them in the closet. The fabric of her dress slid over her body, slightly cupping the curve of her bottom, and his muscles clenched in reaction. Lord, what was he thinking of, coming here? He should have insisted on going on to his own place, or sleeping on the Metro. Anything would have been smarter than this.

He knew he would have sought her out here in Washington, to try to repair the friendship he'd shredded. It meant too much to him not to try; she meant too much to him. But he'd intended to wait a little longer, to arrange the encounter to the last detail, to plan what he wanted to say and how to say it. To have a better grip on his emotions. To have some chance to prepare for the impact of looking up and seeing Tris. And wanting her, instantaneously and incessantly.

She glanced at him and he quickly turned away, pretending an absorbing interest in her living room's decor. Soft earth tones, a cushy couch pulled up in front of the brick fireplace along with an overstuffed companion chair, built-in bookcases, lots of mellow wood, spaces flowing into each other and big, airy windows.

It was pure Tris. "It's a great place. I can see all the work you put in it."

His eye caught the twin framed photos on the bookcase—the four friends in college, then captured twelve years later in the same pose. She'd chosen to frame the first of the two pictures Bette had taken in August, though he knew Bette had sent out copies of each shot. He could understand why Tris had chosen that photo; the other one was too raw, his hunger for her too clear. He turned away without comment on the display, and had the impression she'd been watching him. If so, she avoided the topic, too.

"Thanks. It's not as challenging as your Victorian must have been, but it gave me plenty to handle."

"When were these places built?"

"In the twenties. You want some coffee? Or would you rather have tea? Hot chocolate?"

"Coffee would be great." Strangely, her slightly nervous rendition of the perfect hostess eased some of his discomfort. He followed her through the dining area and into the kitchen, prepared to help, prepared to make this as unawkward as it could be. Maybe their friendship could yet be salvaged.

They'd both left their wet footwear at the front door, so their steps barely sounded, even on the hardwood floors. He watched her stockinged toes curl into the cotton throw rug in front of the sink as she filled the coffee maker's pot with water. An unconscious reaction to the soft texture of the rug, he knew. A mere reflex. But he couldn't stop it from triggering a series of memories of how she had tested and tasted and seemed to enjoy the different textures of his body.

She looked over her shoulder at him questioningly, and he knew he'd missed something she'd said. What? "I'm sorry. What did you say?"

"It wasn't anything. I just—um—said I couldn't imagine how people got along before coffee makers."

Her cheeks had grown pink and her movements jerky as she started the coffee, shouting her self-consciousness. She must have caught the direction of his preoccupation, and it made her uncomfortable. Lord, making her ill at ease was the last thing he wanted. Friendship, Dickinson. Friendship, not hormones.

Doggedly he began plying her with questions about her house as she poured the coffee and arranged cookies on a plate. He noticed her glance at the sofa, and knew when she decided against having their coffee there. She probably considered it too intimate a setting. Instead, she set the coffee and cookies down on the tiny breakfast bar that separated the kitchen from the dining and living rooms, gesturing for him to take one of the cushioned stools. He complied. Drinking his coffee, eating his cookies and expanding on his questions regarding her house's renovation, its history and its neighborhood. A nice, safe topic, interesting but not personal, and he pursued it relentlessly. Even when her answers dwindled to nearly nothing.

But finally, there were no more questions to ask.

He let out a long breath and glanced out through the dining room's bay window. The snow was coming down as hard as ever and the light was fading rapidly.

"Maybe I should get a start on the shoveling before it gets dark."

Tris jumped, as if her mind had been on something else entirely. "Tonight? Oh, no. I thought we'd shovel tomorrow. The snow's not supposed to stop until noon and there's no sense doing it twice, and it's nearly dark anyhow and—" her eyes skimmed over him in a way that made him wish it meant half of what it looked like it meant "—you're not dressed for the job."

He looked down at his suit a little ruefully. "I'm not going to be any better dressed for the job tomorrow."

She frowned at that. "I have some men's things in the spare room closet. I'm pretty sure there are some sweats, and a pair of sneakers, though I don't know if those will fit. Maybe some jeans."

"Oh?" Jealousy and doubt and possessiveness—how could a syllable give so much of himself away? She'd run from him for sure. At least emotionally.

Instead she raised her chin and locked eyes with his.

"I don't know what you're thinking, Michael," she challenged him directly. "But they're Paul's things. He left them here on one trip through and decided he likes having them here so he can pack lighter. Now, I think I'll change and go check on Mrs. Jenkins before dinner, and you can look through the things and see what will fit."

As she spoke, she cleared their few dishes and stowed them away in the dishwasher. She had reached the door before he could get a word in.

"Tris."

She stopped, but didn't turn. "Yes?"

"I apologize. It wasn't any of my business." He saw the line of her shoulders ease at his first words, then almost appear to slump.

She mumbled something he couldn't make sense of, because it had sounded to him as if she'd said, "Not since you don't want it to be your business." Then she said more clearly, "C'mon, I'll show you the spare room."

Upstairs minutes later, he stood at the window in the spare room she obviously used as an office and watched her, head lowered into the slanting snow, make her way to her neighbor's house. She'd briskly pointed out the location of his room, the bathroom and the closet holding Paul's clothes, then left him on his own. He'd stood there for quite a while, listening to the sounds of her moving around in the room across the hall.

God, he'd missed her. The breath he let out as she disappeared up her neighbor's walk clouded the window with instant frost. Which was harder, not seeing her at all, or seeing her and not having the right to touch her? His mouth twisted at the question. He was about to find out.

Turning from the window, he strode to the closet and jerked it open, ignoring the clench of his stomach muscles. The dim light picked out Tris's out-of-season clothes neatly hung in plastic bags. And in a corner a couple of hangers' worth of men's casual clothing. What had he been expecting? A collection of mismatched men's outfits, silent legacies of relationship after failed relationship?

He reached out to touch the worn denim of a pair of jeans. No, he hadn't expected that so much as remembered it. In that moment she'd said she had some men's clothes upstairs—even while the twist in his gut had presumed they were Grady's—he'd seen just such a closet in his mind's eye, only it wasn't in Tris's house, it was in his mother's.

He shook his head at himself and his memories as he pulled the jeans free of the hanger. Tris wasn't his mother, or his father, for that matter. Tris didn't fall in and out of love with the passing of the seasons like some people did. She'd known what she wanted from the time she was a freshman in college—Grady Roberts. There'd been only two sidetracks in that devotion. Terrence, and he'd understood that relationship for the substitute it was from the first time he'd laid eyes on the tall, blond, handsome charmer so like Grady. And himself, a trusted friend who took advantage of her vulnerability and lonesomeness to act out his own fantasies.

Jerking on jeans that were a shade tighter than his usual style, he cursed himself with the thoroughness of practice. His mouth twisted as his repertoire wound down. He'd gotten into a verbal rut since August. What he had to do now was stop chiding himself and find some way to once again give Tris the friendship she'd always counted on from him.

He pulled a sweatshirt over his head, and emerging from it came face-to-face with something on the bulletin board above her desk. The second picture Bette had taken of all of them on the library steps five months ago. Right in the middle of the bulletin board, right at eye level for anyone sitting at the desk. A memo tacked up next to it half obscured Grady and Paul, but he and Tris were shown clearly. He saw the questioning in Tris's smile as she gazed down to where his hand grasped hers as it lay on his chest. And even with his face averted from the camera, longing etched lines into his expression for any perceptive observer to see.

Why had she put it here? Didn't she see what was in his face?

His eye caught a name on the papers spread over the desk and he jumped at the chance to divert his mind from those questions. The facility in Cincinnati she'd mentioned, the one that had inspired her proposal. He picked up the brochure, reading of how a once derelict building had become a place where the homeless could get a haircut, a shower, a shave, a change of clean clothes—and a dose of renewed dignity.

He sat down, looking at the papers more closely, recognizing Tris's handwriting in the scrawled notes on how other old buildings could be converted to this use. She had target sites and possible funding sources and rough operational budgets. Impressive, very impressive. It had taken a lot of work—a lot of hard, practical work, not just the wishful thinking of an idealist leading with her heart.

He wondered at the short, sharp twist inside him at that thought. There was no reason for this to bother him. He'd said he'd help her if the proposal warranted it, and she'd obviously been making sure it did. A vision of Tris from twelve years ago formed in his mind: Tris pleading that the money from the Phantom party should go to the denizens of skid row, Tris passionate and impractical.

The vision faded as he focused again on the papers in front of him. Had she really grown up so much, changed so much? Deliberately, he forced the muscles drawing his brows together to ease.

Someone would only put this kind of work into a project that was very important to them.

"Michael!"

He started at her voice shouting up the stairs, realizing abruptly that his mouth was watering from the smell of broiling chicken. When had she come back? He hadn't even heard her come in. How long had he sat there?

"Michael, are you ready for dinner?"

"Yeah. It smells great. I'll be right down."

They ate dinner informally in front of the fireplace, with her on the couch and him in the armchair. He insisted on doing the cleaning up, and bringing her a cup of coffee as they watched television reports on the snowstorm and the havoc it was causing in the nation's capital. She reported that her neighbor seemed fine, and he told her about the last, wild days of the campaign. They laughed at memories and silly jokes on the sitcom that followed the news.

And then their eyes met, the laughter fading as he felt the shift. For a while, they'd recaptured the ease of all the years they'd know each other. Then, in a moment, it had been replaced by another memory. Would they ever stop being betwixt and between—not just friends anymore, not really lovers? God, to be her lover— No, that wasn't what he could give her, that wasn't what she needed from him.

A scene flashed on the television screen, an update on plans for the upcoming inauguration celebration, and he grasped at the topic.

"I—uh—got tickets . . . I mean our office has got extra tickets to some of the parties and things."

"That's great. Even some of the movers and shakers have been maneuvering to get their hands on tickets this time around. You're lucky."

"I guess so. Sharon always seems to come up with things like that—Sharon's Joan's confidential assistant," he explained. "She just gave me a batch this morning. For the gala at Kennedy Center a couple days before the inauguration, then the swearing-in and parade and one of the balls."

"They're definitely the hot tickets in town."

"Yeah."

He glanced at her, then quickly away. She almost sounded as if she were having as much trouble coming up with something to say as he was. Actually, he knew what he wanted to say. He just wasn't certain how to say it . . . or whether he ought to even try.

"I thought Paul and Bette and Grady would enjoy all the hoopla, so I called them right away. They're coming next weekend. And I was wondering . . . I mean, I was going to call you. I got your office number from Paul this afternoon, and I thought tomorrow morning...but then when I saw you on the Metro..."

His words wound down and he wondered what the hell had happened to the times he and Tris had understood each other so well that he never would have had to spell all this out. She would have understood halfway through his first sentence, and by now she'd have been saying, "That sounds great, Michael. I'd love to come. It'll be terrific, all being together." That was what Tris would have said twelve years ago. So why did she just look at him now with that small, stiff smile on her face?

"Would you like to join us?"

"Would I like to?" she repeated as if her likes in the matter might not be the key factor, which didn't make much sense. Had giving in to his desire and making love to her five months ago also made a stranger of her?

"It wouldn't be the same without you, Tris."

"Thank you, Michael. I'd love to come."

Even the formality of the words couldn't still the triumph that flowed through him for one, ungovernable moment.

Tris weighed the risks at the same time her arms gauged the heaviness of a shovelful of snow.

She'd listened to Michael stumble over the invitation last night, and wondered why she didn't help him out. She'd known what he was trying to say. But she'd also known she needed him to say it. She'd tried to tell herself that her accelerated heartbeat resulted simply from the prospect of being with her favorite group of people in the world once again, that it had nothing to do with knowing that it would guarantee her several more chances of seeing Michael over the next week or so.

Then he'd said *It wouldn't be the same without you, Tris,* and she'd stopped lying to herself.

So here she was, shoveling snow in the blinding-white of a finally clear early afternoon, and considering the risks to her heart.

In the months since she'd walked out of his room over the garage last August, she'd accepted that he had realized after making love to her that he could never feel anything but friendship for her. Spending more time with a Michael who saw her only as a friend would be self-punishment of the hardest sort. But what if she could change his mind? Or better yet, his heart? Until yesterday, she hadn't thought there was a chance of that.

But, even granted that he had never liked changes, she thought she'd seen signs. The way he'd looked at her in the Metro, the feel of his hand guiding her, his words at her front door, the snap in his eyes at the thought of other men's clothes in her closet, even his fumbling over the invitation to join everyone for the inauguration events. If she gave him time, maybe the desire he'd certainly felt for her back in August would find its way to the surface again, would convince him of the possibility of more than friendship for the two of them.

"Leaning on your shovel and staring into space does not constitute shoveling."

They'd started off side by side on Mrs. Jenkins's porch, working their way down her walk and across the front to Tris's. But Michael had shoveled ahead of her, so now he'd nearly reached the front steps while she lagged two yards behind. Her cheeks burned with more than the chill, because she knew she hadn't been staring into space, but at the foreground—where Paul's jeans fitted Michael snugly enough to form a fascinating picture as he bent, straightened and twisted with load after load of snow.

"I—um—was contemplating the glories of the inauguration next weekend," she improvised, quickly filling and dumping her shovel twice.

"I hope the snow doesn't ruin it." Now Michael had taken up leaning on the handle and staring.

"It'll probably be gone by then."

His eyebrows rose as he looked around at the midcalf-high expanse of snow that extended into a street as yet untouched by plow or salt truck.

"Really," she answered his unspoken doubt, as she uncovered two more feet of walk. "That's one of the things about D.C. weather. The snow can catch you off guard, but then it'll go from winter to spring in a blink."

"I'll take your word for that, since you're a veteran Washingtonian. You and Leslie were certainly right about how this town reacts to snow, so I'll count on you being right again. I'd hate for the rest of them to be disappointed. You should have heard Paul on the phone, already planning how he was going to casually let it drop at lunch with one of his highbrow competitors."

"Now that's true friendship, giving him something to brag about." Of its own accord, her grin softened into a smile. "Really, it was nice of you to invite them all. And it was nice of you to include me, Michael."

Close enough now to touch, she couldn't resist resting one thickly mittened hand on his arm. He'd insisted on coming out with only a couple of layers of Paul's sweatshirts over his own shirt, but he showed no signs of chill now as she looked into his eyes.

He shifted slightly, breaking the contact between her hand and his arm, and cleared his throat.

"I thought it would be...uh, fun, all of us here. I realized how much I'd been missing that when we got together for the wedding."

"Yes." Was that all it had been? Fun? A case of nostalgia and old times gone too far? Was that what he was trying to say, in a voice that sounded more uneven and rough than usual? She found a part of her couldn't believe that any longer.

"Of course, I know you've been seeing Grady since the wedding, but still, I figured you'd enjoy being together next weekend, even though it'll be a bigger group."

"Seeing?" Where did that come from? She blinked against the brightness, trying to see him more clearly. "What do you mean?"

But he seemed to have gotten up a full head of steam now, and her questions didn't slow him.

"I imagine you took him by surprise at the wedding. I think you took a lot of people by surprise." He flashed a grin at her that didn't seem to quite fit his face, but then quickly looked away and bent to the shovel again. "Seeing you all grown-up and so much a woman instead of the girl we knew. It probably took him a little while to adjust. But nobody's ever accused Grady Roberts of being stupid."

"You think Grady and I..."

"I know he's visited you here, Tris." He said the words softly, without looking at her. Then his voice strengthened, though his eyes did not meet hers. "I think it's great."

"Great?" She felt as if the world's spinning were grinding to a wrenching stop, so that everything went in slow motion, with her mental processes the slowest of all. Did he want her to be with Grady? Because he didn't want her? But what about what she'd seen in his eyes? The signs she'd seen? "But you...you and I—"

"Don't worry about that, Tris. I know it's been awkward, but we have too many years of friendship behind us to let that be permanent. As long as we understand how it happened, so it won't..." He cleared his throat, but didn't bother to finish that sentence. "It's pretty natural when you think about it. You thought he was rejecting you, and I was there and we'd always been friends. What shouldn't have happened is my letting it get so carried away. I don't know how to tell you how sorry I am that I failed you there."

"*Sorry.*" That damn word again. She felt the burning cold of outrage settle into her. "You thought I turned to you because I was upset about Grady." She didn't question, she summed up.

"Of course you turned to me," he said, and she supposed the words were meant to be heartening. "You always had, and I'd always been there. But this time I let you down and—"

His words broke off as she turned her back on him, stalking up the first three steps to the porch.

"Are we going in now?" He looked around at the porch and steps still waiting to be shoveled.

She spun back to face him. "I am. But if I had my way, you could stay out here forever and freeze to death for all I'd care. But I suppose then I'd be arrested for cruelty to idiots."

"Tris—"

She stomped down a step to stand just above him, thumping one multimittened hand against his hard chest. "How dare you! How dare you think I would be that, that cheap?"

"Tris, I never—"

"Cheap! Or worse. For months I've racked my brain and my heart. I knew, *knew* that you couldn't think I still had any feeling for Grady, because I had made an utter fool of myself making it crystal clear exactly how I felt about you! So I accepted that you just didn't care for me that way, that in the light of day you realized friendship was all there was for us. And all the time you were thinking this!''

She pulled in air, trying to steady her breathing, but the cold oxygen only fueled her anger.

''What kind of woman do you think I am to make love to one man when I was longing to be with another? If that's what you think of me, Michael Dickinson, you can just go to hell!''

She shoved with both hands against his chest. His heel caught a slick patch and he toppled back into the snowbank they'd built up from shoveling the walk. She didn't wait to see how he extricated himself, but stomped into the house and slammed the door behind her.

Stripping off her snow-dampened clothes haphazardly on her way to the bathroom, she jolted her chilled body with the shower's warm stream. Tears leaked from the corners of her eyes as the steamy moisture enveloped her. She could cry her heart out here and no one would hear. The pounding of the water against the tile would mask any sobs that might escape her, even if someone cared to listen.

But she *wouldn't* cry. She'd cried enough. And this hurt might have gone too deep for tears.

He didn't know her at all. Not really, not if he thought she could do that. He thought she was some giddy young girl, perhaps the image he'd formed of her when he first knew her. That hurt deeply. But what frightened her the most was the niggling voice suggesting that maybe he didn't want to know her—the woman that the girl he'd known had grown up to become. The person she was now.

It hurt. It hurt terribly. And worst of all was that Michael—Michael, who'd always been there for her—not only couldn't ease the ache this time, but was its source.

The water was edging toward tepid before she finally turned off the shower. She dried herself quickly and pulled on a soft sweater and knit pants, her favorite outfit for curling up on the couch and enjoying a three-hanky movie. Even with no such movie to watch, the clothes suited her mood.

Michael wasn't in the house. She knew that without looking. Still, she couldn't keep herself from crossing the hall to the room that already seemed to have taken on some imprint of his presence. She'd been so aware of him lying here in this bed for all the hours of the previous night. She had practically been able to feel him listening when she went downstairs for some late-night water. Even when she'd finally slept, the awareness of his nearness had crept into her dreams, where he'd been so much closer.

He'd made the bed, but imperfectly. Unconsciously, she trailed her fingers over the rumpled spread where it exposed some of the pillow. She caught herself caressing the material and snatched her hand back.

If she had to be touching something, she'd be better off cleaning things up. She pulled open the desk drawer and scooped in some earlier drafts of her homeless proposal. No sense in letting Michael see this. He might actually begin to glimpse the real Tris, and heaven knew she wouldn't want to confuse him that way. She grimaced down at the cleared desk top and wondered if her feeling fell under the heading of bitterness or self-pity.

Impulsively, she snatched the picture of the four of them off the bulletin board, tearing it a little where the thumbtack wouldn't let go. How many times had she stared at his face in that picture, telling herself that the emotions were simply a trick of shadow and light, and not totally believing it. Well, believe it now, kid.

Movement drew her gaze to the window, and she saw Michael, across the street, clearing the walk in front of the Grabowskis' while young Mikey plied a shovel nearly as big as himself and chattered happily, apparently undeterred by his audience's grim expression. Good, let him shovel the entire neighborhood for all she cared.

She spun away from the window and tromped down the stairs. The ringing telephone saved her from having to decide what to do with herself.

In response to her muttered hello came Paul's voice, vibrant and amused. "Hey, Tris, how're you doing in the Great D.C. Blizzard?"

"Hi, Paul. I'm fine."

"Yeah, you sound it. What happened, cousin, get caught in a snowbank overnight?"

That would have explained the sensation of ice encircling her heart, but it wasn't that simple. "How'd you know about the storm?"

"I was talking to Michael and— You did know he was in Washington now, didn't you?"

"Yes."

A pause followed her syllable. She could almost imagine Paul sitting in his office, chair tilted back, feet propped on the desk. He would recognize her unwillingness to talk. Considering it, he might let his eyes wander to the photo of the four of them he kept in his office, now joined by the more recent edition as well as several pictures of Bette. Then he'd make up his mind, straighten his shoulders and plunge ahead.

"Yeah, well, I was talking to him on the phone yesterday morning—" her lips tilted up slightly as he spoke right on cue, and some of the tension left her "—and he men-

tioned it was snowing some. Then it was all over the news
last night how our nation's capital had ground to a halt
because of a little white stuff. I've been trying to get
through all day. You and Michael. All I get are recordings
at the offices, and the telephone company saying your
phone was out of order until just now. But there's no answer at Michael's.''

''He's here.''

''He's . . . he's *there*? With you?''

She couldn't deny a small thrill at nonplussing her un-
flappable cousin.

''Yes. With me. Although right now he's outside with
Mikey Grabowski. Still, I think that qualifies as being here
with me.''

''Hot damn! That's terrific!''

She wanted to laugh. She wanted to cry. She did neither. She sighed, deeply and wearily, sank down on a stool
and rested her elbow on the breakfast bar.

''I've known it for years. Years! I told Bette, and she
just said to leave you two alone because—''

''Oh, Paul.''

The silence was abrupt and complete for all of three
seconds. ''*Oh, Paul?* That doesn't sound good.''

''It's not.''

''You don't still have a thing for—''

''Don't you start, too!''

''All right, all right. What happened?''

Telling him came surprisingly easy. And somehow, saying the words out loud, the problems didn't sound quite so
insurmountable.

''Sounds to me like you just have to talk out this Grady
issue, and the two of you will be all set.''

''I don't think it's that simple.''

''Why?''

Wondering if she'd imagined an indecipherable note in Paul's voice, she shifted her shoulders in frustration. "I don't know. There's something... It's like there's something he knows that I don't, but somehow I'm being held accountable, or judged or... Oh, I don't know. I don't even know what that means."

"What are you going to do about it? Give up?"

"No." She hadn't honestly known what she was going to do until she heard her heartfelt answer. Heartfelt. That was the key. She couldn't give up, not the way she felt about Michael. Her heart wouldn't let her. She had to follow these emotions to wherever they led. Even if that meant heartbreak.

"Cheer up, kid. I seem to remember you telling me over and over how true love could conquer all."

"When did I say that?"

"When Jean Marie Rustin broke up with me."

She made a sound of disbelief. "You were a freshman in college and I was a sophomore in high school at the time, Paul. Are you holding me accountable for what I said then? People change, grow up."

"Yeah, people do." Tris thought she caught an echo of something in his voice, but then it disappeared. Had the same thought occurred to him, that Michael didn't want her to grow up, that he was still stuck on the girl of twelve years ago? "So, what about now? You still think love should automatically be perfect?"

"No."

"Don't you?"

He asked the question almost absently, as if his mind had started on another track. Did she? Maybe it was a question to consider. Did she expect an easy solution, a painless transition from feeling friendship for Michael to feeling... what?

"I gave the proposal to that contact I told you about last week. He said he'd get it to Joan Bradon this week." Honesty might force her to recognize her blurted words as a detour from considering the proper label for what she felt for Michael Dickinson, but it made sense—a high-rates long-distance phone call wasn't the time to get into such thorny questions.

"Does Michael know?"

"No."

"Why not?"

"Because I haven't told him."

"That much I'd figured out myself. What I want to know is why you haven't told him?"

"It just seemed to complicate things. And he's got enough to worry about, with getting settled in on the Hill and moving and everything."

"Is that really the reason?"

Was it? The proposal was part of her adult life, far from the Tris that Michael knew in college, the one he might still care for in a way he didn't care for the new her.

"I bet your accountant would love to know you're calling long distance to play Twenty Questions."

"My accountant's thrilled that I'm going to be in D.C. next weekend making important contacts with important people. Although he won't be half as green-eyed as Judi. She was practically spitting bullets she was so mad. But she's got some big test coming up in school and can't get away."

"She must be disappointed." But Tris knew she wasn't disappointed her young cousin wouldn't be coming, although that made her feel a little guilty. She'd always liked Judi, but having her around, flirting with Michael, was more than she could take right now. Especially if he flirted back.

While she'd been thinking along more personal lines, she realized Paul had returned to the subject of getting ready to come to D.C. for the inauguration. "And he'll understand perfectly that I need to call to make arrangements for such a high-powered trip."

"Uh-huh. Like what arrangements?"

"Like checking to see if Michael's asked you to all these party things."

"Yes."

She decided to ignore his self-satisfied chortle. "Anything else?"

"Yes, asking if Bette and I can stay with you. Grady can rough it at Michael's, but I don't want Bette sleeping on the floor, and Michael's furniture probably won't arrive in time."

Tris smiled a little to herself. She wasn't the only one of their group who'd changed. Come to think of it, there were differences in all of them. Commitment-shy Paul had a wife he loved and looked out for. Self-centered Grady fretted about two friends' problem. And Michael . . . the changes in Michael were much more difficult to define. Maybe because she was still discovering them.

"Of course you can stay with me."

"Good. That'll give me more time to ask questions, too."

Chapter Eleven

She'd polished two-thirds of the wooden kitchen cabinets, punishing her arm and shoulder muscles with harder and harder strokes each time her mind threatened to stray to Michael Dickinson, when she heard the front door open and close.

About time. Not that she'd really been concerned about him out there without a proper jacket and with the winter sun rapidly losing strength. Pneumonia would serve him right.

She rubbed the cabinet front vigorously when she found herself envisioning Michael stretched out in bed—her bed—with her as his very devoted nurse.

"Tris."

A cool glance over her shoulder revealed him leaning against the doorjamb, cheeks ruddy with the cold, hair whipped by the wind, and looking incredibly healthy and vital.

"You'll freeze," she said coolly. "You'd better go change out of those clothes. If they're wet, the dryer's in the closet across from the bathroom."

"Are you worrying about me now because you don't want to be accused of cruelty to idiots?"

She refused to respond to his lopsided smile. "Right."

He pushed his right hand through his hair, and she had to turn away before she did something stupid like burst into tears. Or throw herself into his arms.

"Tris, I'm sorry. I was an ass."

"You've got that right."

"Dammit, Tris, are you even going to listen to me?"

Fairness demanded that she give him that much. She turned around, but she crossed her arms across her chest and leaned against the counter at the farthest point from his position. She could see him read her body language and she heard his sigh. He moved into the kitchen, but stayed more than an arm's length away.

"I never meant to hurt you, Tris. Not by anything I said, not by anything . . . we did."

His voice was low, and a little husky. There was no doubting his words. He cleared his throat. "It was just that as long as I've known you, you've wanted Grady Roberts, and I just thought— All right, I didn't think." He held up a hand, palm out, as if he sensed the words welling up in her and wanted to stop them.

"Maybe I'm a little slow adjusting. Maybe I don't always like changes, like you said."

She watched his brows draw together and saw a shadow pass over his face, something more than puzzlement. Something almost like pain. Her arms came uncrossed, and she stopped herself from reaching to him only by gripping the edge of the counter at either side of her hips.

"But let me tell you, it takes some adapting to get used to you." He glanced up quickly at the involuntary sound she made, his frown disappearing into a rueful grimace. "I didn't mean it quite like that. For someone who's supposed to be pretty good at stating political positions, I'm really making a mess of this."

His sigh carried a load of frustration.

"What I'm trying to say is I knew this leggy, impulsive girl, knew her through and through. And then it seems as if I blinked and she was transformed into this woman—this lovely, warm, sensuous woman." His eyes met hers for the space of a long exhaled breath that forced thought out of her and replaced it with the remembered sensations of his arms around her, his body moving against hers. And for that instant, her heart soared with the hope that he did cherish the woman, not just the girl. Then he looked away, and rationality returned. "But I still see flashes of the girl and I don't know..."

His hand worked a path through his hair once more. "I just don't know, Tris. Maybe you have a better idea what's going on."

Maybe, maybe not. Was friendship all he could feel for her? Was it the memory of her as she'd been or the person she was now that he cared for? The possible answers frightened her. But one issue held no terrors for her, one issue was absolutely clear.

"I don't deny I had a longtime crush on Grady. There'd be no sense in denying it even if I wanted to, because you were there to hear all about it. And I wouldn't want to deny it. It was part of my growing up. But I grew out of it long ago, Michael. I'd discovered a long time ago that Grady wasn't the man for me. That week we were all together just confirmed it for me."

The question of what she'd discovered about Michael during that week hung in the air between them, unspoken. She could try to tell him now. But she wasn't entirely sure of the answer.... And she could see from his face that he was even less sure.

"And I would never, ever use somebody the way you accused me of using you."

"Tris, I—"

She didn't want to hear him say he was sorry again. Not now, with undeniable hope surging in her. In his whole explanation, he'd never once said that all he felt for her, all he could ever feel for her, was friendship. With that to build on, hope was already reaching skyscraper heights.

"You better get that shower. Then I could use some help getting dinner."

And a lot of help chasing memories out of her head. About the way he'd looked coming out of a shower in August in Illinois, and her wonderings about the taste and feel and scent of his shower-clean body. About the fact that she'd experienced those sensations. Just once.

She said she'd gotten over Grady Roberts. What did that mean to him? And why the hell wasn't he elated?

Michael stared at his reflection in the shower-fogged mirror and asked himself the questions that had been echoing in his head since he'd plucked himself out of a snowbank several hours earlier.

She said she was long over Grady. Infatuation, she'd called it. A college crush.

He toweled off vigorously, and pulled on his clothes.

There'd certainly been no mistaking her anger at his belief that she'd seen him as a substitute for Grady that night in the bedroom over the garage. He caught the image of his wry expression in the mirror as he picked up the discarded clothes. But that would mean that all she'd given that night was really given to him—for *him*. He saw again the concentrated desire on her face, a face framed by the silken sweep of her hair that tangled and teased his hands. He heard again her voice, saying his name in a way that made him know he gave her pleasure. He felt again fingers that curled into his shoulders in urgent desire, fingers that held on to him with a wonderful tightness as the body below his rose to meet his demands. Lord... Tris.

He scooped up his damp clothes and headed to the dryer across the hall. The clothes inside, he absently twisted the knob to set the timer, then started the machine up. It hummed and whirred under his hand. If only his mind, this roiling mix of fear and hope, were as easy to turn on... and off. Instead his thoughts tumbled with about as much order as the clothes being dried.

Tris had always stood for dependability to him, for affection and caring that would never waver. She gave her heart and never took it back. Knowing that about her, admiring that about her had made it possible for him to accept that she would always want Grady. But now... What now?

She had thought she loved Grady and then Terrence. She certainly had cared deeply for them. He didn't doubt that. Yet now she thought she cared for him. How long would it last? How long before he, too, was in the past tense in her heart?

She would never hurt him on purpose, but many people in this world hurt without intention. Many people did not equate love with permanence. They took the moment's emotion and left it behind when the moment ended. But he wasn't one of them. He'd sworn he'd never be one of them. He'd been certain Tris wasn't, either. All these years he'd believed that she would always care for Grady, knowing with total conviction that she was not the type to move on from one "love" to another.

What if he was wrong? What if he'd been wrong all this time? What if the person he'd given his heart to twelve years ago turned out to be that kind? What then? Because he very much feared that his heart at least had never strayed in twelve long years.

"So you like living here?"

Michael's murmured question broke a silence that had been long and comfortable. They were both sitting on the floor, backs supported by the couch and legs stretched toward the flickering fire, the remains of their dinner on the coffee table they'd pushed aside to better enjoy the fire. Tris felt mellow with the aftereffects of the day's exercise, the food, the wine and most definitely the company.

"It's a great neighborhood. Quiet. Safe. Wonderful neighbors, but still near everything."

"Yeah, I was surprised to find it so suburban-looking this close to downtown."

"That's me, just an old suburban matron." She twisted a little, feeling a twinge in her shoulders from the double strain of shoveling and polishing.

"Sore?"

"Mmm. A little."

"Here, turn around." As she complied, he sat up straighter and shifted so he was behind her, close enough that she felt the warmth of his presence, but touching only where his hands kneaded her shoulders.

She clutched the pillow that had been supporting her head and let out a hum of satisfaction, not bothering to speculate how much came from the easing of groaning muscles and how much from the delicious tightening of other muscles at his touch.

"Better?" He didn't wait for an answer. "I wouldn'
worry about being viewed as a suburban matron if I were
you. I have it on the best authority that you're the hottes
thing in the neighborhood. Especially in the summer when
you wear shorts."

"What? Who in the world said that?" She turned to
look over her shoulder at him, chuckling despite the utter
seriousness of his expression.

"Mikey Grabowski."

She laughed outright. "Mikey? Mikey's all of nine years
old!"

"Uh-huh," he agreed with no abatement of solemnity.
"But Mikey has a sixteen-year-old brother whom he cites
as his source, and there is no greater authority on women
on the face of this earth than sixteen-year-old boys."

"Good heavens. Chris Grabowski? He's just a—"

"Don't say it. And don't ever let him know you think it.
He'd be crushed."

"Lord, I will never be able to garden in shorts again. I'll
feel like I have to wrap myself up in a sheet every time I
walk out the front door!"

"Ah." His breath of satisfaction whispered at her ear,
even as his fingers traveled from her shoulders to the tops
of her arms, still soothing the muscles. "Then this little
talk hasn't been wasted."

"Why, you manipulative...manipulative politician!"
She twisted around to land a blow with the pillow.

"Just trying to keep this fine neighborhood safe from
hot women gardeners."

"Oh, yeah?"

She landed another pillow blow, and another. He interrupted his laughter for a pro forma "ow" after each one.
Then, as he dodged a fourth strike, the "ow" sounded
different, and his hands instinctively went to his neck.

"Aha! Sore?" She pounced on the sign of discomfort, but stopped her attack.

"A little." He shot her a sheepish smile as he echoed her earlier words, and she felt her heart constrict in a most distracting way.

"Well, turnabout's only fair, so turn around," she said lightly.

He sent her a look hard to decipher, then turned with a trace of reluctance. She knelt behind him, contemplating the broad shoulders under the old sweatshirt, narrowing to where the snug jeans molded to him, and decided that turnabout could also be taken a step further. She scooted closer, until her knees enclosed his hips. His back straightened as if his whole body had just been called to attention, but before he could protest, she put her palms to the tight muscles at either side of his neck, rocking and pressing so effectively that she heard his small groan of reaction almost immediately.

Leaning forward, she spoke into his ear, trying to imitate his earlier conversational tone. "I have it on pretty good authority that you're not so bad yourself."

"Tris." His tone was admonishing, but his head dropped forward under her questing fingers, so she figured that outweighed any warning.

"'Hunk,' I believe, was the description. Not, perhaps, as strong a term as 'hot.' But then there was a member of the older generation present, and their sensibilities had to be taken into account." She brushed against him, not quite sure herself if the touch of her breasts to his back was deliberate or not, but most pleased by the sound he tried to swallow.

"And this judgment came from someone considerably older than nine, or sixteen. For that matter, I believe I saw the opinion reflected in the eyes of several women last August.''

''Tris—''

Oh, she knew the dangers of not heeding his cautions, of turning the conversation from the teasing of a moment earlier. But somehow, even with all that had happened between them, she knew that Michael would not let her fall if she took a misstep on this tightrope.

''And I realized they were right. I was the one who hadn't been seeing clearly.'' Her fingers slipped into the sweatshirt neck widened by age and fanned wide across the smooth, tight skin of his upper back. She wanted more.

''I'd always thought you so calm, so rational. I didn't recognize the heat underneath. Until...until you held me. You surprised me, Michael. I thought I knew you so well but you surprised me.''

She wanted to touch him more, to slide her palms across the well-remembered contours of his back, but he surprised her again, twisting around abruptly and catching her wrists in a hard grip.

He bit off a word even before he'd spoken it, but she knew it was going to be ''don't.'' She couldn't quite meet his eyes, instead watching the rapid rise and fall of his chest. His hands on her wrists hurt a little, but she didn't want him to let go. She might fall completely if he did.

''It was an artificial situation, Tris.'' He'd regained most of his calm when he spoke. That irritated her. Why should he be calm when she felt such confusion? ''I understand that.''

''I don't. What are you saying, Michael?''

''It wasn't real. The whole week. A wedding's a pretty emotional time anyway, and then there was all the emotion of all of us together, and remembering the past, and the way things were and...''

She knew Grady had edged into his thoughts from the tenor of extreme reasonableness in his voice.

"And the way things weren't," she finished for him.

"Yeah, that, too."

"And you think that's why I made love to you?"

"It's natural, Tris. All those emotions . . . Old emotions and new emotions. Changes."

"If you're going to say again that I used you as some sort of substitute—"

He held up a palm in a peacekeeping gesture. "No. No, I promise. Besides, you can't push me down this time. I'm already down."

He recaptured her hands, one in each of his, and she found something hopeful in that.

"Okay." She let her ire subside. If he could be reasonable, so could she. And they'd just see where reason led. "So you think I made love to you out of an excess of emotions that I didn't know how to deal with."

He grimaced at her summation. His slight shrug could have acknowledged her accuracy or the uselessness of trying to explain further.

"All right, so let's say that's why you think I made love to you." She drew a deep breath and he seemed to still suddenly as if he sensed a danger. She issued her challenge. "Then why did *you* make love to *me?*"

Motionless, he stared into her eyes. But she could read nothing in his. She controlled the urge to shiver at their blankness, and met his look as steadily as she could, very aware that he still held her hands where they rested on her knees.

When he shifted his weight and grinned at her, she felt as if he'd crossed a line of some sort. But her heart sank at the unfamiliar slant of his mouth. There was no hint of a dimple, and this wasn't his usual little-boy grin. It was an impostor.

"Well, you got to admit you came on like gangbusters. A guy would have to be crazy to pass up..." He started off fine, but it didn't last, and soon his voice faded into nothing. She offered up a silent prayer of thanks that he had been made so incapable of lying.

He lifted his hand, taking hers with it, to brush a lock of hair back from her cheek with his knuckles, then let a pent-up breath escape in the sound of a small defeat. "I made love to you because you were so damn beautiful. Because you're you, Tris. And I have never been able to resist that temptation."

"I don't want you to resist, Michael." She wanted the words to be strong and assured. They were a whisper. Her laugh came out shaky and low. "I've done my best to show you that. Good heavens, I've brazenly thrown myself at you every time trying to show you that."

"Not every time." In that low-voiced denial she heard the gruffness of desire, and she remembered how he'd awakened her during the night in the bedroom over the garage, and how he had shown her how much he did want her, needed her. His words now and the memory of his loving then gave her the courage to say more.

"There's no one else around this time," she said. "No other emotions complicating our feelings. No nostalgia for the past, no sentimental journeys home. Nothing artificial about the circumstances this time. Just you and me, together. It's very simple."

She lifted her hand to his face, taking his hand along as he had hers.

When she cupped her palm to mold it to his cheek, Michael spread his hand atop hers to press it tighter to his face, then turned to touch his lips to the delicate skin at the base of her fingers.

He knew she was wrong. Lord, she was wrong. Simple? When had there ever been anything simple about the two of them? And nothing artificial? What could be more artificial than being insulated by drifts of snow and warmed by a roaring fire and good wine? No other emotions? How about longing and need and passion?

"Michael?" In her voice he felt the remembered vulnerable timbre of her questions five months before. *Will you dance with me? May I come up to your room? Will you kiss me?*

He looked into her eyes and saw the uncertainty and the desire. And more, he saw the need. Tris needed him, and that, as always, was the temptation he stood no chance of resisting.

"Yes, Tris."

He freed his hands from hers and set them on her jawline, sweeping his thumbs across the soft sharpness of her cheekbones. He bent to touch her lips, gently, slowly. Then he slid his fingers farther into her hair and curled his hands more securely around her head to pull her tightly against his mouth, so that her lips parted and her tongue met his. He loosened his hold when they were both breathless and lifted his head enough to look into her eyes again. The desire and the need were there, stronger and darker. The uncertainty was gone.

He'd force himself to take it slow this time. Not to let the passion pull them under too quickly. To let it build gradually, so that if the uncertainty returned... If the uncertainty returned, he'd go crazy, but he'd stop. God help him, he'd stop.

"Slow," he murmured against her mouth. "Slow."

She mumbled something, but slow or not, he was too greedy for her taste to let the words escape her lips.

Still sampling the dark sweetness of her mouth and tongue, he let his hands glide slowly, so slowly, down the length of her neck, feeling the arch of it under his fingers as she bent back to receive his kiss.

His caresses spoke of infinity as he explored her through the medium of her sweater. Under his hands, the knit became an erotic abrasive. She longed to have it gone, to erase all barriers between them, but when at last—at long, lazy last—he languidly removed the sweater, she found no release. Only more need.

She wondered hazily how he could keep his loving so slow on the surface while she could sense—and share—the surging urgency underneath. The passion they had experienced five months ago had been almost alien to their relationship. Tonight, she felt something new. As if elements of their easy friendship overlaid the desire, creating a third stage. A new level, distinct and very potent.

His mouth, long journeying from her chin to her nipple, at last reached its destination, and he opened his mouth to pull on it through the lace of her bra. She arched, in pleasure and frustrated longing to draw him closer still, to draw him into the closest of embraces. Now.

But she couldn't gather enough wits to express any of that until he broke contact to start another joltingly languorous exploration of her other breast.

"Michael, please."

"Slow."

She took a quick, deep breath, trying to steady herself. She didn't consider the resulting movement of her breasts until she heard Michael's rumbled groan, and then she allowed herself a small smile.

"All right, slow. But only after you catch up with me."

With some regret, but also a dose of self-preservation, she broke away.

He let her go, a horrible doubt slicing into him for the instant before he saw her eyes. Then he relaxed. Momentarily.

She slipped her hands, wide open, under the sweatshirt, managing to caress a couple hundred million nerve endings while lifting the shirt over his head. She leaned forward to circle him with her arms and stroke her hands over his back.

"I love your back."

He mimicked her action, sweeping his hands along the delicate indentation of her backbone. "Me, too."

Encountering the encumbrance of her bra, he quickly unhooked it. The lacy material swung loose between them and he felt it like a teasing feather against his chest. Reflexively, he pulled her to him, relishing the way her soft breasts pressed the lace against his skin. "But I like other parts, too."

"Me, too."

She sounded a little breathless, although he knew for a fact that she was breathing, because he could feel the movement of her lungs under his hands and could feel the effects of her breaths against the skin where she was nibbling along the cord of his neck. Could feel it there and in every square inch of his body.

She backed away enough to let him look into her eyes. The desire and the need shone in her, flaring as brightly as the fire before them.

"Yeah? What else do you like?"

With a motion so slow he could hardly bear it, she pulled the straps of her bra down on her arms. Deliberately, she set the bra aside, then put her hands, warm and soft, on his chest. Their progress down his chest was wickedly languid. A slow-motion torture of pleasure as she tempted his nipples with gentle touches, then too soon deserted them to slide lower and lower over ribs and muscles that battled not to tremble.

At the snap to his jeans, her fingers fumbled long enough for him to wonder if she really was nervous or just prolonging his agony of anticipation. Then the rasp of the zipper came in time to his breathing. He captured her hand and brought it to the waistband of his briefs.

"Touch me, Tris. If you want to, touch me."

"I want to."

And from her touch, he knew she did.

He knew it was her hands that freed him, that stoked the fire so hot that he had to still them once, twice. But he wasn't aware of stripping off the rest of her clothes and the rest of his until he was settled between her legs.

"Oh, God. Tris."

"It's okay. Michael."

"Slow. Going . . . to give you . . . slow."

The tinge of desperation in her soft laugh did nothing to cool him. "Somehow I'd forgotten you were the one saying slow."

He eased slightly away from her, bowing his body to open his mouth over her stomach and take a mockingly gentle bite of the soft flesh there. "I meant it. Something must have made me forget that resolve—temporarily."

He set about proving to her just how firm his resolution could be, determined to stretch their communication, their knowledge of each other. Courting familiarity by listening to her body, tuning himself to what she needed, where a touch would make her tremble, how a kiss could make her sigh. And he knew she was doing the same. She had to be, because she would touch her lips to his collarbone, her fingers to his hip, her breasts to his chest, and only then did he realize he had wanted that touch above all other touches at that instant.

The exertion of patience left its sheen on their bodies when he finally acceded to the pleas of her soft voice and urging fingers and positioned himself above her. He looked into her eyes as he gradually brought himself into her body. She lifted her hips to take him more deeply, and they stilled.

He wanted to hold this moment forever. He wanted to extract every millisecond from it. He wanted the simple rightness of this sensation to last forever. But a movement started in one of them, and echoed to the other, then back, growing stronger and faster with each exchange until there was no knowing where one ended and the next began. The movements became shudders, and then cries, and then boneless, nerveless exhaustion and small sounds of content.

Michael shifted some of his weight off Tris, but did not break their union. Time passed, but the increments weren't important to him. She was right; what there was between them was simple, as simple as this. And she was wrong, because what there was between them was also as complex as this.

"I'm glad their flight comes in before rush hour. That way I can get off a little early to pick them up at the airport and have Grady settled at your place and Paul and Bette here, before we meet you at the restaurant for dinner. You're sure you'll be able to get away in time?"

"I'm sure." He automatically shifted to one side to give her better access to the mirror as she brushed her hair.

"Did I tell you I invited Leslie?"

"Uh-huh," he grunted as he lifted his chin to pass one end of his tie over the other.

"Seven-thirty, okay?"

"Okay."

Tying his tie, he could still watch her, and marvel at how in the seven days since the heavens had dumped a snowstorm on Washington, D.C., they had meshed their daily lives.

In the mornings they equably shared the bathroom as they got ready for work, leaving together to walk—through snow that melted as rapidly as Tris had predicted—to the Metro headed for downtown and their jobs. In the evenings, they put together dinner from the basics Tris had on hand and some specialties one or the other of them happened to pick up during the day. And in the nights . . . ah, the nights.

Tris swung away from the mirror and headed back to the bedroom. Peering at his image as he straightened his tie and shirt collar, Michael caught a glimpse of the sly grin on his face.

The nights were what had him smiling stupidly all through the days, and thinking ahead to the time when he could go home to Tris.

Home.

The word caught him off guard. Was he considering this narrow brick house his home? He had a key, yes. And Tris had certainly made him welcome. He'd hardly been back to the small apartment farther up Connecticut Avenue for more than changes of clothes.

But home. That implied things he wasn't sure he wanted implied. Things like counting on permanence, like staking your future on the steadfastness of someone else's heart.

They said the desire for a home was inbred, but he might be better off ignoring that and honing some of his other instincts. Like self-preservation.

"Michael? What's wrong?"

"Nothing."

He stood in the doorway and watched Tris smooth the stocking over her leg and felt the clutch of another instinct. The instinct to return her to that warm, mussed bed and use only a small slice of its wide surface.

"I wish you could come with me to the airport to pick them all up this afternoon."

"It's an important meeting."

"Oh, I know. And we've been very lucky that you've had so much free time this week." She looked up at him through her lashes as she buttoned her blouse, and he felt his body tightening, despite the shared shower—long and steamy and most satisfying—that had already put them behind this morning.

He talked to divert his mind in hopes his body would take the hint. "It's the inauguration. Everybody has so many social obligations there's not much time left for work."

"I've heard that some senator once said it was a lot less work to govern than to inaugurate." She fastened her skirt and pulled her shoes from the closet.

"I believe it."

He knew what could happen. How many times had he seen his mother or father go through this euphoria with a new partner? How many times had they told him that this time, this person was really *it?* How many times had he believed them and gotten involved in their latest loves' lives? And how many times had those people—nice people, generally, good people—disappeared along with the supposed never-ending love? And there he'd be, turning around to be introduced to someone new.

The only way he'd learned to cope was to not let the changes permeate the fabric of his life, to let them skim over him and to hold on to the certainties he did have with both hands. To cultivate those certainties, like his ability, like his regard for Joan Bradon and a few others, like his friendships with Grady, Paul . . . and Tris.

There was no way to avoid all changes, so he'd felt the pain of some, like having Laura go out of his life last year. But he knew that pain would be nothing compared to what would happen when Tris moved on. He knew—he feared—she would move on, as she had from Terrence and Grady. And he had to make sure he survived it.

"Did I give you the name of the restaurant?" she asked as she put gold hoops in her ears and reached for a gold chain.

"Yes."

"And the address?"

He had to forcibly restrain himself from giving in to the temptation to take the chain from her hands and fasten it around her neck, knowing full well that that would lead to kissing her vulnerable, velvet nape and that would lead to so much more. "Yes. You wrote it all down, and I have the paper here in my pocket. You're treating me like a kinder-gartner. You want to pin it to my coat?"

Her smile was a little quizzical and he knew his rough tone was the cause.

"No. I just want to be sure you'll be there. I'm sure Paul and Bette and Grady and Leslie will want to see you. And I know that after twelve hours I will be more than eager to see you." She passed him on her way out the door, paus-ing to brush a kiss both promising and fleeting across his lips.

"C'mon, I think we have time for one cup of coffee if we hurry." She made the words sound like an invitation of an entirely different sort.

He clenched his hands at his sides to keep from reaching for her as they headed down the stairs.

Chapter Twelve

"Michael's place is on the sixth floor." Tris led the way into the small elevator, and caught the look Bette and Paul exchanged as she turned around to press the button. "He told me when he gave me the key," she added.

That was true. She'd never been to his apartment, because he'd been at her house for all this short, idyllic week. She felt her stomach give a little lurch as the elevator started a sluggish ascent, but she didn't think her reaction was to the motion.

Was the idyll over? Was that why he'd been acting so odd this morning? He'd seemed both more intense and more removed somehow. There'd been an emotion so strong in him that she'd felt its waves halfway across the bedroom. But she couldn't define it. Wariness? Uneasiness? Perhaps those could be explained if he still had a lingering doubt about her feelings for Grady and he was keyed up by the prospect of them all being together again.

But what about the other possible labels her mind had come up with for his mood? Like fear. Or distrust.

"C'mon, Tris. We need the key to open the door."

Shaking her head free of her questions, she followed the rest of them out of the elevator. She unlocked the door to 605 and swung it open wide. "Michael said to leave your stuff anywhere, Grady."

Grady, followed by Bette and Paul, walked to the center of the room before thunking down his suitcase on the carpeted floor.

"Yeah, anywhere," he muttered.

"Great decorator," commented Paul, looking from the uncurtained windows to the bare walls to the small stack of unpacked boxes.

"His furniture hasn't arrived yet." Tris bristled on Michael's behalf at the implied criticism. But a whispered question in her mind about whether the unsettled air had a deeper cause than all the time he'd spent at her house sent a shiver down her back. It almost looked as if he weren't sure he would like the transition to D.C., and he wanted to be ready to pick up and leave, to return to where he'd been before this change in his life.

"But he did order a bed," she added for Grady's benefit, and perhaps, a little, to sidetrack her own thoughts.

She set off purposefully down the short hall that obviously led to the two bedrooms and bath. In the larger bedroom was a sleeping bag on top of a pallet. Tris wondered if it was her imagination that made it seem so obvious that this wrinkled arrangement hadn't been used in a week. In the other room was the brand-new bed, the box spring and mattress still enclosed in plastic.

"Guess he hasn't had a chance to settle in much," commented Grady.

"It does look unlived in," agreed Bette, innocently—too innocently. "As if he hasn't spent much time here."

Paul emitted a sound of choked laughter. Tris lifted her chin as she met grins from Bette and Grady. All right, so they all knew, or had a pretty good idea, where Michael had been spending his time. She wasn't ashamed of it. Quite the opposite. And she wished like the dickens that he could be spending his time in her bed these next few days instead of returning here to be host to Grady.

"He hasn't," she said boldly. "And frankly, you're all putting a definite cramp in our style."

The easy laughter that followed her declaration seemed to wash away any traces of awkwardness in adjusting to the newness of her and Michael being more than friends. By the time they'd prepared the bed for use, stowed Grady's belongings, then done the same with Paul and Bette's at her house and made their way to the restaurant, Tris felt that she and Michael were accepted as a couple as surely as Paul and Bette were.

At the restaurant, she discovered there might be one exception to that. Michael.

Her heart seemed to take an extra beat when she saw him making his way through the crowd to them. He really was, in a most understated way, a hunk. And that was even with the conservative dark suit and white shirt hiding the attributes she had come to know and enjoy intimately over the past seven days.

The glance he sent her seemed a little constrained. He accepted a kiss and hug from Bette and exchanged warm handshakes with Paul and Grady. But she quickly realized that he was keeping distance—and often a couple other bodies—between the two of them, as if he were afraid that she might grab him and kiss him in front of their friends. Was he uncomfortable about their relationship? Ashamed?

The stab of hurt at that possibility weakened her enough that she'd been maneuvered into a corner seat before she realized exactly what he had in mind.

Grady sat at her right. And Michael was at the opposite corner of the table from her, as far as he could get at a cozy table for six in a crowded restaurant.

What did he think he was doing? Trying to force the clock back to twelve years ago? Was this some sort of test? Or worse. Was some part of him trying to make her return to what, to who she had been, because that was who he loved?

Wasn't that a kick? she thought, when she allowed herself to think. The girl Tris had thought she was in love with Grady. The woman Tris knew she loved Michael. But Michael was still caught up with the girl Tris. All it would need to be a complete mess was for Grady to fall for her, now, as the woman she was. That would make all three of them miserable.

But, despite her own troubles, Tris was observant enough to believe that Grady, long the oblivious corner of this triangle, was far from miserable when Leslie came hurrying up to the table.

At least someone was happy, she thought, with a swell of self-pity. Amid the easy banter of old friends and somewhere between the salad and the main course, anger started chipping away at the self-pity. Who did Michael Dickinson think he was? How dare he push aside the past week as if it hadn't existed? Because it sure as hell had existed, and so did she. And she wasn't about to let him pretend otherwise.

By the time the waiter had cleared the main course and Leslie started to excuse herself from the table, temper had enough strength to push Tris out of her chair and slap her napkin down on the table as if it were a gauntlet as she glared at Michael.

"I'll go with you." She had a sense that everyone looked at her a little strangely then, but the only reaction that really interested her was the startled uncertainty in Michael's eyes. Good. Let him wonder what was going on in her mind. Let him be concerned just a fraction as much as she had been. Let him worry about how she felt about him for a change.

She was still considering exactly what she would do to him when the wonder and the concern and the worry finally wore him down enough to break through all his barriers, while she and Leslie stood before the mirror in the ladies' room, reapplying lipstick and combing their hair. It abruptly struck her that Leslie had been talking earnestly and watching her intently for a couple of minutes. She struggled to catch up with the thread of the conversation.

"...since we've been friends for so long, and your friendship's very important to me, I think being honest is best. So if you tell me hands-off, that's the way it'll be. Not that there's been any hands-on. Nothing like that, it's just sometimes I get a sort of vague impression.... It's just that I'd rather head it off beforehand than wait to see if it's my imagination. I mean, I wouldn't want you to think I was trying to infringe." Leslie's uncharacteristic babbling had Tris staring at her friend, who wouldn't meet her eyes. "Never mind. I think it's all my imagination."

"What's your imagination, and what are you talking about, infringe? Infringe on what?"

Leslie took a deep breath. "Not 'what,' 'who.' Grady."

Tris stared at her a moment in the mirror, then turned to face her. "Oh, God. Not you, too. Not one fool. Two."

Leslie's expression froze. "I know you think you were a fool to care about Grady when you were in school, Tris. But I am not getting involved, and I'm not a fool—"

Tris shook her head. "Yes, you are, but not the way you think. I don't mean you and I are the two fools. I mean you and Michael."

Leslie's stiff dignity evaporated instantly. Curiosity could do that. "Michael? How are Michael and I being fools?"

"By thinking I still have a thing for Grady," Tris said tartly.

"I never said—"

"No, you never said. But why else would you start talking this junk about 'infringing'?"

"I just thought... I mean, we've been friends a long time and I wouldn't want you to think..."

"To think you were trying to cut me out with a guy." Leslie started to protest, but Tris stopped it with a wave of her hand. "See what I mean? Lord, it's bad enough getting it from Michael, but you! Leslie, I don't know how to say this any more clearly than I already have. I don't love Grady Roberts. I never did, not in the way I understand love now. I had a severe case of unrequited infatuation, but that was years ago. Whatever you want to call it, it stopped a long time ago. I know it was gone by the time I met Terrence. And I can tell you that by the third day with Grady last August, I knew with total, utter, absolute certainty that there'd never be anything other than friendship between Grady and me. That other feeling was like a ghost—a pleasant, friendly ghost of a long-gone memory."

Leslie smiled at her a little sheepishly. "I knew that. I really did. I knew it when you came back from Illinois in August, and I would have had to be wearing a blindfold

not to know it when I saw the way you and Michael wer
looking at each other that day on the Metro. Otherwise
never would have interfered that way.''

"Oh, no, you never would have interfered," said Tri
with affectionate sarcasm.

Leslie pretended huffy indignation. "I might interfer
now and again, but it's only top-quality interference. An
you can't tell me any different. I've seen you come in ever
day this week with dark circles under your eyes and thos
turned-inside grins that say that you've found somethin
a darn sight better than sleeping to occupy your nights!''

Tris abruptly turned away to return her comb and lip
stick to her purse.

"Tris? What is it? Is something wrong? Oh, Lord, hav
I put my foot in it? Was I totally wrong about how you'v
been looking this week?''

"No. You weren't, but now..." She raised her head to
meet Leslie's searching look.

"But now you're not sure," Leslie supplied, and Tri
nodded. "I've got to admit I wondered a little at the seat
ing arrangement tonight. That's why I was asking about—
well, you know. So what's happening?''

"I don't know. That's what's so frustrating. Last nigh
everything was fine. Then this morning, when we wer
talking about everybody coming in, and the plans for th
weekend, it was as if he backed up about a hundred miles.''

"Why?''

"I don't know. I honestly don't know.''

Through the rest of the meal, and even when everyone
returned to her house for a nightcap, she had no opportunity to confront Michael with that question of "why,''
because they were always in a group, with no chance for
private conversation. Almost as if Michael had planned i
that way. And through the weekend rush of sight-seeing

and party-hopping that absorbed them all, she had the
distinct impression he meant to keep it that way.

Emerging from the dim, cozy restaurant into the
brightness of a sparkling winter day, Michael watched
Senator Joan Bradon and their two business-lunch companions blink their eyes against the cold dazzle of the sky,
trying to get their bearings. He didn't need to do that because he knew exactly where he was. A block and a half
from Tris's office. *Tris.*

He flagged a taxi and enclosed the other two in it, then
turned to search for another cab to take the senator and
himself back to Capitol Hill.

"Joan! Joan Bradon!"

Michael watched Joan's face crease into a smile as a
gray-overcoated man separated himself from the flow of
the sidewalk traffic. Even the expensive tailoring didn't
mask that this man had a burly enough build to match the
deep voice.

"Hello, Morton. How are you?"

"Same as always. But how are you? Welcome to Washington, Senator Bradon. Congratulations!"

"You already congratulated me, or didn't you know
your secretary sent me flowers the day after I won the
election?"

"Of course I knew, and I sent them, not my secretary.
But I thought you might have forgotten."

"Not a chance. But of course, you were just covering all
the bases, weren't you?" She turned to Michael. "Michael, you remember Morton Treen, don't you?"

He did. As he shook hands, he contemplated the man.
Truly a political animal, with no official title or power, but
with plenty of clout. Gray suited him. Michael knew
Morton Treen had done enough expedient, self-serving

deals to dim any white hat he'd try to wear, yet he'd ac
complished enough good to prevent anyone from eve
painting him black. He fit Washington perfectly.

"Good to see you again, Michael. And Joan, this is ab
solutely providential running into you this way. I hav
something I'd like to throw your way. It could get you of
to a flying start on the Hill, really make a name for your
self right away. Do you have some time?"

Michael met Joan's look and gave an infinitesima
shrug. With the city gearing up for the inauguration fes
tivities, work was rather piecemeal.

"Certainly, Morton." She turned to Michael. "I'll mee
you back at the office. Or better yet, why don't you tak
the afternoon off? I know you have friends in from out o
town, and you're looking a little tired. You need to rela
more, enjoy yourself."

She gave him a small push, and turned to take Morto
Treen's arm, heading back into the restaurant.

Michael smiled a little as he watched them. Morto
Treen might be a tough political animal, but he'd put hi
money on Joan any day.

He'd walked a block and a half before his consciou
mind acknowledged what his subconscious apparently ha
known all along. He was going to see Tris. He'd misse
her. These past few days, wrestling with his doubts an
seeing her only in the midst of crowds, he'd really misse
her. He paused outside her office building, considering th
words emblazoned above the door. One word caught hi
attention—*Preservation*. That was what he should be
thinking about. Self-preservation. Preserving his heart.
Ensuring that when she moved on from him, there was stil
some of him left. Anything left.

He stared at the word. Preservation. Self-preservation.
Hell, who was he kidding? There wasn't anything left of

is heart to preserve. She had it all. Probably had since her freshman year in college, twelve long years ago.

He pushed open the plate-glass door and went in.

The quick knock on her half-opened door hardly penetrated Tris's mind.

"C'mon in," she called and started to turn around without disturbing either the half of her mind occupied by a Midwestern group's convoluted efforts to save a landmark inn, or the half occupied by the complex man who was driving her crazy... and who was standing in her doorway with the most curious expression on his face she'd ever seen. As if the desire to smile at her made him frown.

"Michael." The tightening of her throat softened the word into a whisper.

"Hi, Tris. Busy? The woman up front said to come on back."

"Yes. I mean, no, I'm not busy. And I'm glad you came on back."

She crossed to the door, and he stepped into the room as she closed it. She watched him survey the small office, taking in the bookshelves, the open folders on her desk, the orderly clutter of a space well organized and well used.

"I've missed you, Michael."

He completed his circuit of the room and stood before her as she leaned against the door. Something in him wouldn't allow him to make the same admission. "You just saw me last night."

"Mmm-hmm. Me and approximately three thousand other people at Kennedy Center."

"Didn't you enjoy the gala? All those stars, all those dressed-to-the-nines celebrities?"

"It was all right."

"Just all right? I thought you were the one telling me a week ago that those were the hottest tickets in town."

"They were. But there are other things I'd rather do. Things you can't very well do at Kennedy Center with three thousand people around."

"Other things? Like what?"

"Like this." She slid her hands up his chest, burrowing under the open topcoat and suit jacket so only the fine cotton of his shirt separated her palms from his skin. At his shoulders, she moved her hands higher, reaching around his neck to pull herself close, at the same time urging his head down to hers.

He required little urging. She felt the taut need in him an instant before his mouth found hers. His tongue thrust between her lips as his body pressed her firmly against the door. Welcoming the weight and heat of him, she shifted to accommodate the knee he slid between hers, spreading her legs apart until he bent a little to turn his hips into the cradle that awaited him. She tightened her legs against his. Ah, it felt so good . . . and it could feel so much better. She felt his arousal pressing against her, hollowing out her insides with the ache he'd created.

He lifted his head, too soon for her desire but nearly too late for her lungs. She gulped in air and joy and relief. Everything was all right. Everything had to be all right.

"God, you feel good, Tris." He muttered the words against her neck, so they thrilled her both as sound and touch.

She moved against him, and he responded by pressing his hips into her, and finding her mouth again and again. Until they both had to gasp for air and enough self-control to keep from slipping down to the floor and completing what they both craved.

He'd eased away from her some, so her forearms rested on his shoulders, and he watched her intently. She smiled into his multicolored eyes, and spoke the words she couldn't hold in any longer.

"I love you, Michael Dickinson."

She felt the change in him immediately. His eyes dropped and he shifted his shoulders as if they carried the weight of her arms on them as a burden.

"That's quite a word to throw around." He spoke very quietly, very reasonably. The flatness chilled her.

"Throw around?" The jolt of fear stopped her heart, then hammered its beats so fast she felt breathless once more. He didn't want her love. Oh, Lord, he didn't want her love.

"You've thought you were in love before, haven't you, Tris?"

It was more accusation than question. She couldn't decide if her reaction was sadness or anger. "You're never going to get over the fact that I once thought I was in love with Grady Roberts, are you?" she asked. "That I had a youthful infatuation with him. You'll never get past Grady."

"Listen. Grady isn't the issue. I wouldn't give a damn if you'd married the man and had five children by him. Since you say it's really over—"

"Over? There wasn't ever anything there. Not anything real. Just my infatuation."

"And is that over? Your infatuation for him?"

"Yes!"

"Good! Because I want to get married. And I only intend to do this once."

She sucked in a breath for her next retort, and it stuck in her throat. How could the right words sound so wrong? How could the right man be so wrong? At last the air hissed out of her as she considered Michael's belligere[nt] face. "That's a hell of a proposal."

"Then it suits the situation just fine, because I'm in [a] hell of a fix."

"What's that supposed to mean?"

"It means I'm in love with you, probably have bee[n] since you were a freshman in college, but I don't know you love me."

Very quietly, very dangerously, she spoke. "I've said [I] love you, Michael, haven't I?"

"Yes."

"But you don't believe it."

"I don't know. I don't know what to believe. All thos[e] years—"

"All those years *ago*, Michael. That's the importan[t] word you keep forgetting." But something inside of he[r] wondered if Grady was all that bothered him. "Yes, [I] thought I was wildly, unrequitedly in love with Grady When I was seventeen years old. And yes, I held on to tha[t] belief for a while. But I grew out of it."

"Is that what happened with your marriage, too? Yo[u] grew out of it?"

She stilled at the harshness of his words. She remem[-]bered her uneasy feeling during her telephone conversa[-]tion with Paul the week before. The uneasy feeling tha[t] there was something standing between her and Michae[l] that she didn't know about. Something deeper than he[r] long-ago crush on Grady Roberts. Did her marriage an[d] divorce have something to do with it? What if it was she not Grady, that he couldn't get past. The changes in her If he still loved someone she no longer was. She felt [a] clutch of something as cold as panic at her heart. *Lord[,] please let it be Grady that's the issue here. I know, even[*

tually, I can convince him that's no threat to us. But if it's something else . . .

"I made a mistake marrying Terrence. A terrible, unfair mistake. But people do make mistakes, Michael. Especially young people. I grew up. I don't think you've seen that yet—"

"What if this is another mistake?"

She felt as if the breath, the life, the love, had been sucked out of her. "You don't know. You really don't know. You don't know me. And you don't trust me. Or my love. God, I thought if there was anybody in the world who would understand . . ."

"Tris—"

"No." She pulled her arm away from his touch, afraid she wouldn't get through this if he touched her. "I very much fear that the Tris you say you're in love with, the Tris you proposed to just now, is no longer the Tris I am. So I must decline, with very great regret, your flattering proposal."

He stared at her so long that she feared the tears would come before he left. Then he muttered a curse word that would have shocked her coming from him, if she'd had any emotion left over for shock.

He spun on his heel and jerked open the door, almost colliding with Leslie, whose hand was raised in preparation to knock.

"Oh!" She stepped back in obvious surprise, started to smile a greeting, then stopped. "Michael."

He didn't acknowledge her, but he did alter his route enough to avoid running her down as he strode out. Leslie seemed to be grateful for that courtesy, muttering something dryly about "nice seeing you, too" as she looked in the direction of his departure.

Then she turned to Tris and, after one long, searching gaze, she swung the door closed behind her and stood there a full minute before breaking the silence.

"Anything I can do?"

"No."

"Anything anybody can do?"

"No." Nobody except that stubborn, pigheaded man who'd just walked out.

"Maybe you should take the afternoon off."

Tris sank into her chair, tension abruptly giving way to exhaustion. "No. At least here I have a chance of keeping part of my mind off it."

Leslie came across the room to perch on the low bookshelves under the window. She didn't say anything, but Tris felt her concern. She had to talk to someone. Who better than Leslie?

"It's the same old thing, Leslie. Every time I think he's past it, it comes back to that whole silly thing with Grady." She gave a laugh devoid of amusement. "You know the weird thing? I never even so much as kissed Grady Roberts. I've shown Michael every way I can think of that I don't care for Grady as anything more than a friend. If someone had told me that Michael Dickinson would be a jealous man, I wouldn't have believed it. It just doesn't fit him."

Leslie's expression became very thoughtful, but she said nothing.

"You know what makes me the saddest, Leslie? I used to feel that Michael could look right into me and see all the way to the bottom of my heart. It used to make me feel so safe, too, because here was someone who knew everything about me and still accepted me, still liked me. But if that's true, why doesn't he see or believe that I love him? Or was I just wrong all those years about him, about us?"

Asking the question, Tris felt a swell of loneliness rising in her. She didn't want to consider the hole in her life that would be left without Michael there. She found some comfort from the emphatic shake of Leslie's head.

"You don't really think you were wrong, Tris. You know you and Michael have something very special. But it's changed. You were friends a long time, and now you're something else. You've got to give yourselves time to adjust to all these differences—the differences from each of you growing up, and the tremendous differences from a new kind of relationship."

"I guess my mind knows that," Tris acknowledged. "But it's hard, and a little lonely. And when he starts acting this way, so unlike himself, with this jealousy—"

"Are you sure it is jealousy?"

Tris looked up at her friend. "What do you mean?"

"I've just wondered... You say it doesn't fit him, and I'd have to agree. It doesn't fit the man he seems to be, or how he acts."

"What do you mean?" The words came out again, although she wasn't sure she wanted the answer.

She could tell Leslie how Michael had brought up Terrence, too. That would prove his jealousy... wouldn't it? *Is that what happened with your marriage, too? You grew out of it... ? What if this is another mistake?*

She remembered her doubts, her impressions that there was something deeper bothering Michael. Be honest, Tris. You fear that it was something deeper. She wanted it to be jealousy, because jealousy seemed straightforward, relatively simple and perhaps fixable. While the unknown could very well be unsolvable.

"I watched Michael yesterday with Grady, and it doesn't seem to me that Michael treats Grady like someone he's jealous of. And then I thought about how he is with you, how he looks at you. I'd be willing to bet my last Southern drawl that he loves you. But he looks at you as if it's all going to be taken away from him any moment. And you're the one who's going to do the taking away.''

Leslie's words dogged Tris for twenty-two-and-a-half hours.

They ran continuously in her mind through the rest of a long, unproductive afternoon at work. And during a dinner with Bette, Paul, Leslie and Grady that Michael had excused himself from at the last moment. And through a restless, unhappy night that turned into a dull, unhappy day.

At first she tried to assess Leslie's words rationally. Did she see any proof for such an observation? Had he said anything that might support Leslie's contention? Soon, however, she found herself wondering why he might feel that way, and she knew that she'd accepted the truth of the words.

But that didn't bring her any closer to an answer. Why would he think that she would take her love away? Why didn't he—couldn't he?—believe in her love?

Staring out her office window, she wondered if it was because she hadn't fallen in love with him in college. Could it have hurt him so much that she hadn't returned his love back then? But she hadn't even known about his feelings. Of course, hearts weren't always reasonable, or just.

"Can you take the afternoon off?"

She twisted around so fast at the deep, familiar voice just behind her that her foot came out of her shoe.

"Michael!" He looked awful. Even more tired than he'd looked election night on television. She wanted to fold her arms around him and bring him rest and contentment. But could she, when he didn't seem to trust her?

"I got the afternoon off." His face shifted to a grimace. "Actually, I was thrown out of the office and told not to come back until I could be human. If you can get off, we could go somewhere."

She felt disoriented by the suddenness of his appearance. Go somewhere? Like a date?

"Where?" Why?

"I know Paul, Bette and Grady are spending the day in Annapolis, so I figured your house would be empty. We could have some privacy there." He pulled in a quick breath and let it out. "We need to talk."

Chapter Thirteen

Terse refusals had been his only response to her offer of something to drink or eat. Silently, Michael sat beside her on the couch, elbows on his knees and his lightly clasped hands extended in front of him. His stillness conveyed tension as clearly as pacing would have, until, abruptly, he started talking.

"I've never told you much about my parents, have I, Tris?"

"No, you never have."

He hadn't had to. She'd often wondered if he'd tell her what she already knew. But at this moment, another issue overrode all else. Why was he telling her now?

"My parents divorced when I was nine. Lots of kids go through that, I know. And it wasn't a particularly bitter divorce. There was never any trouble with them sharing custody or anything. In fact in some ways they understand each other very well. They're very much alike." She heard the harsh note in his voice at that, and even with only his profile to judge from, she saw a deep disappointment in the lines of his face.

"By the time I was out of high school I'd been to four of their weddings. And there have been more since that I haven't bothered to go to. My mother's been married four times, my father three times. And those were the 'successful' relationships. Each time they're sure it's going to be the one that lasts forever."

He made a rough sound that caused burning in Tris's throat. If only she could touch him. If only she didn't fear that touching him was the last thing he wanted right now. "Forever's gone by so fast and so often it makes my head spin to think of it."

She wanted to gather him in her arms, to comfort him, to protect him from the pain he must have felt in those unsettled, unsettling years. But she didn't. The questions wouldn't let her. *Why have you chosen this time to tell me all this, Michael? What does this have to do with me? With us?*

"I have half brothers and half sisters, not to mention a slew of ex-stepfathers and ex-stepmothers. I honestly don't think I could name all my various ex-stepbrothers and stepsisters—they came and went too fast. But some I remember. My junior year in high school Mom met the father of this girl I was dating and the next thing I knew, my girlfriend had become my stepsister."

He glanced at her, then returned his stare to the empty fireplace. She wondered if he'd been expecting her to look shocked. "Not exactly the kind of sane, stable childhood you had, huh?"

"No." She spoke very carefully, waiting. "I was very lucky. It must have been difficult for you, Michael."

"Yeah. Difficult." He slowly turned to face her, and Tris thought that he was forcing himself to let her see all the way into him, down to the bedrock of determination he'd founded himself on. "I swore I would never be like them, Tris. That when I said forever I'd mean it and I'd stick to it. No equivocation, no backing out. Forever."

Her heart thudded heavily against ribs that suddenly seemed too delicate to hold this assault. Was that the way he felt about her? She knew that was what she wanted from him, with him. It was the certainty, the reliability she'd always felt in his friendship. Now she wanted it from a deeper emotion. If he'd loved her all these years, as he'd indicated he had, didn't that qualify as the kind of love he was talking about? Wasn't that the kind of feeling she'd sensed from him?

Then why was the ecstasy of that thought flavored with this unknown terror?

"And I swore that was what I would have in return. That's what I have to have in return. I have to know that other person will be there for me forever. That her love will be constant."

Her lips parted on the words that would tell him that was how she felt. Words like marriage and children and home and growing gray together. Words like love and forever. Then the words dried in her heart and her lips closed.

He wouldn't believe them. She could already see the wall of disbelief in his eyes. And she understood. Understood, why he'd told her this now, understood his reluctance to love her, to make love with her. He believed that she would break his heart, that she would be as inconstant as his parents. He believed, as Leslie had guessed, that Tris was going to take everything, all her love, away from him.

And even while her heart tried to cry out to him how wrong he was, her mind acknowledged that he could jus-

fy his disbelief. He could point to her infatuation with
Grady, to her short-lived marriage, and he could see them
as proof of her changeability.

Her hand reached to him, hovering by the small indentation in his cheek, but not touching him. He shifted on the
couch, bringing them face-to-face with their bodies not
quite making contact.

She thought of all she longed to say. I've grown up, Michael. I was young, and I didn't know. I thought I knew
about love, but I didn't. Now I do. I've grown up and I
love you. And I know it's forever.

But he didn't know that. And no matter what words she
gave him, she couldn't give him that knowledge, that certainty. It could only come from him.

What if it never came? She couldn't think of that,
couldn't consider it.

"Michael." Only his name and already the tears threatened to stop her words. "Michael, I do love you. I can't
deny that I thought I was in love with someone else when
I was younger. I wouldn't deny it even if I could make you
believe it. Those people, those relationships are part of
who I am now. If I could make you see that... But I know
it doesn't matter what I say to you, because nothing I say
is going to convince you."

She leaned forward and placed her right palm over his
heart, feeling the rhythm of its beat and taking comfort
from it. Such a strong heart. Surely it would be strong
enough to believe in her.

"This is the only place you can be convinced. Listen to
what your heart tells you about my love, Michael."

Holding her look, he lifted her palm from his chest and
brought it to his lips, wondering at the softness of her skin
and her eyes.

He'd been so sure his words would drive her away. He'd
made his demands clear, and he'd let her see his skepti
cism that she could meet them. Fear or anger—or both—
that was what he'd expected. Not the clear, strong light of
desire in her eyes.

He stood, drawing her with him, and led her toward the
stairs without speaking.

If she desired him, that was what he'd take. He'd gone
long past the point of self-preservation. He couldn't stop
himself from loving her. He couldn't protect himself from
the pain when she left. This had been his last weapon to
buy himself the safety of driving her away. But she hadn't
been driven away. And now there was no safety, no pro-
tection for him.

The bedroom door shut behind them, and he moved to
her, skimming the zipper down the back of her dress.
Pushing aside the material, he cupped her breasts from
behind. His hands absorbed the sensations of the teas-
ingly slick material of her bra and slip and the sweet weight
of her breasts, as his mouth gently traced her backbone
down from her nape.

He felt the shimmer of her need just under her skin, and
he welcomed it.

He'd take whatever she gave him for as long as she chose
to give it, and he'd give everything in return. Everything
except the belief that she could give him forever.

Why didn't she cry? Her eyes and throat held the hot
ache of tears, but no tears fell.

Maybe tears seemed too small. Or maybe the feel of
Michael's leg, heavy and intimate, thrown across hers, and
the warmth of his arm, resting just beneath her breasts,
and the rhythm of his breathing, communicating itself to
her through the periodic whisper across her skin and the

ise and fall of his chest against her shoulder, all com-
ined to make her feel too right, too cherished to cry.

How could he doubt the feeling between them when
heir bodies were so right together? When they found each
ther and brought each other joy every time they made
ove?

She tipped her head to see his face and confirm what she
lready knew; he was asleep. In the fading winter light, his
air and eyebrows and lashes stood out darkly against his
kin. Carefully, she shifted so she could bring her right
and up to brush back his thick hair from his forehead.
he smiled to herself as she thought of his characteristic
esture, and mimicked it with gentle fingers. Touching the
larkened skin under his eyes that betrayed his weariness
ind the fan of grooves that seemed to be cut more deeply
han they had been just a few days ago, she frowned.

He looked tired, worried. And she knew she was the
ause. That seemed so wrong, so very wrong—that loving
iim the way she did she was somehow causing him pain.

He mumbled something in his sleep, and his arm and leg
ightened around her, bringing their bodies into more se-
ure contact.

Her heart swelled at the unconscious movement, be-
ause she thought she understood the instinct that
rompted it. She thought—she hoped—it was the same
ossessive, protective emotion that was welling in her.

Love. The forever kind.

The kind that could leave a scar forever, too.

Grady had been an infatuation, as unreal as a teenager's swooning for a rock star. Even the failure of her
marriage to Terrence, embarked on too young and for the
wrong reasons, hadn't hurt her the way Michael could.
Because Michael was passion and companionship, can-

dlelight and sunlight, seduction and security...lover and friend.

At least now she knew what she had to conquer. At least now she knew what he needed—certainty. The utter, complete belief in her love. The girl she'd once been might have thought that would be easy to give him. She knew differently.

In the years since college she'd learned very well that achieving the bright, shining goals of idealism required the hard work and hard head of realism. From wanting to save the world, she'd come to the challenge of trying to preserve one small part of it for future generations. She'd learned that succeeding at that could bring an abiding satisfaction. But she'd also learned that, even with the hardest work and the hardest head, for some buildings—and perhaps for some hearts—the endings weren't always happy.

He didn't trust her love. Didn't trust it not to evaporate, to disappear overnight as he had seen "loves" disappear from his parents' lives. She couldn't force him to trust her love. There was no final test, no hurdle she could jump and then have Michael Dickinson convinced once and for all that she would love him for as long as she breathed.

It was her personal catch-22. If the girl Tris had fallen in love with him all those years ago, he might have believed in the reliability of her love. But she knew that it had taken the experiences, and especially the mistakes, of the past twelve years to mold her into the woman who could love Michael Dickinson as deeply, as completely as she loved him now.

All she could do was endure. And keep loving him. There was no choice about that.

* * *

Michael turned in from the quiet hall where his footsteps had echoed hollowly, and heard voices coming from the senator's office. He wasn't surprised to find he wasn't the only one who'd stopped by to slip in an hour or so of work before the Inauguration Day festivities.

The next few weeks were going to be hectic and draining; at least he'd start them with a clean desk. Anyhow, that was a better use of his time than staring at the unfamiliar ceiling of his apartment bedroom and wishing for things that weren't going to happen. Such as he'd be magically transported back to Tris's bed. Or she'd be magically made to love him for the rest of her life.

He'd left Grady sleeping soundly in the new bed in his spare room, with a message that he'd meet all of them at the Metro stop nearest the Capitol in plenty of time for the swearing in.

His desk was nearly empty and he was twenty minutes from leaving to keep that appointment when a voice spoke from the doorway.

"She wants to see you."

He looked up to see Sharon Karik, the senator's confidential secretary and general assistant, leaning against the jamb. He was one of the few people who knew she'd met the senator many years ago when she was a battered wife and the senator was a volunteer counselor with no political ambitions. They'd both come a long way, but he knew the trust built in those first encounters had never wavered. Some relationships were built to last. The thought stung on his raw doubts about Tris's feelings for him.

"How'd she know I was here?"

"Radar, I guess. You know how she is."

"Yeah, I know." They exchanged grins mixed of pride and accomplishment. They'd really made it to Washington. "Any idea what's up?" he asked as they walked the short corridor to the inner office, but without much expectation of an answer. If Sharon had thought he should know she would already have told him.

"Nope. Go on in." She swung the door wide. "Here he is."

"Good morning, Senator."

Joan Bradon glanced up from the papers on her desk with a swift smile, then finished jotting a note even as she started talking. "Morning, Michael. Have a seat. I'm glad you stopped by today. I have something I'd like your opinion on."

"Certainly, Senator."

She pulled her dark-rimmed glasses off impatiently, ruffling her smooth cap of gray-sprinkled hair. "Enough of that 'Senator' stuff, Michael. The first few days it was fun, but it's been Joan for five years, let's leave it that way." She didn't wait for an answer, tossing a folder to his side of the wide desk. "Here, look at this."

He picked up the folder, but wasn't surprised that she kept talking as he opened it; people who couldn't do two things at once didn't last long around Joan Bradon.

He looked at the title page and felt a curious shifting in his chest. It couldn't be.... But if it was ... why? Why did she do it this way?

"This came to me from Morton Treen. He doesn't often steer me wrong, either. I found it quite impressive. Well thought out, well presented. And certainly the idea of two benefits from the cost of one project has a lot of appeal. In fact, I thought you'd mentioned something similar to me back before the election. But then you didn't follow up on it. Wasn't there a project you wanted me to look at? Something similar to this?"

Michael raised his eyes from the pages he'd first forced himself to look at, then couldn't help himself from examining. "Yes, there was, Joan. But it wasn't similar—it was the same project. But with some changes in the proposals for how the funding would be accomplished."

"The same project, hmm?" She studied his face a moment longer, then put her glasses up to her eyes to check a note on a scrap of paper at her elbow. "Morton says someone named Tris Donlin is the brains behind this. You know her?"

"Yes, I know her." At least he'd thought he did. But she'd gone to Morton Treen with her proposal instead of bringing it to him. He felt as if he'd been kicked in the gut. Hadn't she trusted him?

"She'd talked to you about the project before and then decided to approach me from another direction, hmm?"

He hardly needed to answer since she obviously was certain she'd pegged the situation correctly, but he forced himself to say the word that confirmed what he didn't want to acknowledge. "Yes."

"This funding looks pretty reasonable, like she knew what might fly. You say the funding proposal was changed?"

"Yes."

"Sometimes changes are for the better, Michael." Her voice was soft, but her look seemed to pierce right through him to his soul. He didn't look away. "I know you don't always care for change, but— What is it?"

He didn't think he'd betrayed his reaction, but she was sharp. "Someone else has said that to me recently."

"Ah." She looked from him to the papers in front of her and back to him. "Someone perceptive. Someone who knows you well."

His brief nod accepted her words.

"I was a little concerned about you when you were talking this fall about not coming with me here to D.C., Michael. I've been glad to see you seeming more settled the past week." Her hand moved over the paper with Tris's name on it. "Just remember, you're a skeptic and not a cynic. I need your talent for seeing the holes, but don't ever forget that there can be damned fine cheese surrounding those holes. Don't focus on the holes to the exclusion of the cheese, Michael."

This time she didn't wait for him to respond, putting on her glasses and briskly rearranging the papers before her. "Anything involved here that will prevent your review of this proposal from being objective and fair?"

"No, I don't think so." If anything, he might be a tougher judge, knowing Tris had chosen to bypass him with her heartfelt project. Why, Tris?

"Good. I'd like you to take a look at it and leave me something brief with a preliminary opinion." She consulted her slim gold watch. "Not now. It's time to leave for the swearing in. But maybe after the parade this afternoon?"

She left just enough of a question in it that he knew he could beg off if he wanted to. He didn't. He nodded.

"Good. I know you men don't need as much time to get all dressed up, so I thought you would have time before tonight's ball. Leave a note on my desk and I'll look at it in the morning. If you like the idea, we can get a few other people involved in it right from the start. It never hurts to make people think they were in on the discovery of something great. See you tonight, Michael."

"Okay, Joan."

"I have never seen so many horses! Not since the day my great-uncle took us all to the Kentucky Derby in Louisille." Leslie emphasized her exhaustion by flopping on 'ris's couch. Tris had long envied Leslie her ability to flop racefully. "And let me tell you, the jockeys' outfits at .ouisville were a darn sight more conservative than some ve saw today."

"Where is that you said? Lu'ville? Is that somewhere in Kentucky?" Grady perched on the couch arm by her side and handed her a cup of coffee.

"That is how we in the South pronounce it," Leslie intoned, but her eyes gleamed at the teasing.

Tris had a momentary vision of Leslie and Grady sitting on a wide, white veranda in the dress of a century and a half ago, and Leslie rapping him on the knuckles with her an. But rapping gently enough to encourage him to go ight on with his flirting. She tried to stifle a grin as she set lown a tray with cream and sugar and a plentiful supply of cookies and added her review of the parade they'd just .een.

"I thought the horses were fine and the marching bands sounded great, but you could have cut out all the smiling politicians for my taste."

"Try to remember that all those smiling politicians are he reason for the whole thing in the first place," recommended Michael, bringing in the last two cups. "Coffee, Bette?"

"No. No coffee for Bette." Paul answered for her. 'Don't you have some milk?"

Tris tried to remember the contents of her refrigerator. 'Uh, I guess so. You want milk, Bette?"

"Or hot chocolate?" Paul asked his wife.

She patted his hand. "No, thanks. No milk, and no hot chocolate. I'll just have a cookie."

She leaned toward the tray, but before she could reach it, Paul had jumped up, snagged the cookie plate and brought it back to her.

"You sure you don't want something hot to drink? It was awfully cold out there this afternoon."

"It was fifteen degrees warmer than most January days in Chicago, Paul."

"But the wind was raw, and we were out a long time, with the swearing in and then the parade. Maybe we should have come back earlier. It's a long day, and with the ball tonight... Maybe we should skip the ball tonight, stay home and rest."

"I'm fine. Honest. And if you think I'm going to miss my one and probably only opportunity to go to an official inaugural ball you're crazy."

"Then maybe we should all clear out now and let you take a nap before you get ready. You really should rest some."

"I'm not tired enough to take a nap. Sitting here like this is just fine, Paul. Besides, I want to talk to everybody."

Tris listened to the exchange with growing amazement. She couldn't resist seeing if anyone else thought Paul was acting out of character. The stunned expressions of Grady and Michael told her they agreed.

Bette obviously also had been checking out her audience because she gave a giggle. "Paul, I think your friends are suspecting I've had your personality altered while they weren't looking."

Paul colored a little, but gruffly intimated that he didn't care. "Husbands are supposed to look out for their wives," he mumbled.

"Especially when they're looking out for two," added Bette. She surveyed the blank faces around her, and prompted, "You know, as in eating for two."

"A baby." Michael was the first to get it.

"A baby."

"Congratulations!"

"That's wonderful!"

"When are you due?"

"How long have you known?"

"Is everything all right?"

"Have you picked out names?"

"A boy or a girl?"

"We won't know that for a while yet, Grady," said Bette with a laugh, then started separating the spate of questions. "Everything's fine. The baby's due in mid-August. So that leaves us several months to thrash out the name issue. But we know a few we're considering," she added with a big smile at all of them.

"This calls for champagne, and I just happen to have a bottle in the fridge."

"I'll help." Michael followed her into the kitchen.

"No champagne for Bette," Paul called out after them.

"That doesn't seem fair," Tris heard her protesting.

Michael had the glasses out by the time she'd retrieved the bottle from behind items in daily use. She peeled the foil off from around the bottle's neck. An effervescence bubbled into her bloodstream as she remembered another bottle of champagne, and what had followed it. Was Michael remembering?

"You want me to open it?"

Tris looked up and met his intense eyes. He remembered.

"Yes. Please." Her voice seemed oddly breathless for such a mundane request.

Or maybe it wasn't so odd, she decided as she watched him wrap one strong hand around the bottle and the other around the towel-covered cork. How hopeful she'd been that night. It had all seemed so simple, so inevitable. She'd discovered a bright, new feeling for Michael Dickinson and had been certain, deep in her heart, that he shared that feeling.

Now she knew the name for that feeling—love. She also knew that simple and inevitable were not among love's guarantees.

He filled the last glass and put down the bottle, two drops from the lip of the bottle dropping to his finger. She followed his automatic motion as he brought his hand to his mouth, reaching out quickly to stop him short. He stood very still. Meeting his eyes, she slowly brought his hand to her lips instead, sipping those two precious drops slowly and carefully.

He finally moved, twining his fingers into her hair and bracketing her cheeks with his palms, holding her face so his eyes bored into hers. She felt, as she had before, that he was searching for something in her face, in her look that would answer forever his questions. She opened her eyes and her heart to him, hoping it would be enough.

When he abruptly ended the look by bringing his mouth down to hers, she couldn't help a feeling of sadness at the same time she relished the feel of his lips and tongue and teeth. He hadn't found the answer he'd been seeking.

Michael, if I could give you certainty I would. But only you have the power to believe in me, in my love.

"Did you say you were going to find out what's taking so long? With the champagne? In the kitchen?" Leslie's raised voice of warning penetrated through the mist of desire Michael so easily raised in Tris. She backed away quickly and was fussing with the tray when Grady and Paul came around the corner.

"Good. Here, you each carry a couple glasses and then we won't need a tray." She handed them the glasses and hustled them out of the kitchen, taking one covert look at Michael before heading to the living room with him following.

The look told her that he had been as affected by their kiss as she was. There were so many emotions in it. So many questions. So many declarations. She knew she couldn't begin to sort them out.

She looked from Bette to Paul. She was thrilled for them, and she envied them.

They hadn't always had a smooth road, she knew. But they'd passed that. They'd been sure enough to marry, and now sure enough to have a baby.

She wanted a baby. She wanted Michael's baby, with Michael's warm eyes and tousled hair and errant dimple. But how could that be, how could a marriage work for them if he didn't truly believe she loved him?

"A toast," Michael announced.

Everyone raised a glass, turning to Michael to say the words. His eyes never wavered from Tris. "To Paul and Bette, to old times, old friends and . . ."

She remembered the words she'd added to this same toast he'd made in the small room over the garage five months before. Would he remember? Would he give her hope by using them?

" . . . and new beginnings."

"Hear, hear," came the voices around her.

Michael leaned forward to clink his glass softly against hers. She saw him through a mist of tears. If only he could truly believe in the power of new beginnings.

Tris stared at her image in the bathroom mirror, and wished Michael's were next to hers.

He'd said he was going to his office for a while before returning to his apartment to dress for tonight's ball. Then he and Grady would pick up Leslie before coming here to get her, Paul and Bette.

She had already put on her dress, a shimmer of garnet red that rippled with light when she moved. But she'd never be ready if she didn't stop staring into the mirror making useless wishes. She picked up her brush with determination.

If Michael were beside her, the wishes wouldn't seem so useless. If she could keep him beside her all the time, maybe his doubts would finally be eased.

But that wasn't very realistic. Just as her first expectations five months ago that the new feelings they'd discovered for each other would be perfect weren't realistic. How could she have expected them to switch from years of friendship to being lovers without any hitches? That was the foolishness of someone who, indeed, led with her heart, and she wasn't that person anymore.

It made sense that Michael had doubts and concerns. It was reasonable and understandable, especially considering his family history and what he'd seen of her track record with relationships. She couldn't blame him for not feeling the absolute sense of rightness that she experienced every time they touched. She might wish he could feel it, but she couldn't blame him if he didn't.

No, what she had to do was work to overcome his doubts until he did feel it.

And work she would…until he couldn't do anything but believe she loved him. And when that happened, then … then, she'd take about two seconds to say yes if—no, when, *when* he again asked her to marry him.

"If you keep sighing like that you're going to fog up the mirror." Paul grinned at her from the doorway before being scooted aside by his wife.

"Why don't you go wait for us downstairs? You're all ready, but we have a few more finishing touches. Just a few minutes."

Paul groaned as he went down the stairs but was wise enough not to question Bette's time estimate.

Pulled from her reverie, Tris rapidly finished arranging her hair and checking her makeup. Gradually, she became aware of Bette watching her in the mirror. She met the look and saw sympathy and understanding there.

"Ready?"

"Ready," Bette confirmed, but stayed where she was a moment longer. "Hang in there, Tris. It'll work out, and he's a wonderful man."

"I know he is."

"It'll work out," Bette repeated with a brief squeeze of Tris's shoulders before they headed downstairs.

It had to. Please, it had to.

Chapter Fourteen

He closed the report slowly, not wanting even the rustle of paper to disturb the total quiet of the office or the acceleration of his thoughts.

Tris had done an impressive job. Her proposal sold itself. It was solid and professional—not the work of a wide-eyed, idealist girl, but of a pragmatic, resourceful woman. He'd responded to the former when she'd first talked about the proposal back in August. He'd seen glimpses of the latter in the notes on her desk ten days ago. Which had he been expecting to encounter within the pages of this report?

He'd checked the phone number and was dialing before his mind acknowledged the impulse.

"Hello." The voice was familiar and—yes, for all the faults—loved.

"Hello, Mom."

"Michael! Dear, how wonderful to hear from you! Is ~erything all right? It's been so long! Are you enjoying ~ashington? So exciting! Tell me what you've been do-~g. Are you going to all the parties?"

At the characteristic mixture of exclamations and ques-~ons, he found himself smiling a little as he complied. ~hen he listened to her enthusiastic description of the ~idower she'd seen every night since she'd met him the ~eek before in the grocery store.

She was still like an exuberant teenager, still a kid. And ~r all his smooth sophistication, so was his father. To give ~em their due, he knew they'd done their best to love and ~are for him. But they'd never really grown up.

They'd never really grown up.

The phrase seemed to slam into his mind, pumping an ~drenaline mixture of hope and fear so strong that his ~and shook a little as he said goodbye and hung up the ~hone.

They'd never really grown up.

But Tris had.

The proposal under his hand was the solid proof of that. ~ut he shouldn't have needed that. His fear had made him ~quate her with his parents, but she'd never been like them. ~ven as the seventeen-year-old he'd first met. And cer-~ainly not as the woman he'd made love to five months ago ~nd over the past two weeks.

Only now could he look into the past and see how his ~raving for permanency had blinded him. He'd seen Tris's ~outhful infatuation for Grady, and because he wanted her ~o be so different from his parents—needed her to be so ~ifferent—he'd imbued it with the trappings of a lifelong ~ove. Even her marriage he'd twisted into some sort of echo ~f the one love his view of her had allowed. To meet his ~eeds she had to be perfect, could make no mistakes of the

heart. Because if she did, then the fear lurking in hi
would pounce, and would convince him she was like th
other undependable, unenduring loves he'd seen his pa
ents go through.

He'd left her no middle ground, no room to be first
girl, trying out her heart, and then a young woman, mak
ing her mistakes and learning her way, and now a woma

She was a woman now. *Wasn't she?* A mature woma
who would know her own heart. *Wouldn't she?* Who,
she said she loved somebody, truly did. *Didn't she?* She'
been telling him that, and showing him, but he hadn't be
lieved it—he'd been afraid to believe it.

Afraid of the change?

What about her accusation that the person he loved wa
the girl Tris had been, not the woman she'd become? Wa
he so afraid of change that he couldn't accept the change
in her? Or was he so afraid of being his parents' son tha
he refused to admit that his own love might have changed
might have grown out of a young man's infatuation an
into something deeper and richer?

"This was a definite tactical error, letting the three o
them go to the bathroom together."

Despite himself, Michael grinned at Paul's grousing
Since the ladies' cloakroom was inside the ladies' lounge
they'd agreed to meet the three women at the base of th
broad marble stairs that led from the entry level to the ex
pansive ballroom. He, Paul and Grady had quickly she
their coats and now stood at the bottom of the stairs
waiting.

"Now, this is my idea of a ball."

Michael turned from where he'd found an open spot b
the turn-of-the-century-styled light post that flanked th
bottom step, and followed Grady's gaze, surveying th

ene lit by chandeliers and the sparkling of silver and ystal. Tuxedoed men and expensively gowned women rcled the packed dance floor, while more of the same atched from the gallery that hugged the sides of the oom.

Paul's waiting was less than patient. Michael thought he nderstood that. He'd known that Paul and Bette had omething special since the first time he'd seen them to-ether. But now, when he saw them looking at each other, e saw something more, deeper. Something that spoke of marriage that would last, and a commitment strong nough to rejoice at bringing a new life into the world. If ris were carrying his child...

The image hit a velvet, heated blow to his heart. God, to ave Tris carrying his child. He'd never let her out of his ght.

"Here they come."

He heard the undercurrent of unreasoning relief in aul's voice, and felt a small echo of it in his own heart.

Turning back, he saw Tris immediately. She and Leslie anked Bette with a faint air of protectiveness about them. le recognized that, along with the incredible picture the aree women made, especially Tris, tall and straight and lond. But those impressions were pinpricks compared to ae burst of awareness in his chest. A kaleidoscope of im-ges overlapped, blurring time and geography as he saw ris, long-haired and coltish, red-cheeked and irate, aughing and innocent, sleepy-eyed and wise. All Tris. All is woman. All the woman he loved. All the woman who oved him.

He watched her gaze slide past Paul and Grady with a aint smile on her lips. And he watched her continue her earch for something—or someone—else. Another image ame into his mind, a double image of Tris coming down a church aisle toward him. Of the way she'd smiled from man to man at the altar until her eyes had met his, and how the impact of that look had rocked him. And how he' forced his eyes away from her so she couldn't see to deeply into him.

Not this time.

This time he had to risk it, had to risk seeing what wa really there, had to risk letting himself believe in her love

He made a slight movement toward her, and saw he find him. And he saw.

She lit up from within with the love.

It washed over him, cleansing long-ago scars, healing hi wary heart with a belief strong enough to base a life on. H felt his heart expand within his tightening chest as she cam into his arms unquestioningly.

He hugged her hard, trying to remember not to crush her. He'd tell her, he'd make her see what he had finall seen. Somehow. And he'd do it tonight, but not now. No with a couple thousand celebration-minded reveler around them. For now, he'd just indulge in an hour or two of the kind of pleasurable pain known only to a man i love.

He nuzzled the intricate curves of the delicate ear ex posed by the curve of her hair, and felt her answering shiver like a tingle of electricity in his own nervous sys tem.

"Let's dance," he breathed into her ear. "All the slow dances. Real slow."

"Michael. How nice to see you this evening."

He stifled a small groan as he loosened his arms from around Tris. Never in his life had he been less thrilled to hear Joan Bradon's voice. He had no idea of how many dances they'd danced, but he knew it had grown harde

th each one to remember that they were in a public place,
pecially since Tris had shown no inclination to object
nen he'd found this secluded corner devoid of chande-
rs.

Grown harder. His mouth twisted a little at his mental
oice of words. He slipped his arm around Tris's waist,
lfheartedly hoping her wide skirt would help mask his
ndition. Ah, well, Joan Bradon was the mother of three
d grandmother of one, so she wouldn't be particularly
ocked. Besides, he had the feeling she'd sought him out
this secluded corner, and probably had a good idea of
hat she'd find.

"Joan. Nice to see you, too. I'd like you to meet Tris
onlin. Tris, this is Senator Joan Bradon."

"It's an honor to meet you, Senator Bradon." Tris ex-
nded her hand and Joan met it immediately, then held on
it.

"Tris Donlin," Joan repeated. As if she hadn't already
nown who Tris was before she approached them, Mi-
hael thought with wry knowledge of his boss. "I've seen
ur proposal. Very impressive. I'll call your office to-
orrow to set up an appointment to talk further about it."

"Thank you." To a stranger she'd seem totally com-
osed, but Michael could see that Tris was a little stunned,
nd he felt the worried glance she threw at him.

"I understand you and Michael went to college to-
ether." Now it was Michael's turn to be surprised. Joan
ust have made it her business to find that out in the past
w hours. "You strike me as a very perceptive woman.
Michael's not an easy man to know, is he? But he's worth
e effort. It's good to meet you, Tris. I'm sure we'll be
eeing more of each other—over the proposal and—" she
ave the two of them a significant look "—in more social
ircumstances."

Well past surprise, Michael knew the meaning of fata
ism when Joan turned her bright eyes back on him. Sh
wasn't done yet.

"Don't bother to come in until after lunch tomorrow
Michael. I have a feeling the entire Hill is going to spen
the morning recovering. And remember, Michael, enjo
the cheese."

She strode away, a little ripple of head-turning follow
ing her purposeful passage.

"Michael, I was going to tell you about sending her th
proposal. I had this contact, and he said—"

"It's all right, Tris."

"I just thought that with things, so...unsettled be
tween us that it would be better..."

"I know. I understand."

"I'm sorry. I should have told you before it had a chanc
to get to Senator Bradon's desk. And to find out lik
this—"

"I already knew. Joan showed it to me this morning."

"She did?"

"Yes. I recommended she throw her support behind it."

"You did?"

"Yes. It had nothing to do with you, Tris." He tried t
be stern, but looking into her blue eyes, he couldn't main
tain it. "I admit I was a little hurt at first that you'd by
passed me, but I do understand, Tris. When I read th
proposal, I realized what you've probably known al
along—that I'd been treating you like you were still sev
enteen. You were right to give it to someone who judged i
on its merits. When I did that this afternoon, I knew it de
served all the support we could give it. You did a great job
The proposal sells itself."

Her smile was wide enough to encompass a love even a
large as his. "I did, didn't I? Do a great job, I mean."

"Yes, you did," he said with mock gruffness. "Now 's get back to dancing. We're missing a slow one."

She went into his arms willingly, but he could tell her nd wasn't totally with him.

"The proposal really sells itself."

"Yes, it really does." He whispered the words against r temple where his tongue made a small circle.

Another moment of quiet passed as he felt their movements meshing.

"Michael?"

"Hmm?"

"That was an odd comment she made about cheese."

"Mmm-hmm."

"What do you think it meant?"

Who could think? "Maybe she's confused, thinks Wisnsin elected her instead of Illinois."

Tris chuckled a little. Then he felt first her lips, then her ±th, soft but sharp, on the turn of his jaw. A definite admonition. "Will you tell me someday?"

"Yes, someday. I promise. Just not right now. Right w, I want to dance with you."

He shifted their bodies closer and heard her sigh of intent coursing all the way through his reheating bloodream.

Tris unlocked the door and the others trooped in bend her, stamping their feet clear of slush and cold.

"What does everybody want? Coffee? Brandy? Milk for e mother-to-be?"

Bette smiled at the last offer, but Paul seemed to conder it seriously as he took off his wife's coat and laid it ith his on the back of the couch, then guided her to a seat n the other side of the room, away from the door's draft.

"I don't think you should have stood outside watchin the fireworks like that. You might have gotten chilled."

Bette smiled at him and answered patiently. "I was fin Paul. I had my wrap and your coat on, I could have with stood a blizzard."

"Thanks, but nothing for us, Tris," said Grady. "I' talked Leslie into going to a jazz club over in Georg town."

"Okay, see you guys later." Tris met Leslie's eyes for moment, trying to convey both encouragement and ca tion. She wanted Leslie to have a wonderful time; sl didn't want her to get too hooked on Grady Roberts. Sl knew from Leslie's arched-brow smile that the message wa received and understood.

Good-nights were cheerfully exchanged with Grady an Leslie, but when she turned to hang her coat in the close she found Michael not a foot away from her, watching he face intently.

Lord, he was at it again—worrying that she'd be hurt b Grady's "defection." Her surge of disappointment at tha thought was a physical pain.

For all her lectures to herself about being patient an reasonable, she'd let herself imagine that everything wa all right. It had been very easy to pretend that Michael a ready believed in her love. Especially after the way he' held her tonight when they danced, after the way he' stayed by her side all night long, after the way he'd stole a brief, heated kiss in the temporary dark betwee fireworks, the way he'd held her hand during the taxi rid home.

When she'd seen that look on his face when she cam down the ballroom stairs to meet him, she'd thought... she'd hoped. Now, having the hope not fulfilled hurt.

She'd be patient, she'd endure, she'd show him her love was lasting. But that didn't mean the waiting didn't hurt.

"What?" she demanded of him, the pain edging her voice.

"Just wondering if you—"

"Michael, please don't start."

"I just—"

She growled a little at him, trying to ease her frustration. "You are so stubborn."

"I was just going to ask what *you* wanted to drink, but if it comes to being stubborn, how do you think I stayed in love with you all these years?" he muttered.

Her anger melted at his words, and that left room for her renewed resolve to be patient and understanding. To be realistic about the adjustments in their relationships. To love him the way he deserved to be loved.

"Michael, I do love you," she said softly.

He met her eyes directly, just a hint of a smile in his. "I know you do."

She felt as if one of the fireworks they'd watched earlier had just gone off inside her, complete with pinwheels and sparklers.

"You do? You do! You...know... You really believe it."

Instead of answering her, he swung away and grabbed Bette's and Paul's coats from the back of the couch, strode across the room and shoved them into Paul's unresisting arms. Then he dug in his pocket and pressed his key ring into Paul's hands, while Bette and Tris gaped at him.

"Paul, here are the keys to my car and my apartment. Use anything you want, eat all my food, use my phone to call New Zealand, use my credit card for a TV shopping spree, but please, please get the hell out of here. Now."

Bette recovered first, and was tugging on her husband'
arm at the same time she started pulling on her coat
"C'mon, Paul, I can tell when we're not wanted," she sai
with a splutter of warm laughter.

"But... But what's going on?" Paul protested. "Wha
are you going to do?"

"It's none of our business," his wife informed him a
she gave Tris a warm hug that Tris felt too stunned to re
spond to.

"Tris and I have some things to prove to each other
Monroe. Okay? You've been saying it for months and nov
we're agreeing, so get the hell out of here, will you?"

"Oh." Paul pulled on his coat along with a self-satisfie
grin. "Oh! All right. All right. We're outta here." H
shepherded his wife out the door, but paused just befor
closing it behind him. "'Bout damn time, you two."

Tris turned to face Michael. His hands cupped her face
his fingers tunneled into her hair as he looked down at her

"Are you—"

She didn't have to finish the question because she sav
his certainty in his eyes. Still, he gave her the answer i
words, too.

"I'm sure. Very, very sure."

He kissed her, just his lips touching hers, and she taste
the answer there, too.

Backing away only enough to look into her eyes, h
smiled at her. "Do you know how long I've loved you?"

"Do you know how long I'm going to love you?" sh
countered softly. "I think it's the same answer to bot
questions."

She saw the puzzlement in his eyes, then it disappeare
and, with it, her own last tiny bit of worry.

"Forever?"

"Forever."

He looked at her a long, lingering moment, as she discovered both the warm light of her friend and the bright, hot light of her lover firing his eyes. Then he touched his mouth to hers, softly, hungrily, demandingly, strongly. All the emotions in each of a dozen kisses that explored and declared until kisses, even these kisses, were not enough.

She wound her fingers into his thick hair and pressed herself against him, loving the different feel of his hardness.

Climbing the stairs was slow and distracted, with stops to touch and kiss and unclothe. At the top landing, his fingers fumbled to find the secret to her dress, and she couldn't still a throaty chuckle.

"Damn dress . . . Where do you . . . ?"

"Here." She guided his fingers.

"Promise me something, Tris."

"Anything."

"No more dresses that take an engineer to figure out. I don't have the patience. From now on, only easy dresses to get you out of."

"Ah, Michael, you don't know yourself. You're a very patient man. And very stubborn. I don't believe there's a dress in the world that could defeat you."

He growled something as he slid the dress away from her, and found her skin.

"But I promise," she said on a soft gasp, with her lips touching the top of his head as he bent to take her into his mouth. "Only easy dresses."

She awoke to the feel of his body next to hers, as she had before. Several times. And each time was an awakening of passion for both of them. Only this time, it was broad daylight and Michael was propped on one elbow, staring

down at her intently, the lines at the corners of his eye
etched in solemnity. With no preliminaries, he asked.

"Will you marry me?"

"Yes."

"Will you love me forever?"

"Yes."

"Even when I'm stupid and stubborn?"

"As long as you're not stupid about worrying that
don't love you, and as long as you're stubborn about
staying in love with me."

"I think that can be arranged."

He dropped a kiss on her chin as he stroked down her
body with a possessive hand. She found she enjoyed his
possessiveness, his wordless declaration that he knew she
was his.

At the sound of the phone, their eyes met in an ex
change of good-humored grimaces.

"I wonder who that could be?" said Michael with ab
solutely no wondering in his voice.

She grinned at him and rolled on her side to reach the
phone.

"Hello. Oh, good morning, Paul."

Tris listened for a minute, then turned to Michael with
eyes bright with laughter and love. "Paul says he's checked
with Grady and Leslie, and June would be a great time for
all of them."

"Great time for what?"

"Great time for another reunion—at our wedding."

Michael leaned across her body to take the receiver ou
of Tris's hand and spoke very firmly into it. "We'll let you
know what we decide, Monroe. And no matter when it is
you'll all be there—come hell or high water. Now good
bye."

He hung up, but he stayed where he was, the length of his body blanketing hers. She felt the heat between them building. Not flaring like something short and intense, but readily welling to an enduring flame. "And what are we going to decide, Michael Dickinson?"

"We're going to decide which day in June," he said, shifting against her to find his place in her. "And then we're going to decide if we can stand to wait until then."

* * * * *

Silhouette Special Edition

is pleased to announce

WEDDING DUET
by Patricia McLinn

Wedding fever! There are times when marriage must be catching. One couple decides to tie the knot, and suddenly everyone they know seems headed down the aisle. Patricia McLinn's WEDDING DUET lets you share the excitement of such a time.

December: PRELUDE TO A WEDDING (SE #712) Bette Wharton knew what she wanted—marriage, a home...and Paul Monroe. But was there any chance that a fun-loving free spirit like Paul would share her dreams of meeting at the altar?

January: WEDDING PARTY (SE #718) Paul and Bette's wedding was a terrific chance to renew old friendships. But walking down the aisle had bridesmaid Tris Donlin and best man Michael Dickinson rethinking what friendship really meant....

Silhouette Special Edition

salutes

MOMENTS OF GLORY

from Lindsay McKenna

In a country torn with conflict, in a time of bitter passions, these brave men and women wage a war against all odds ... and a timeless battle for honor, for fleeting moments of glory, for the promise of enduring love.

February: RIDE THE TIGER (#721) Survivor Dany Villard is wise to the love-'em-and-leave-'em ways of war, but wounded hero Gib Ramsey swears she's captured his heart ... forever.

March: ONE MAN'S WAR (#727) The war raging inside brash and bold Captain Pete Mallory threatens to destroy him, until Tess Ramsey's tender love guides him toward peace.

April: OFF LIMITS (#733) Soft-spoken Marine Jim McKenzie saved Alexandra Vance's life in Vietnam; now he needs her love to save his honor....

SEMG-1

NORA ROBERTS

Love has a language all its own, and for centuries, flowers have symbolized love's finest expression. Discover the language of flowers—and love—in this romantic collection of 48 favorite books by bestselling author Nora Roberts.

Starting in February 1992, two titles will be available each month at your favorite retail outlet.

In February, look for:

Irish Thoroughbred, Volume #1
The Law Is A Lady, Volume #2

Collect all 48 titles and become fluent in the Language of Love.

LOL192

THE LANGUAGE of LOVE